V. A. STUART

V. A. Stuart is an acknowledged expert in British military and naval history, and is the author of more than sixty books and countless magazine articles. The excitement, authenticity and flavor in V. A. Stuart's writing is due in part to a colorful career as a world traveler and as an officer with the British Army in Burma, Japan, India and Australia during World War II.

The major part of V. A. Stuart's recent writing has been concerned with the periods surrounding the Indian Mutiny of 1857 and the Crimean War. It is in this latter area that this volume, the third in the saga of Phillip Horatio Hazard, continues what is planned as a series of at least twelve books.

The first book in this series, THE VALIANT SAILORS, was acclaimed by critics in England and America. *Publisher's Weekly* reported that "this meticulously recorded adventure novel is a worthy successor to the Captain Horatio Hornblower series, and make no bones about it." Here, then, is superb writing about the exciting days of iron men and wooden ships.

The next volume to be published in the series is HAZARD OF HUNTRESS.

HAZARD'S COMMAND

by
V. A. Stuart

PINNACLE BOOKS • **NEW YORK CITY**

For
Captain Harry Hamilton, R.N. Retired,
with the author's affectionate good wishes to the "Little
Admiral's" grandson.

HAZARD'S COMMAND

Copyright © 1971 by V. A. Stuart

All rights reserved including the right to reproduce this book
or portions thereof in any form.

A Pinnacle Book, formerly titled *Black Sea Frigate*, published by
special arrangement with Robert Hale Limited, London, England.

This edition has been completely reset in a type face designed
for ease of reading. It was printed from new plates and contains
the complete text of the original, high-priced edition.

First printing, March, 1972

Printed in the U.S.A.

PINNACLE BOOKS, 116 East 27 Street, New York, N.Y. 10016

AUTHOR'S NOTE

With the exception of the Officers and Seamen of
H.M.S. *Trojan,* all the British Naval and Military
Officers in this novel really existed and their actions are a matter of historical fact. Their opinions
are also, in most cases, widely known and where
they have been credited with remarks or conversa-
tions—as, for example, with the fictitious charac-
ters—which are not actually their own words, care
has been taken to make sure that these are, as far
as possible, in keeping with their known sentiments.

The main events described are historically accurate
and did actually take place, as described, according to books published, soon after the Crimean
War ended, by those who took part in them.

PROLOGUE

THE day dawned bleak and misty over the Crimean
Upland, heralded by the boom of cannon, as first one
battery and then another opened fire on the well-fortified
Russian city of Sebastopol. The Russian gunners replied
with spirit.

In the small, sparsely furnished room which, in his
farmhouse headquarters on the Upland, served him both
as office and sleeping quarters, General Lord Raglan sat
in front of a makeshift wooden desk, shoulders wearily
bowed. As always, the British Commander-in-Chief was
dressed in the plain blue frock coat to which he had
become accustomed when, as Military Secretary to the
Duke of Wellington and later as Master General of the
Ordnance, he had occupied a much more impressive desk
at the Horse Guards in Whitehall.

It was cold in the low-built farmhouse, with its damp,
stone-flagged floors and ill-fitting windows and the fire,
which his German valet had lit in the tiny grate the
previous evening, had long since burned to a heap of dead
ash that did nothing to ward off the dank chill seeping in
from outside. His nephew and aide-de-camp, Somerset
Calthorpe, aware that he intended to work late on his
despatch to the Duke of Newcastle, had placed a blanket
about his knees before leaving him but Lord Raglan,
finding that it impeded his penmanship, had let it slip to
the floor.

He sighed, feeling its yielding softness beneath his feet and, for a moment, let his gaze go longingly to the bed beside him, wishing that he might sleep and, in sleep, find relief from the torment of his thoughts, if only for a few hours. But there was the dispatch to be completed, checked carefully and signed . . . a hand in front of his mouth to stifle an involuntary yawn, he started to re-read what he had written to the Secretary for War in London. Headed "Before Sebastopol" and dated 8th November, 1854, the report was lengthy. In it the British military commander had endeavored to describe the bloody, hand-to-hand battle fought on the Inkerman Ridge three days before, employing the stilted, tactfully worded phrases and bestowing the meaningless praise his political chief expected of him upon their French allies.

"My Lord Duke," the despatch began, *"I have the honor to report to your grace that the army under my command, powerfully aided by the corps of observation of the French Army, under the command of that distinguished officer, General Bosquet, effectually repulsed and defeated a most vigorous and determined attack of the enemy on our position overlooking the ruins of Inkerman on the morning of the 5th instant. In my letter to your grace of the 3rd, I informed you that the enemy had considerably increased their force in the valley of the Tchernaya. . . ."*

The attack had been by overwhelming numbers—estimated at between fifty and sixty thousand men—on the vulnerable British right flank, Lord Raglan thought bitterly, skimming quickly through the first page. The French aid, which he had described as "powerful" had, as it usually did, come too late. Indeed, he reflected, the battle need never have been fought had General Canrobert, the French Commander-in-Chief, acceded to his repeated requests for troops to share responsibility for the defense of the exposed position above the Tchernaya Valley, which his men had been compelled to shoulder alone. Canrobert had over 40,000 men to his own 24,800— which included the Naval Brigade—yet the Frenchman had insisted that he could spare none of them, even for so urgent and essential a task.

Lord Raglan's mouth tightened in remembered exasperation. With the small force under his command, it was becoming increasingly difficult to bombard Sebastopol into submission from the Upland and, at the same time, hold the port of Balaclava and the extended line of defense on the undulating ridge, known as Inkerman, on which the right of his line rested so precariously. Canrobert's right, on the other hand, was protected by the British main body and his left by the sea, where the Allied Fleets reigned supreme and he had two excellent and accessible ports in Kamiesch and Kazatch—both secure from land attack. Whereas Balaclava ... Lord Raglan turned impatiently to the second page of his dispatch. He had always intended Balaclava to be a temporary expedient; neither he nor Admiral Sir Edmund Lyons, when they had chosen the tiny, landlocked harbor—seven miles from the besieging troops on the Upland, which it had to supply—had seen it as anything else but a stepping stone to the capture of Sebastopol. Once Sebastopol fell, Balaclava could be abandoned, since the captured city would provide not only a large harbor and well-equipped dockyard but also winter quarters for the Allied Armies, now under canvas and exposed to steadily worsening weather.

He and Canrobert—and, before him, the late Marshal St. Arnaud, his predecessor in the French supreme command—had agreed that their primary objective must be the capture of Sebastopol. They could have walked into the Russian base, virtually unopposed, within three days of their victory at the Alma and the flank march which had brought them to the south side of the city. But they had not done so. . . .

9

He had wanted to make that final assault, Lord Raglan reflected. He had wanted with all his heart to advance when the Russians were reeling and had retreated from Sebastopol, and his own soldiers were flushed with the victory they had so gallantly won but ... the French had insisted that the siege trains must first be landed. An assault without the support of heavy guns and a preliminary bombardment was so entirely contrary to the French concept of war that Canrobert had declared the mere suggestion of such a course to be a crime. Lord Raglan had recognized that he could not attack with the British army alone. Despite the almost contemptuous claim, by General Sir George Cathcart, that he could take the city with his Fourth Division and with "scarcely the loss of a man," the British Commander-in-Chief had regretfully decided that this was a gamble he dared not risk. General Sir John Burgoyne, his Chief Engineer, had agreed with the French view and advised against an attack and so ... Lord Raglan expelled his breath in a long sigh. He had ordered the landing of the siege guns and, in the three weeks which it had taken to drag these into position on the Upland, the enemy had reinforced and re-fortified Sebastopol, with the result that now the place defied all efforts to capture it.

The Allied Armies, while technically besieging the city had, perforce, to leave the north side unguarded. Through this open door Prince Menschikoff, the Russian Commander-in-Chief, was able to pour all the troops and guns he needed for its defense and, having done so, was in a position to attack the besiegers from beyond the River Tchernaya, using for this purpose the seemingly inexhaustible reinforcements reaching him from all over Russia. The obvious point to attack was the weakest and ... for a moment, Lord Raglan covered his eyes with his hands, looking back, recalling the decisions which circumstances —and the demands of his Allies—had forced him to make.

One of these had been greatly against his better judgement, for it had involved still further weakening the defences along the line of the Inkerman Ridge but ... Canrobert had assured him that, at last, the French were ready to join the British in a full-scale assault on Sebastopol which, he suggested, should be made on 7th November. Sebastopol *had* to be taken, if a long winter campaign were to be avoided and the French, heaven knew, had kept him waiting for long enough so, as he had to the landing of the siege trains, Lord Raglan had agreed to the French plan for the attack. Leaving his right flank to be defended by only the Second Division and the Guards Brigade, he had concentrated all his depleted force on the preliminary bombardment, on which the French still obstinately insisted, and had been busy preparing detailed orders for the assault when—two days before the date agreed by Canrobert—the Russians had struck.

They had struck shortly before daylight on the morning of 5th November and ... the British General bent once more over his report.

"The morning was extremely dark, with a drizzling rain," he had informed the Secretary for War, *"rendering it almost impossible to discover anything beyond the flash and smoke of artillery and heavy musketry fire. It, however, soon became evident that the enemy, under cover of a vast cloud of skirmishers, supported by dense columns of infantry, had advanced numerous batteries of large calibre to the high ground to the left and in front of the Second Division, while powerful columns of infantry attacked the Brigade of Guards.*

"Strong columns of the enemy came upon the advanced pickets covering the right of the position. These pickets behaved with admirable gallantry, defending the ground, foot by foot, against the overwhelming numbers of the enemy, until the Second Division, under Major-General Pennefather, with its field guns, which had immediately

11

been got under arms, was placed in position. The Light Division, under Lieutenant-General Sir George Brown, was also brought to the front without loss of time; the 1st Brigade, under Major-General Codrington, occupying the long slopes to the left towards Sebastopol, and protecting our right battery, and guarding against attack on that side; and the 2nd Brigade, under Brigadier-General Buller, forming on the left of the Second Division, with the 88th Regiment, under Lieutenant-Colonel Jeffreys, thrown in advance. The Brigade of Guards, under His Royal Highness the Duke of Cambridge and Major-General Bentinck, proceeded likewise to the front and took up most important ground to the extreme right on the alignment of the Second Division, but separated from it by a deep and precipitous ravine, and posting its guns with those of the Second Division.

"The Fourth Division, under Lieutenant-General Sir George Cathcart, having been brought from their encampment, advanced to the front and right of the attack; the 1st Brigade, under Brigadier-General Goldie, proceeded to the left of the Inkerman road; the 2nd Brigade, under Brigadier-General Torrens, to the right of it and on the ridge overhanging the Valley of the Tchernaya. The Third Division, under Lieutenant-General Sir Richard England, occupied in part the ground vacated by the Fourth Division, and supported the Light Division with two regiments, under Brigadier-General Sir John Campbell, while Brigadier-General Eyre held the command of the troops in the trenches. . . ."

Set out thus, the battle sounded as if it had taken place according to plan but, as he re-read his account, Lord Raglan knew that this was very far from being the case. He had, of course, expected a Russian attack on his right flank; had, in fact, as he had endeavored to impress on Canrobert, lived in hourly dread that it would come, for he was constantly receiving reports of a massive build-up of enemy troops across the Tchernaya. When, however, the attack was launched on his thinly held positions, the "dense columns" of Russian infantry he had described in his despatch had been met only by pickets of the Second Division and that Division, by itself, had had to fight a delaying action, until such time as he could order his other divisions down from the siege-works to its aid. And this had taken time, not only because of the distance involved but also because, in the swirling Crimean mist, the battle had become confused. Men were fighting in thick brushwood and on precipitous slopes, among ravines, using the bayonet rather than musket fire, since visibility was, at times, so poor that to fire into the fog might have meant firing on friends, unrecognizable in the swaying tide of battle.

Two feint attacks, one on the French left, the other in the direction of Balaclava, had been launched by the enemy simultaneously with that on the Inkerman Ridge. These diversionary sallies had achieved their purpose, in that they delayed the French aid for which he had asked—General Bosquet, from his vantage point on the Sapouné Ridge, refusing to move for over an hour until assured that they were, in fact, diversions. No one could possibly question Bosquet's personal courage, Lord Raglan reminded himself . . . once in the battle, he and his splendid Zouaves had fought with admirable gallantry. Nevertheless, the stout French General had waited with all save two regiments of his *Corps d'Observation,* for a further two hours after bringing them down from the Heights before, at Lord Raglan's personal request, ordering his troops to the aid of his hard pressed allies.

One of the two regiments he had sent in to support the depleted British 55th Regiment had refused to continue its advance without artillery cover and, himself and his staff under heavy fire, the British Commander-in-Chief had watched them retreat, seemingly indifferent to the fate

13

of the unfortunate 55th. Only after Colonel Warren's scant hundred men had followed him in an heroic bayonet charge had the Frenchmen halted and turned to face the enemy and, even then, Lord Raglan had had to send a staff officer to upbraid their commander before the 7th Léger could be persuaded to take an active part in the fight, this time in support of the brave and already exhausted British 77th Regiment.

None of this could, of course, be stated in an official dispatch. Lord Raglan read his reference to the incident, a wry smile curving his lips.

"Additional batteries of heavy artillery were also placed by the enemy on the slopes to our left, the guns in the field amounting in the whole to ninety pieces, independently however, of the ships' guns and those in the works of Sebastopol. Protected by a tremendous fire of shot, shell and grape, the Russian columns advanced in great force, requiring every effort of gallantry on the part of our troops to resist them.

"At this time two battalions of French infantry, which had on the first notice been sent by General Bosquet, joined our right, and very materially contributed to the successful resistance to the attack, cheering with our men, and charging the enemy down the hill with great loss. About the same time a determined assault was made on our extreme left and for a moment the enemy possessed themselves of four of our guns, three of which were retaken by the 88th, while the fourth was speedily recaptured by the 77th Regiment, under Lieutenant-Colonel Egerton. In the opposite direction the Brigade of Guards, under his Royal Highness the Duke of Cambridge, was engaged in a severe conflict."

The gallantry of the Guards defied description, their Commander-in-Chief thought, conscious of a warm glow of pride as he read again his all-too-inadequate account of their magnificent part in the action. Firing with steady and

14

telling accuracy whilst their ammunition lasted, they had attacked again and again with the bayonet when powder and musket balls were exhausted, driving the massed Russian columns before them in terror. They had fought for, lost, recaptured, lost again and yet again retaken a two-gun emplacement, known as the Sandbag Battery, with matchless courage, fighting on despite appalling casualties, finally putting the enemy to rout in a desperate charge down an overgrown slope. They had, it was true, charged too far in the confusion, with the unhappy result that another enemy column had advanced rapidly across the high ground above them in order to cut them off from their commander, the Duke of Cambridge, whose position had, for a time, been in grave danger. But, rallied by their officers, the Guardsmen had reformed and clambered back to the plateau where, joining the heroic handful who had remained with the Colors, they had fought off several Russian attempts to capture these and had, finally, managed to escape from the trap.

General Sir George Cathcart, the Divisional commander, had not been so fortunate, however. Lord Raglan read through the next page of his report, conscious of a sense of loss. He had not liked Cathcart—who, although junior in rank and service to Sir George Brown—had been designated his successor to the supreme command until just before the battle of Inkerman. But ... he had been a brave man and a good soldier and the manner of his dying had been in the best traditions of the British Army. No matter now that he had been difficult and obstructive, forever complaining that he was not consulted when major decisions had to be made, constantly insisting that *his* advice—as holder of the "dormant commission" as Commander-in-Chief—should be sought and acted upon, instead of Sir George Brown's or Sir John Burgoyne's. He was dead and ... leaning forward, Lord Raglan added some lines between two of those already written in his dispatch.

"*Lieutenant-General the Hon. Sir George Cathcart, with a few companies of the 68th Regiment, considering that he might make a strong impression by descending into the valley and taking the enemy in flank, moved rapidly forward, but finding the heights above him in full occupation of the Russians, he suddenly discovered that he was entangled with a superior force, and while attempting to withdraw his men, he received a mortal wound, shortly before which Brigadier-General Torrens, when leading the 68th, was likewise severely wounded.*

"*Subsequently to this the battle continued with unabated vigor, and with no positive result, the enemy bringing upon our line not only the fire of all their field batteries, but those in front of the works of the place and the ships' guns, till the afternoon, when the symptoms of giving way first became apparent; and shortly after, although the fire did not cease, the retreat became general, and heavy masses were observed retiring over the ridge of the Inkerman, and ascending the opposite heights, abandoning on the field of battle five or six thousand dead or wounded, multitudes of the latter having already been carried off by them. I never before witnessed such a spectacle as the field presented; but upon this I will not dwell.*"

In his despatch to London, Lord Raglan thought painfully, that spectacle was one on which it would not be politic to dwell but the terrible sights he had seen, when the Russians at last withdrew from the blood-soaked Inkerman Ridge, haunted him now, waking and sleeping, and he could not drive these or his memories of the battle from his mind. He shivered, remembering how General Strangeways, riding only a few yards from him, had had his leg shot off by a round shot at the height of the action. Brave and courteous to the last, the old artilleryman had politely requested that someone assist him from his horse.

When this was done and the old man lain gently down behind the shelter of a boulder, Lord Raglan had felt the tears come unbidden into his eyes, aware that his old friend and fellow veteran of Waterloo could not long survive his terrible wound. He had died, stoic and uncomplaining, only an hour or so later, and there had been others, so many others—old men, like Strangeways, young men in the prime of life, all of them his soldiers, whom he would mourn and whose faces he would not forget. . . .

Lord Raglan read through the next paragraph of his dispatch, forcing himself to do so, although a mist of tears obscured his vision and had constantly to be wiped away. He had paid more than generous tribute, in this part of his dispatch, to the valor and devotion to duty of his French allies. Bosquet deserved the tribute, in spite of the delay he had caused, if only for the supremely courageous manner in which, caught in a Russian trap below the Sandbag Battery, he had led his Zouaves and Algerians in a brilliantly timed charge. Indeed, he had told the plump young French General so himself, in his halting French and in a moment of emotion, thanking him "in the name of England," while Canrobert, bleeding from a slight flesh wound in the arm, looked on, beaming with pride. Yet the dead—his English dead—might not be lying now in their bloody graves, had Canrobert listened to his pleas and sent him the reinforcements whose presence might well have deterred the Russians from their attack on the Inkerman Ridge.

The British Commander-in-Chief stifled a sigh, as he glanced swiftly through the names of the officers of his own force whom he had commended, knowing these by heart. Sir George Brown, shot through the arm who, as always—stern old martinet that he was—had led his Light Division with efficiency and distinction, doing all and more than was expected of him. The Duke of Cambridge . . . well, if he had, perhaps, yielded to emotion

17

when he had lost contact with most of his Guards in the chaos which had followed their wild charge into the ravine below the Sandbag Battery, his emotion was understandable. The Guards were his pride; he held himself personally responsible for them whenever they were in action and previously, at the Alma, he had displayed a similar concern for his men. Apart from this one incident, His Royal Highness had behaved admirably. Cut off and with his Colours threatened, he had extricated himself and the hundred or so Guardsmen who had remained with him, and had then held his ground until the French, belatedly attacking the enemy on the flank, had relieved the pressure on his position. The Navy, in the persons of the dashing Captain Peel, of H.M.S. *Diamond,* and his aide-de-camp, a youthful midshipman, who had been present in the rôle of spectators, had joined the Guards in the defence of their Colors, earning a warm commendation from the Duke of Cambridge but ... Admiral Lyons would see to it that this was passed on to the Admiralty Board. His own report would be confined to the Army ... Lord Raglan's white brows met in a thoughtful pucker. There were so many deserving of his commendation but in this, his first official communication concerning the battle for Inkerman, he must confine himself to those in command.

In explanation, he had written: *"I will, in a subsequent dispatch, lay before your grace the names of the officers whose services have been brought to my notice. I will not detain the mail for that purpose now; but I cannot delay to report the admirable behavior of Lieutenant-General Sir George Brown ... of Lieutenant-General his Royal Highness the Duke of Cambridge, who particularly distinguished himself; and of Major-General Pennefather, in command of the Second Division, which received the first attack, and gallantly maintained itself, under the greatest difficulties, throughout this protracted conflict; of Ma-*

18

jor-General Bentinck, who is severely wounded; Major-General Codrington, Brigadier-General Adams, and Brigadier-General Torrens, who are severely wounded; and Brigadier-General Buller, who is also wounded. . . .

"Lieutenant-General Sir George de Lacy Evans, who had been obliged, though a severe indisposition, to go on board ship a few days previously, left his bed as soon as he received intelligence of the attack, and was promptly at his post; and, though he did not feel well enough to take command of the (Second) Division out of the hands of Major-General Pennefather, he did not fail to give him his best advice and assistance. . . .

"It is deeply distressing to me to have to submit to your grace the list of the killed, wounded and missing . . . it is indeed heavy, and very many valuable officers and men have been lost to Her Majesty's service. Among the killed your grace will find the names of Lieutenant-General the Hon. Sir G. Cathcart, Brigadier-General Strangeways, and Brigadier-General Goldie. . . ."

Once again, as he read through the brief tribute he had paid to each of his general officers, the British Commander-in-Chief had to wipe the tears from his eyes with his single hand. The face of the gallant old Strangeways still haunted him, caught and held in his memory with such poignant clarity. It had been a strange battle, he reflected, to have cost the lives of so many brigade and divisional commanders and he supposed he was fortunate, in that it had not claimed his own. He read the final page of the *dispatch.*

"It is difficult to arrive at any positive conclusion as to the actual numbers brought into the field by the enemy . . . but judging from the numbers that were seen in the plains after they had withdrawn in retreat, I am led to suppose that they could not have been less than 60,000 men. Their loss was excessive, and it is calculated that they left on the field near 5,000 dead, and that their

casualities amount in the whole, in killed, wounded and prisoners, to not less than 15,000. Your grace will be surprised to learn that the number of British troops actually engaged little exceeded 8,000 men, while those of General Bosquet's division only amounted to 6,000, the remaining French troops on the spot having been kept in reserve. I ought here to mention that, while the enemy was attacking our right, they assailed the left of the French trenches, and actually got into two of their batteries, but they were quickly driven out in the most gallant manner with considerable loss, and hotly pursued to the very walls of Sebastopol. . . ."

Lord Raglan picked up his pen, carefully signed the despatch and, attaching the casualty list to it, laid both ready for General Airey, his Quartermaster-General and Chief of Staff, to attend to when he came on duty. All in all, he thought wearily, perhaps a casualty list of 2,575 was not excessive, in view of the nature of the ground on which the battle had been fought, the poor visibility and the numbers involved. No doubt Canrobert, in his despatch to the Emperor, would claim the ghastly shambles as a victory for the arms of France . . . and Prince Menschikoff, too, despite his appalling losses, might well inform the Tsar that his forces had made a successful sortie from their beleaguered fortress. In fact, he probably would consider it thus—as one young British captain had commented, "the Russians could well afford to lose men" . . . even twenty thousand of them. The British could not and the flower of his two best fighting divisions, Lord Raglan reflected sadly, had been lost at Inkerman in defence of a ridge of barren rocks, which would not shelter them when the harsh Crimean winter set in.

In defence of the inadequate and already over-congested port of Balaclava, a scant two weeks before, all but a handful of the Light Cavalry Brigade had also perished, thanks to a criminally stupid misinterpretation of his orders and ... thrusting aside his papers, the British Commander-in-Chief rose and started restlessly to pace the floor of his room. So many lives sacrificed in these actions and to the terrible ravages of cholera and all to no purpose, he thought wretchedly. Had they been lost in a successful assaut on Sebastopol he might, perhaps, have been conscious now of a sense of achievement, might have felt that they had not been uselessly thrown away. But Sebastopol still stood, as impregnable as it had ever been to land or sea attack, and he could already feel the chill of winter in his bones.

While he himself had never experienced a Russian winter, one of his interpreters—British Consul at Kertch until the outbreak of war—had given him a vivid description of what might be expected. *"Bleak winds, heavy rain, snow and bitter cold ... a cold so intense that if a man touches metal with an uncovered hand, the skin adheres to it."* These, with his troops under canvas and on trench duty, added up to a daunting prospect. But what was the alternative? Lord Raglan's bowed shoulders lifted in a helpless shrug, as he silently replied to his own question. To abandon the Crimea and return, with the remnants of his army, across the Black Sea to Varna, there to wait until spring, when the whole complicated maneuver would have to be repeated ... that, surely, was unthinkable? The British Government would never hear of it, there would be a public outcry at home, the morale of the brave soldiers he commanded would sink beyond the power of any General to restore it ... no, no, he dared not even suggest such a course. To retire to Eupatoria was also out of the question.

He could, however, order the evacuation and abandonment of Balaclava ... Lord Raglan's frown relaxed. Balaclava, after all, was not essential and he had never intended it to be used as a permanent supply base. The siege troops and their guns could, by arrangement with the

21

French, be supplied from Kamiesch or Kazatch—the latter, probably, if Canrobert were reluctant to permit him the use of the better equipped of the two ports. Although, in this case, the distance involved might be greater, the steeply rising track from Balaclava to the Upland was already, through over-use, a sea of churned-up mud. In winter, under snow and ice, it might well become impassable. Besides, the port was always vulnerable to attack from the Tchernaya Valley, as past experience had shown and, if spared from the necessity to defend the place, he could consolidate his position on the Upland plateau, shorten his over-extended perimeter and use the men he had left under his command to the best advantage.

Suddenly revitalized, Lord Raglan went back to his desk fumbling, with his single hand, for the maps he kept there. Finding the one he wanted, he spread it out in front of him and subjected it to a careful scrutiny. It was a sketch map, drawn by a member of Sir Colin Campbell's staff, in order to show the position of the defenses for which his commander was responsible. Lord Raglan was conscious of a lifting of his earlier depression as he noted each of these and realized how many men and guns were now required to ensure the continued possession of Balaclava, not to mention the warships in and outside the harbor itself, which included a ship-of-the-line, the *Sanspareil*, commanded by Captain Dacres.

To the sleepy-eyed servant who, roused by the sound of his movements, came in to inquire whether he wanted breakfast, he nodded absently, and went on planning the evacuation of the port and the uses to which he could put the seamen and soldiers whose services would be available, once Balaclava was abandoned. A winter campaign would be difficult in the extreme, but he had always known that it would be, always been painfully aware that his troops were not equipped for one. Nevertheless, it would have to be accepted now as inevitable—they had lost their last chance of taking Sebastopol before the weather changed. Canrobert had made it abundantly clear, after the Inkerman battle, that he had no intention of joining his British allies in an assault on the enemy stronghold during the next few weeks and, within a few weeks, winter would be upon them.

If only the Russians had delayed their attempt to break through his right flank by two days, Lord Raglan thought regretfully, the assault on Sebastopol—to which the French Commander-in-Chief had, at long last, agreed—would have taken place and would, in all probability have succeeded. It had been the devil's own luck that Menschikoff should have chosen to make his sortie on 5th November, more especially since his first attack on the Inkerman Ridge, on 26th October, had been so decisively beaten off . . . and this, in spite of the fact that the battle for Balaclava, with its appalling butcher's bill, had been fought the previous day. By all the laws of civilized warfare, the Russian Supreme Commander should have learned his lesson but . . . he had not and now, with the shelter of Sebastopol denied them, his own men would have to face all the rigors of winter—and an indefinite prolongation of the siege—as best they might.

Lord Raglan bent once more over his map, his tired eyes troubled. Balaclava must be abandoned, he decided, there was no help for it. Without the ceaseless drain upon his, alas! all too limited resources, which continued defense of the port entailed, victory might still be possible once the winter was over. Whilst the cold weather lasted the Russians, too, would find their overland communications disrupted and Sebastopol could not be supplied by sea, as his own army was, since the Allied Fleets held undisputed command of the whole of the Black Sea.

Balaclava could not, of course, be abandoned without the loss of part of the stores already landed there but the

Navy would have to take off as much as they could and the port be kept clear of transports and supply ships from now on, to enable them to do so. Sir Edmund Lyons would not like his decision, he knew. The Admiral had been obstinately determined from the outset to hold the place and it had been on *his* insistence that the useless little port had not been evacuated on 25th October, when all that stood between it and the Russians had been Sir Colin Campbell and his "thin red line" of 93rd Highlanders. He would have to talk the Navy's second-in-command round to his point of view, Lord Raglan thought, not relishing the prospect. He liked and admired Lyons whose courage and enterprise, as well as his administrative ability, had impressed him immensely. He would succeed his present Commander-in-Chief, Vice-Admiral Deans Dundas, within the next two months and Lord Raglan—who had found Dundas as obstructive and overcautious as any man could be—was looking forward, with an eagerness he made no attempt to conceal, to the day when the British Fleet would be led by its present second-in-command. He ... the servant entered, with his breakfast, followed by an orderly bearing a load of green wood, with which he lit the fire, not without difficulty. It spluttered, eventually, to reluctant life and, while giving out little warmth, had at least the effect of making the small room seem more cheerful.

General Airey came in a few minutes later, as always with an air of purposeful energy.

"Your staff sleep late, my lord," he observed, referring to the absence of aides.

"Poor boys, they are tired." Lord Raglan smiled his gentle, understanding smile. "I won't have them disturbed before I must. They need their sleep."

"And you do not?" General Airey gestured to the pile of papers on the desk and, from these, to the unslept-in

24

bed. "You take too much out of yourself." His tone was reproachful. "That dispatch could have waited, surely?"

"So that *The Times* correspondent's report might reach London first? No, Richard." The British Commander-in-Chief spoke with bitter emphasis. "You know as well as I do that Mr. Russell's pen is inclined to run away with him and I shudder to think what he may have written about the Inkerman Ridge attack. I have had to accept the fact that, since *The Times* reaches and is read in Sebastopol, his reports of the number and disposition of our troops are of material assistance to the enemy. But I will *not* permit the Duke of Newcastle to hear the first news of a major engagement between our forces via *The Times*!"

Richard Airey inclined his good-looking head. "I understand your anxiety, sir, on that account. But even so, your health is of great importance to the army under your command and to the successful prosecution of this war. It behooves you to take some care of it and to work throughout the night. . . ." he shrugged helplessly. "Why did you not call on me? I am ready and anxious to serve you and—"

"I know that, Richard. And you serve me as no other man could." The gentle, affectionate smile was again in evidence. "Nevertheless this was a task only I could perform and, since it is done, let us say no more about it. You'll see that my dispatch goes off this morning, won't you?"

"Of course, sir." His Chief-of-Staff gathered up the documents, glancing at them, his brows meeting in an anxious frown. But he offered no comment and Lord Raglan, aware that his decision regarding the future of Balaclava would be received with approval by Airey, if not by everyone else, hastened to make it known to him.

"Ah!" The younger man's face lit with relief. This was what he had advocated, stressing his view as vehemently as Admiral Lyons had put forward one that was com-

25

pletely contrary. "I am sure you are right, sir. Balaclava is too small to serve as our base. Already it is reduced to chaos, with half the perishable stores which have been unloaded rotting where they lie . . . and the rest rot in the holds of ships that cannot be unloaded! But you do not need me to tell you what a shambles the place is and must remain, since we cannot enlarge its facilities. It will be an immense weight off my mind to be rid of it."

"Those are precisely my sentiments," the military Commander-in-Chief agreed.

"Do you wish me to make out orders for the evacuation?" Airey asked. "Captain Dacres already has instructions to permit no more supply ships to enter, so that the harbor is as clear as it can ever be. But Dacres, I feel sure, would appreciate a preliminary warning, because there will be pressure brought to bear on him by ships' masters anxious to discharge their cargoes and there are still wounded to be taken off. . . ." he was all eagerness, his quick brain busy with the problems that might be expected to arise and, in his enthusiasm, he was prepared then and there to act upon this most welcome decision. But, to his dismay, Lord Raglan shook his head.

"Not yet, Richard. I must first discuss the matter with Admiral Lyons who is, after all, at least as concerned with it as I am. It is the Navy's responsibility to keep us supplied and, for this reason, the Admiral must be allowed his say."

"Your lordship knows *what* he will say," the Quartermaster-General objected.

"Indeed, my dear fellow, I do. In fairness, however, I am bound to listen to him when he says it and he will, I understand, be here during the course of the morning. Besides, there are others with whom this question will have to be discussed—General Canrobert, for one. He may not welcome us at Kamiesch or even at Kazatch, and it is essential that we find an alternative to Balaclava

26

before we decide finally to relinquish it." Lord Raglan's tone was dry. "Inadequate though the place is, it is the only supply base we have at present."

"True, sir. But——" Airey began. His Chief interrupted him. "Officially Admiral Dundas will have to be consulted also. We can do nothing without his approval and I think we should call a conference of the Divisional Commanders—although that, perhaps, might wait until I have put my suggestion tentatively to the French. You could ride over to the French headquarters this morning, if you like, and get an idea of how the suggestion that we share Kamiesch with them will be received. Then you can call a General Officers' conference for this afternoon."

"As your lordship pleases," Richard Airey acknowledged. He scribbled some notes on his pad and let the pen fall adding, as if it were an afterthought, "Sir Edmund Lyons' son is due here in a day or so, he told me."

"His son?" Lord Raglan frowned, in an effort to remember. "The one in the Diplomatic Corps?"

"No, sir, the younger—Jack Lyons—who is in the Navy. He is in command of the *Miranda* steam frigate and distinguished himself, the Admiral told me, when serving with the Baltic Fleet earlier this year. The *Miranda* and the *Valorous* sailed in company with the *Jura* transport from Plymouth, with the 46th Regiment and the rest of the reinforcements we are expecting." He smiled, the smile lighting his freshly shaven face and making him look younger than his fifty-one years. "It just occurred to me, sir, that the subject of Captain Lyons' impending arrival might—ah—well, it might possibly be introduced *before* your lordship mentioned Balaclava to Sir Edmund."

"To little purpose, I fear," Lord Raglan demurred. "But rest assured, my dear Richard, that I shall use all the powers of persuasion I possess in order to convince Sir Edmund. We. . . ." he broke off, hearing the clatter of horses' hooves outside and Airey, crossing to the window, exclaimed in surprise, "Here *is* the Admiral in person, my lord! He is early astir, is he not? I wonder what that portends."

"Instruct our good Hans to serve breakfast to him," the Commander-in-Chief requested. "While he is partaking of our modest fare, I shall endeavor to talk to him informally. And, Richard——"

"My lord?"

"See that we are not interrupted. And I think, perhaps, you had better have Nigel wakened."

"Very good, my lord." The Quartermaster-General gathered up his commander's despatch, glanced curiously at the sketch map of the Balaclava defenses and then spread it out, using an inkstand and a paperweight to keep it flat. This done, he took his leave as Lord Burghersh, the Commander-in-Chief's nephew and senior aide-de-camp— unshaven but alert and wakeful—ushered in Sir Edmund Lyons.

"Ah, Sir Edmund . . . it is a pleasure to see you." Lord Raglan advanced to greet his visitor, his left hand extended in welcome, his handsome, patrician face wearing its accustomed warm and charming smile.

"And you, my lord. . . ." Rear-Admiral Sir Edmund Lyons accepted the proffered hand, his own smile also warm. A deep and sincere friendship had grown up between the two men dating, on Lord Raglan's part, from the weeks preceding the embarkation of the British Expeditionary Force from Varna to the Crimea, the entire organization of which had been undertaken with faultless efficiency and minute attention to detail by the Rear-Admiral. They were of an age and, if Lyons lacked the aristocratic background and breeding of his military contemporary, his twenty years' distinguished service in the Diplomatic Corps—to which he had been seconded from

28

the Navy at the age of forty-five—gave him intellectual equality.

He had served as British Minister to the Court of King Otho of Greece from 1835 until the summer of 1849 and his knowledge of the Balkans was extensive so that, as an adviser, he had proved invaluable. As a young officer in the Navy, he had also won fame and rapid promotion and, when commanding H.M.S. *Blonde*, the 46-gun frigate which had been chosen to convey Sir Robert Gordon to Constantinople as British Ambassador in 1828, he had contrived to obtain permission from the Sultan to embark on a cruise in the Black Sea. His had been the first British warship to pass through the Bosphorus, with the full knowledge and consent of the Turks, since the signing of the Treaty of Unkiar Skelessi, twenty years before ... and Lyons had not wasted his time there. With the enterprise that was typical of him, he had visited and drawn careful plans of the defenses and fortifications of both Sebastopol and Odessa and, in addition, had made an extensive survey of the Black Sea coast.

For this reason, the Board of Admiralty had recalled him on the outbreak of war with Russia and appointed him as second-in-command of the British Black Sea Fleet ... a wise choice, Lord Raglan reflected, as young Burghersh drew up a chair for the Admiral facing his own. It would have been wiser still, of course, had Their Lordships appointed Lyons in place of his present superior, Admiral Dundas. Whilst his last active command might have been that of a frigate in 1835, Edmund Lyons had proved again and again since his arrival in the Black Sea, that he had lost none of his professional skill. It had been he, in his fine steam-screw ship-of-the-line H.M.S. *Agamemnon*, who had demonstrated with great courage and resource, when the Allied Fleets had bombarded Sebastopol's formidable sea defenses on 17th October, just how such an operation should be fought and led. His senior, in

29

the *Britannia,* had stood off, virtually out of range of the Russian guns, and had then had the effrontery to claim, in an acrimonious note addressed to himself, Lord Raglan recalled, that the action had been *"a false one . . . with which, as a naval officer of fifty years' experience,"* he had been *"profoundly dissatisfied and which he declined to repeat."*

Small wonder, the British military Commander-in-Chief thought with bitterness, that he had sought Edmund Lyons' opinion and taken his advice on naval matters, in preference to those of Admiral Deans Dundas who, in any event, never came ashore or did him the courtesy of offering either, save in notes entrusted to his second-in-command for delivery—and even these usually belated and bluntly critical. How could Admiral Dundas, lying off-shore in his comfortable and well-provisioned flagship, possibly know or attempt to understand the problems that beset the military command? Living like a king on the pigs and sheep he had crammed into the *Britannia's* ample hold, he cared little that the unfortunate soldiers and seamen, serving their guns on the Upland existed on a diet of ship's biscuit, salt junk and green coffee beans. When asked for Marine reinforcements, Dundas made excuses and delayed landing them for as long as he could and then did so grudgingly, as if the Army had no right to ask for them.

The Admiral had no conception, Lord Raglan thought wearily, of the obstructions and the difficulties caused almost daily by their French allies. He had not troubled to find out, before writing his critical and discourteous note, that it had been General Canrobert—*not* himself—who had, by his completely unexpected refusal to launch the agreed and simultaneous land attack on the city, rendered the naval bombardment of Sebastopol's sea forts abortive. He sighed, glancing across at his caller, his smile faintly apologetic, as if fearing that the other might have read his

30

thoughts. But Sir Edmund Lyons smiled back, murmuring his thanks, as a servant carried in a tray and set it in front of him.

"This is most kind of your lordship. I broke my fast before dawn as, I rather think"—his gaze was concerned, as it rested on Lord Raglan's thin, tired face—"you yourself must have done? You look, if you will forgive my saying so, as if you had not slept well."

"I had some urgent paperwork to attend to," Lord Raglan evaded. The Admiral inclined his head but did not reproach him. He had offered no reproaches following the naval bombardment either, the military Commander-in-Chief reminded himself. Although he had risked his ship, his own life and the lives of her crew by taking the *Agamemnon* to within less than six hundred yards of Fort Constantine, so that he might bring his guns to bear on the towering, stone-built walls, Sir Edmund Lyons had voiced no criticism. The Navy's losses, in men and ships, had been heavy, but unlike his Commander-in-Chief, the Rear-Admiral had not called the action false because no assault from the land had been launched. *He* had understood, because he had had past experience of French vacillation. He knew, because he had been there and had heard Canrobert, at the Allied Councils of War, promise his full support to an attack on Sebastopol, how often the French Commander-in-Chief had failed—often at the eleventh hour—to keep his word.

As if, this time, he had read his host's thoughts, Sir Edmund said, setting down his coffee cup, "It is a sobering thought, is it not, Lord Raglan, that we once listened to and were deterred by Marshal St. Arnaud's estimate of five hundred casualties which, he claimed, would have resulted from an attack on Sebastopol immediately after the Alma?" He spread his small, well-kept hands in a despairing gesture. "What haunts me now is the knowledge that, had I been able to lead my steam squadron into

31

the harbor, I could have done so almost with impunity! It would not have been difficult at that time—the enemy did not sink their infernal line of battleships across the harbour mouth until September the twenty-fourth."

"I know," Lord Raglan agreed, with infinite sadness. "But the French would not have it, Sir Edmund, they would not have it at any price. And now we are paying that price and shall, I very much fear, have to go on paying it until the spring. . . ." he hesitated. This was the moment to mention his desire to abandon Balaclava, although he had planned to introduce the subject after the Admiral had finished his meal and to lead up to it with care and forethought after, perhaps, as Richard Airey had suggested, some passing and complimentary reference to young Captain Lyons of H.M.S. *Miranda*. Sensitive always to the feelings of others, Lord Raglan, in his turn, subjected his caller's face to a searching scrutiny. Lyons was not a robust man. His physique did not match his courage and, like himself, the Admiral worked long hours, dividing his time between his ship and the steam frigate squadron that was his special command, and his liaison duties ashore. He performed the latter conscientiously, as if in an endeavor to compensate for his Commander-in-Chief's failure to do so and he had missed no major land action, save the battle at the Alma River, since the beginning of the Crimean invasion. At the Alma engagement, he had been at sea, his ship's guns protecting the Allied right flank and afterwards, he had organized the collection, evacuation and transport to hospital of the wounded, which . . . the Admiral's quiet, pleasant voice broke into Lord Raglan's thoughts.

"My son is due to join the Fleet in a day or so," Lyons offered. "He has command of one of the new steam-screw sloops, the *Miranda,* of fourteen guns." His pale, high-boned face—which, Lord Raglan recalled, had in his youth been said to bear a close resemblance to Nelson's—

lit suddenly with affectionate pride, as he went on to speak modestly of his son's achievements with the Baltic Fleet, under Sir Charles Napier. "In company with the *Eurydice,* a steamer of twenty-six guns, and the steam-screw *Brisk,* the *Miranda* entered the White Sea in June and there they remained until mid-September, conducting an amazingly successful blockade of the enemy's Arctic ports. The *Miranda* alone boarded over three hundred merchant vessels, my son told me in one of his letters. Landing parties from the squadron destroyed a number of fortifications on shore . . . and Jack seems to have taken a small fortune in prizes."

"It will rejoice you to see him again, I have no doubt," Lord Raglan said. "And I shall be rejoiced to see the reinforcements his ship is carrying." He smiled, aware that he had lost his opportunity to speak of Balaclava but not ill-pleased, as he urged his guest to help himself to more coffee. There would be time enough for what he knew inevitably must lead to a difference of opinion, an argument and, perhaps, even a clash of wills but he was tired and he had always intensely disliked forcing his own point of view upon anyone. Edmund Lyons was a friend, a man whose company he enjoyed and whose professional ability he respected and, for a while, they relaxed together, talking first of the Admiral's son and then of his own favorite daughter, Charlotte, known to him by the childhood nickname of "Puggums."

It was, in the end, Lyons himself who introduced the subject of Balaclava and now Lord Raglan knew that he could no longer avoid it. After describing, with enthusiasm, a new naval gun position he was proposing to build, in order to improve the port's defenses, the Admiral added, accepting a cigar with an appreciative smile, "I should like to permit the *Jura* troop transport to enter Balaclava when she arrives. The harbor has a good depth of water—your lordship will no doubt remember that I brought the *Agamemnon* in and met you on board, after the flank march. The *Jura* has a regiment to unload and it will save time if the men do not have to be transhipped and ferried ashore. At present the port is fairly clear of shipping and——"

"I should be grateful," Lord Raglan put in quickly. "If it could so remain, Sir Edmund."

"I do not understand. . . ." Admiral Lyons was clearly surprised by such a request. "Do you mean that the harbor should be *kept* clear? My lord, there are supply ships which I have held at anchor outside Balaclava for over a week, some for longer than that. If the wind shifts or bad weather blows up, there's no shelter for any of them." Quietly, as one professional to another, he explained the situation, emphasizing the need to provide a safe anchorage for the laden supply ships and stressing the risk, with so many vessels obliged to lie off the port of Balaclava awaiting entry. "At this time of year, there is always the chance of a storm . . . and storms in the Black Sea can be very severe. Anchored so close up to the high cliffs which surround the port, these ships could all be driven on shore and wrecked. Your troops need the supplies they carry, my lord and, in addition, there are still wounded awaiting evacuation from the Hospital Wharf . . . they could be taken to Scutari in the transports, once we get them unloaded."

"I am aware of all that, Admiral." Lord Raglan spoke gently and persuasively. With all the eloquence at his command, he endeavored to explain the reasons for his urgent desire to abandon Balaclava. The Admiral heard him in polite and noncommittal silence but his expression, the military Commander-in-Chief saw, was glum. When he had done, Lyons rose.

"It is for you to decide, Lord Raglan," he said. "Naturally in this, as in all other major decisons, I shall respect your wishes and convey these to my Commander-in-

Chief—who is, I am given to understand, anxious concerning the Fleet anchorage off the mouth of the Katcha should the weather deteriorate. As"—again he spread his hands in the odd little Continental gesture he had acquired as a result of his long stay in Athens—"the glass leads me to fear that it well may. But. . . ." he broke off, his eyes meeting Lord Raglan's in a swift and searching glance.

"But in your view, I am wrong?" The soldier suggested. "Be frank with me, Sir Edmund, as you have always been in the past."

"Then, sir, I must in all honesty confess that I believe this to be the wrong decision, in our particular circumstances," the Admiral answered, his voice vibrant with sincerity. "Oh, I'm well aware of the inadequacies of the port of Balaclava as a permanent base. It is too small for our requirements, both entry and exit are difficult. . . ." he sighed. "You do not need me to detail all its failings and I know that the distance supplies have to be carried puts a great strain on your troops. Many things could be improved, given time." He hesitated and then asked gravely, "Lord Raglan, can you count on General Canrobert to provide an alternative to Balaclava?"

There was a pregnant silence. Finally Lord Raglan broke it. "To be frank with you, in my turn, Sir Edmund, I do not know," he admitted. "I can but hope. I am calling a conference with my Divisional Commanders this afternoon, to discuss the matter, and I shall invite Canrobert and Bosquet to attend. In the meantime, may I ask that you continue to keep Balaclava clear of shipping so that, should it be decided that we abandon the place, this can be done expeditiously?"

The Admiral bowed his white head in resigned assent and took his leave.

Burghersh came in a few minutes later, to hand his Commander-in-Chief a note. "This came, sir, just now. It is Prince Menschikoff's reply to your request for a truce and burial parties to dispose of the enemy dead on the Inkerman Ridge."

Lord Raglan opened the sealed missive, frowning as he slowly digested its contents. "He refuses to send any burial parties," he told his waiting nephew, with a wry twist of the lips. "This work, he tells me, 'is customarily performed by those left in possession of the field of battle.' And he rejects my complaint of his soldiers' barbarity as 'not generally justified.' Particular cases, in which our wounded may have been bayoneted, he assures me were due to 'the outraged piety of an eminently religious people, filled with horror when they learnt that French troops pillaged a Russian Church at Quarantine Bay'!" The A.D.C. said nothing, sensing a deep rage in his normally mild and gentle uncle that both surprised and worried him, for usually Lord Raglan controlled his personal emotions sternly. "The Prince asks," the Commander-in-Chief went on, "if I can confirm the death of Colonel the Prince Andrei Narishkin, an Imperial aide-de-camp, who commanded the Chasseurs of Odessa at Balaclava. Is he on our list, do you know? Can we confirm it?"

"I'll ascertain, sir." Burghersh left the room, to return five minutes afterwards, the required list in his hand. His uncle had not moved; he still stood, gazing into the small, spluttering fire but now his face was devoid of expression. "Well?" he asked, as if puzzled by the A.D.C.'s reappearance. "What is it, boy?"

"The Prince Andrei Narishkin, my lord—his name *is* listed. He died of wounds on October the twenty-sixth and was interred with the dead of the 93rd Highlanders. It seems, from a note against his name, that the prince died after being cared for by one of the Highlanders' women, sir . . . and she reported his death. A Catriona Moray, sir, according to the records."

Lord Raglan nodded absently, his mind clearly on other matters. "See to it that our 'eminently religious' enemy

36

is duly informed. And you'd better send a galloper to General Pennefather to warn him that we—as possessors of the field of battle—are to bury the Russian dead."

"Very good, sir," the A.D.C. acknowledged. He went out, leaving the Commander-in-Chief of the British Expeditionary Force in the Crimea to his own—all too obviously unhappy—thoughts.

Outside an icy wind rose, to blow for several minutes with sudden, savage ferocity, dispelling the early morning mist. It died, as suddenly as it had got up but, hearing it, Lord Raglan found himself wondering whether it was a portend of things to come. . . .

1

HER MAJESTY'S steam-screw frigate *Trojan,* of 31 guns
and 300 horsepower, lay at anchor off the entrance to Constantinople's Golden Horn. She had steam up and her
decks were thronged with red-coated soldiers—some reinforcements, recently sent out from England but the majority
recovered veterans of the Alma from the British Army
hospital at Scutari, awaiting passage back to the Crimea.

From the sternsheets of his gig, which was taking him
out to the anchorage, her acting Captain—Commander
Phillip Horatio Hazard, Royal Navy—studied her with
critical and faintly troubled blue eyes. The *Trojan*'s previous passengers had been wounded from Balaclava, some
of whom had spent many hours on the ill-equipped Hospital Wharf, without food or shelter, before embarking.
Although her crew had worked day and night to remove
the accumulation of blood and filth they had left behind
them, the ship's state of cleanliness left, in her commander's eyes, a great deal to be desired.

It had been a nightmare voyage from Balaclava to
Scutari and one he wished he could forget. The ship's
surgeon, Angus Fraser, and some women of the 93rd who
had volunteered to assist him, had done their best but,
with little in the way of drugs and dressings and the
unfortunate men crammed into every available inch of
space below and even on deck, many had died. And many
more would die, Phillip thought sadly, recalling what he

had seen of conditions in the one-time Turkish barracks at Scutari, now officially converted into a British military hospital. Although perhaps converted was the wrong word . . . it had simply been taken over and re-named.

From the outside or from a ship, anchored some distance from it, the place looked beautiful—a domed palace which the Sultan might well have occupied. But from within—he shuddered. From within it presented a very different picture . . . dank and dark, a maze of long, echoing corridors and large, badly ventilated rooms, the stone floors cracked, the walls streaming with damp. The whole building was dirty and verminous, with no proper provision for cooking and it was deplorably inadequate to house the thousands of sick and injured men who were now beneath its leaking roof, where they lay in long lines, half-naked on the floor, most of them without bedding. Even the arrival of Miss Nightingale and her small band of trained female nurses had, as yet, made very little difference, as far as Phillip could see. The nurses' presence was deeply resented by Dr. Menzies and Major Sillery, the two senior medical officers, and they had been forbidden entry to the wards, where such nursing as there was seemed to be left to a few elderly male pensioners, almost all of whom were untrained and incompetent or, worse still, drunk and quite indifferent to the suffering they were supposed to alleviate.

Phillip expelled his breath in an audible sigh. He had hated leaving the men he had brought from Balaclava in such a place. Those who had survived the rough passage across the Black Sea deserved better than to be transferred from the confines of the *Trojan*'s heaving decks to foul, unwashed stone floors and vermin-infested straw mattresses, which were all that the Barracks Hospital could provide. Yet, he told himself, glancing up at the soldiers being mustered on the *Trojan*'s forecastle for roll call, some did, by a miracle, live through the appalling experience and, having done so, would return once more to serve the guns and man the trenches on the Crimean Upland. Their faded uniforms and pale, glum faces contrasted strikingly with the bright scarlet jackets and healthy, pink and white faces of the newly-arrived men from England and stamped them for what they were. Watching them, as his gig drew nearer to the ship, Phillip wondered how many of his new passengers would live to see the Golden Horn again—or, indeed, their native England.

He was thankful, now, that he had withstood Catriona Moray's plea to take her to visit the Barrack Hospital and still more thankful—having himself paid several visits there—that he had eventually managed to persuade her not to offer her services to Miss Nightingale. He had seen the type of nurses chosen by Miss Nightingale, witnessed the frustration they were enduring, as a result of Dr. Menzies' refusal to permit them to do what they had come to do, and knew that, for a girl of Catriona's birth and upbringing, such service would be difficult, if not impossible. True, she had lived with the women of the 93rd Highlanders in their camp at Kadikoi, following her adventurous escape from Sebastopol, where she had been governess to a Russian nobleman's family. But to the Highland women, she had been one of their own, a laird's daughter, to be protected and sheltered, treated with respect and spared the rigors of camp life on active service, insofar as it lay in their power to spare her.

It was also true that, during the terrible night which had followed Balaclava and the tragic charge made by the Light Cavalry Brigade, Catriona Moray had gone, with the others, on to the battlefield and later to the Hospital Wharf, sharing their toil amongst the wounded. Andrei Narishkin had died in her arms, imagining her to be his wife and comforted because she had encouraged this belief and . . . Phillip's hands clenched fiercely at his sides as he looked back, remembering. Throughout the protracted

41

passage from Balaclava, in strong, often almost gale force winds, she had not spared herself, spending every waking hour among the wounded but . . . this had taken its toll of her. She had not collapsed, as many gently bred young women would have done—Catriona was too courageous to yield to fatigue or allow herself to be overcome by the horrors she had witnessed. So long as sick and dying men had need of her, she had been there, holding a cup of water to parched lips, saying a prayer for the poor fellows who knew their last hour had come, cleaning ghastly wounds and changing befouled dressings. Surgeon Frazer could not praise her or her fellow volunteers enough but all the same . . . Phillip's jaw set obstinately.

He did not regret having taken Catriona to the residence of the British Ambassador and he felt no guilt for having contrived, without her knowledge, to have a telegraphed message sent to her grandfather, Sir Alastair Moray, in Scotland, informing him of her plight. His sailing orders had come before he had had time to do more but he had left her in Lady Stratford de Redcliffe's care, certain that she would be well and kindly looked after by the Ambassador's wife. The *Trojan*'s Master, Mr. Burnaby, had rejoined the ship and so, to make assurance doubly sure, he had also left his brother Graham, with money and instructions to obtain a passage home for her and the widow of a sergeant of the 93rd, who—now that she had lost her husband—was anxious to return to her native Sutherland. They would, in all probability, leave Constantinople within the next day or two, since there were plenty of transports due to sail home almost empty . . . and Graham, detained in any case for a Court of Inquiry in Constantinople, would see to it that she and the sergeant's widow were provided with comfortable accommodation. After which his brother, if the Court found in his favor, would almost certainly be given a Master's appointment and . . . there was a hail from the *Trojan*'s quarterdeck.

"Aye, aye . . . *Trojan*!" The midshipman commanding the gig answered the hail according to custom, his repetition of the ship's name an indication that her commander was aboard the boat.

Phillip, although he had twice previously acted as the *Trojan*'s commander, was conscious of a thrill of pleasure as he listened to the brief exchange and saw the side party mustering at the entry port, ready to receive him with due ceremony. But for how long, he wondered, after they rejoined the Fleet off the mouth of the River Katcha, would he be left in command of his ship? A 31-gun steam frigate was a senior officer's command, as he was well aware, and his own promotion to Commander had been made temporarily by Admiral Lyons, to enable him to clear the last of the wounded from the Hospital Wharf at Balaclava and convey them to Scutari. His step in rank had yet to be approved by Admiral Dundas and confirmed by Their Lordships of the Board of Admiralty and he knew that, even if this should happen, it was unlikely in the extreme that he would be given a command of his own. If Captain Crawford's illness proved to be of comparatively short duration then he, obviously, would resume command of the *Trojan* but if not . . . Phillip rose, as the bowman deftly secured his boathook to the frigate's chains and, waiting his moment as the gig lifted in the gentle swell, mounted the accommodation ladder and swung himself through the entry port with practiced ease.

The boatswain's mates raised their calls to their lips and the pipes shrilled, announcing his return on board. He acknowledged the salute of his First Lieutenant, Martin Fox, who had come to meet him, and together they ascended to the quarterdeck.

"You've completed loading?" Phillip asked formally.

43

"Aye, aye, sir." Martin Fox's good-looking face wore an unusually disgruntled expression, as he made his brief report. A year or two younger than Phillip himself and his closest friend, Fox was normally the most even tempered and placid of men but something, clearly, had upset him now. Whatever it was would have to wait until they were under way, Phillip decided. All was in readiness for sailing, his First Lieutenant assured him, so he said crisply, "Very well. Pipe hands to stations for leaving harbor, if you please. We'll proceed under engines until we're clear of the Bosphorus traffic. . . ." he gave his orders quietly, affecting not to notice Fox's glum face but added, when these had been passed on and the men of the duty watch were scurrying to their stations in obedience to the pipe, "It's Mr. Cochrane's watch, is it not? Well, leave him to make sail—he's perfectly competent—and come to my cabin for a glass of Madeira as soon as we're under way. I have some paperwork to attend to and I want to change out of my shore-going rig, but neither task will take me long."

"Aye, aye, sir," Martin Fox acknowledged. His tone was still formal but, Phillip noticed, it was no longer stiff. Anthony Cochrane, the young red-haired Officer of the Watch, sang out, "Hands to cat the bower anchor, Bo'sun's Mate!" his order echoed in stentorian tones by the petty officer. Cochrane had matured since their arrival in the Black Sea, Phillip thought, watching him as he went efficiently about putting the ship to sea. They had all been affected, in their various ways, after serving under the *Trojan*'s first Captain, the tyrannical Thomas North, but it had, perhaps, taken Cochrane longer than any of the others to regain his natural high spirits and his self-confidence, which Captain North had so persistently sapped.

When opportunity arose, Phillip now gave him responsibility, hoping thus to undo the harm that had been done,

44

and young Cochrane was beginning, not only to accept this but also to display a much higher degree of professional ability and seamanship than any of his brother officers had expected of him. He, more than anyone else on board—with the exception of Phillip himself—had suffered the cruel lash of North's tongue during the voyage out from England. Later he had been subjected to a sadistic bullying and what, at the time, had appeared to be a deliberate attempt on the Captain's part to provoke him into some act of insubordination, which would offer sufficient excuse to have him charged before a court martial and broken. An attempt that ... Phillip's mouth tightened involuntarily. An attempt that had nearly succeeded, both in Cochrane's case and his own. Indeed, the only reason why it had failed had, he reflected, had been North's sudden and completely unexpected death from cholera ... he sighed, seeing again, in memory, as he entered his day cabin, the white, tortured face of his predecessor in command and hearing his agonized cries for help. It was a vision that still haunted him, whenever he used the cabin, after even a brief absence from the ship, for North had occupied it before him and had died in the cot he now slept in.

But ... he thrust the unpleasant memories from his mind and strode briskly into the smaller sleeping cabin where his steward, in anticipation, had laid out his undress uniform. He changed quickly and had almost completed his paperwork when Martin Fox, heralded by a tap on the door, came to join him. He reported the ship's course and position and the orders he had given Lieutenant Cochrane then, at Phillip's invitation, he seated himself and accepted a glass of Madeira, sipping it appreciatively, long legs stretched out in front of him.

"This is a pleasant wine," he observed.

"It was a present from Jack Lyons, after I dined with him aboard the *Miranda* the night before last. He was

45

extremely generous and gave me a cask of it." Phillip signed his name to the report he had been writing and, gathering his papers together, laid them on one side. "Well. . . ." he raised his own glass. "Here's to the Black Sea Fleet! According to Jack, we've seen more action than the majority of the Baltic Fleet although, I gather, his detached squadron had quite a hot time of it in the White Sea. They put landing parties ashore and destroyed enemy fortifications and supplies, occasionally meeting with a very spirited resistance. And with only three frigates, they maintained a successful blockade of the Russian Arctic ports and made raids all along the coastline from Archangel to Tobolsk, besides capturing a most enviable number of prizes. In fact,"—he grinned—"it would seem that all the *Mirandas* have made their fortunes in prize money, though it hasn't yet been paid to them, of course." Warming to his subject, Phillip repeated part of the account Jack Lyons had regaled him with, during their meal, and added thoughtfully, "Jack has the idea that we might do something of the kind with a small steam squadron here. Admiral Dundas isn't likely to agree to it but once Jack's father is Commander-in-Chief, he'll have a much better chance of a sympathetic hearing, I should imagine. Jack's plan is to enter the Sea of Azoff and. . . ." he broke off, suddenly aware that his companion was not really listening. "What is it, Martin?" he demanded.

"What is what?" Martin Fox evaded. But he reddened and murmured an apology. "I'm sorry, Phillip, I . . . oh, it's nothing."

"I think you'd better tell me about it, all the same." Phillip leaned forward, the wine decanter in his hand, to refill both their glasses. "Go on," he encouraged.

The tall young First Lieutenant shrugged. "Very well then. You'll probably think I'm concerning myself unduly with a matter that is not my affair but . . ." he sighed. "I had understood that the troops we are carrying were to be under the command of Major Leach of the 7th Fusiliers. Most of the men are his, with a sprinkling of the 23rd and some N.C.Os of the 19th and 33rd—and they are all men recovering from wounds received at the Alma, like Leach himself, who lost an arm." Martin Fox paused, glumly sipping his wine. "Leach is a delightful fellow," he went on. "He came aboard yesterday, to have a word and to inspect our accommodation and, because he saw at once the state we were in, he sent a working party out—ahead of his main body—to assist in cleaning up and slinging hammocks. So I was very grateful, as you may imagine, because it enabled me to use our men to coal ship and take on water. I thanked him, of course, but he told me to think nothing of it because he owed *you* a debt ... it seems that you and a stretcher party from the *Agamemnon* carried him down from somewhere near the Great Redoubt, after the battle, when he'd been left for dead. And furthermore, Phillip"—Fox permitted himself a quick smile—"he said you'd filled him up with brandy before you attempted to move him!"

Phillip's brows met, as he endeavored to remember the incident. But there had been so many badly wounded officers and men lying where they had fallen beside the Great Redoubt, many of them Colonel Lacy Yea's heroic 7th Royal Fusiliers, who had led the first charge on the strongly entrenched 12-gun Russian battery on the Heights of the Alma.

"I don't recall his name," he admitted, "though I may know his face when I see him again. What are you so concerned about, anyway? With an officer like the Major commanding our troops——"

"Oh, but he's not, Phillip," Martin Fox broke in. "After he and his party came aboard, late last night, and settled in, another boat put off to us ... the Ambassador's *caique,* no less. Laidlaw was on watch and, knowing that *you* were spending the night at the Ambassador's residence,

47

when the *caique* was reported approaching us, he took it into his head that you must be bringing Lord Stratford de Redcliffe on board and that, for some reason, you hadn't been able to warn us. So he turned up the side party and a Marine guard of honor and sent the midshipman of the watch, in a rare panic, to waken me."

"Good Lord!" Phillip smiled. "The Ambassador was entertaining a large party last night, including a number of Turkish Pashas, and it went on until the small hours. I was regaling myself on Turkish coffee and sherbet, in the company of Miss Moray, and listening to a string orchestra until well after midnight, virtually surrounded by dignatories of the Porte." He laughed, enjoying the thought of Martin Fox's discomfiture. "Well, well! And whom *did* you receive with so much undeserved honor?"

Fox set down his wineglass with a clatter, almost knocking it over and his expression, Phillip saw to his astonishment, was anything but amused. His own smile swiftly faded, as his First Lieutenant answered explosively, "We received the most unutterable young swine I've ever had the misfortune to meet in British uniform, Phillip! He came swaggering on board, followed by a sergeant and a couple of orderlies and a mountain of baggage and, with scarcely the courtesy of a greeting, said he felt ill and demanded to be shown to his cabin at once. When he *was* shown to the Second Master's cabin—the only one we had left—he told young O'Hara, who escorted him below, that it was only fit for a pig. Major Leach, who heard this, very decently offered to give up his own, since the fellow was supposed to be ill and, of course, he took it. He's still occupying it and——"

"I'm sure we can rely on Major Leach to teach him his manners," Phillip interrupted, his tone placatory. "In any case, Martin, he's a soldier, isn't he? If so, he's simply a passenger and his behavior is no business of ours. What's his name, do you know?"

48

"His name," Martin Fox replied harshly, refusing to be placated, "is Captain Lord Henry Durbanville. He holds a Guards commission—presumably purchased for him by a rich and indulgent parent—which, according to himself, entitles him to the rank of Lieutenant-Colonel in a mixed force and thus to out-rank Major Leach. So that *he* is in command of our military passengers, not Leach which—ill or not—he wasted no time in pointing out before he retired to Leach's cot for the night."

Still not quite certain why so easy-going a person as Martin Fox should feel so strongly about the new arrival, Phillip said quietly, "He's right about his Guards commission, you know, Martin."

"*Is* he? Do you mean that a little upstart of about twenty, who has never been under fire, is entitled to take precedence over an officer of Leach's age and service, merely because he's a captain in the Guards?"

Phillip nodded. "Strictly according to the letter of the law he is, yes—but in point of fact most of the young Guards officers don't take advantage of it."

"This one has," Fox assured him wrathfully. "And to some tune! Ever since he rose five hours ago, Phillip, he's been throwing his weight about and he's had the troops mustered for inspection twice. The first time, he wasn't satisfied with their turn-out and complained of the filthy state of the uniforms of the recovered men from hospital—as if they could help that, poor devils! Leach tried to explain but Lord Henry wouldn't listen. He ordered them to clean every article of kit they possessed and then mustered them again, with full packs and wearing their stocks, when he kept them standing to attention for over an hour, by my count, whilst he examined each man minutely, from head to heels. Those who didn't pass muster he's put on a charge and threatens to flog."

"To flog?" Phillip echoed, beginning at last to understand the reason for his second-in-command's indignation.

"He won't do anything of the kind on board this ship, don't worry. But surely Major Leach——"

"Major Leach, my dear Phillip," Fox told him, "has been put under arrest and confined to his cabin."

Phillip stared at him, scarcely able to believe the evidence of his own ears. "You can't be serious——"

"I regret to say I am." Martin Fox's expression was grim. "I've been praying for your return because, as commander of this ship, you're the only man who out-ranks the little upstart. I could not interfere—and Leach advised me *not* to—when he was giving his orders to the troops but, in spite of that, I've had a run-in with him."

"Why?"

Fox shrugged his powerful shoulders. "He wanted me to send a boat to pick up his two horses from the Turkish cavalry pound. I refused, on the grounds that we had no space in which the animals could be accommodated and that, in any event, I had no boat to spare for such an errand. He was damned rude to me and the next thing I heard was that he'd sent his sergeant ashore in the duty boat, which went to collect mail—intending, I can only suppose, to try to smuggle the horses on board!" His expression relaxed a little. "The sergeant and the horses hadn't appeared when you returned and ordered me to get the ship under way, so . . ." the ghost of a smile twitched his lips. "We sailed without them, Phillip."

Phillip grinned back at him. "I cannot say that this distresses me unduly, if all you tell me of this young gentleman is true."

"It is, I give you my word. The young so-called gentleman is quite impossible. Er—he intends to report me to my commanding officer, perhaps I should mention."

"For what reason?"

"The reasons are too numerous for me to recall, but they include insolence, sailing without our full complement and being generally obstructive. Thanks. . . ." as

Phillip refilled his glass, Fox laid a hand on his shoulder. "You've almost restored my temper or perhaps it's this excellent wine. But thanks, whichever it was. I confess I was in some danger of losing my sense of humor." He raised his glass, smiling now. "My gratitude, Phillip. You——" there was a tap on the door and he broke off, as a pink cheeked midshipman entered the cabin in response to Phillip's invitation.

"Yes, Mr. Lovell?"

"Sir, the Officer of the Watch requests permission to make sail," the boy announced breathlessly and, eyes half-closed in an effort to concentrate his thoughts, he reported the ship's position. Martin Fox jumped to his feet, but Phillip shook his head, as he dismissed the midshipman with his assent.

"Mr. Cochrane is quite capable of making sail without supervision, Martin," he reminded his second-in-command, when the door closed. "In any case, make sure that your sense of humor is fully restored before you risk another run-in with our double-ranking Guardsman."

Obediently the First Lieutenant resumed his seat. "If you wish. But"—he turned to meet Phillip's gaze—"how do you propose to deal with the infernal fellow?"

"I haven't made up my mind," Phillip admitted. From the deck, he heard the shrilling of the boatswain's mate's pipe and the sound of running feet, as the men on watch answered the string of shouted orders which followed it. "Loose and make all plain sail! Hands away aloft to set tops'ls and jibs! Man the tops'l sheets. . . ." He was silent for a moment, visualizing the topmen swarming up the shrouds, laying out along the yards to let go the topmast halliards and the studding-sail tacks. He hoped that young Cochrane would take care to see that the men were clear in the fore part of the tops and that the outside hands were given time to lay in, clear of the topsail sheets, before he ordered these hauled taut and the sail sheeted home and he waited, instinctively counting the seconds until he heard the order given and again listened to the thud of bare feet, as the men on deck obeyed the shout of "Man the lee braces!"

Soon the pulsating hum of the engines would cease and the ship would take on a new, exhilarating motion as the sails started to fill and Cochrane trimmed her yards. A sailing ship man always, despite his recent familiarity with steam-screw propulsion, Phillip felt his heart lift. Engines were a great convenience, particularly when entering or leaving harbor but there was nothing to touch a fine frigate under sail, nothing in the world and he. . . .

"The glass is falling," Martin Fox observed, distracted from the subject of Lord Henry Durbanville as he too, listened to the sounds reaching them from the deck. "We could be in for a fairly rough passage, if the wind veers to the nor' west. . . ." They discussed the weather prospects and then Phillip said thoughtfully, "Martin, I fancy it might not be a bad idea to invite Major Leach to take a glass of this Madeira with us, before we decide what's to be done concerning his temporary superior."

"The Major is under arrest," Fox reminded him.

"Then he'll require an escort, will he not? Would you care to act in that capacity?"

"With the greatest of pleasure." Again the First Lieutenant got to his feet. "Shall I warn Mr. Cochrane not to set too much sail?" He flexed his feet against the movement of the deck, frowning. "If we strike a sudden squall to windward with what she's carrying now, he——"

"No." Phillip shook his head. "Mr. Cochrane will have seen the glass too and he knows what he's about. Don't wetnurse him, Martin. In any event, Mr. Burnaby will be in the charthouse for some time yet and the boy's not too proud to ask advice from him. If he doesn't, Burnaby will offer it should he deem it necessary." He smiled, hearing the hum of the engines fade and, in the sudden comparative silence, the Master's voice carried quite clearly to them. "There, you hear? Don't worry about Tony Cochrane . . . it is Major Leach we should concern ourselves with, so bring him along, like a good fellow, would you? We may have ruffled feelings to soothe."

Major Leach, however, when he made his appearance in the cabin, did not look in the least ruffled. He was a big man with greying hair, and a tanned, deeply-lined face which betrayed long years of overseas service. As nearly as Phillip could judge, he was in his late forties and he found himself taking on sight to the newcomer. Leach's handshake—made with his left hand, for the right sleeve of his faded scarlet jacket was empty—was firm, his smile cheerful and friendly and, when Phillip invited him to be seated and poured him a glass of Madeira, the smile became an almost boyish grin.

"The last time we met, Commander Hazard," he said, "You made me drunk, for which act of mercy I shall always remember you with the deepest gratitude. This evening, however, I should prefer you to curtail your hospitality, if you do not mind, lest that of insobriety be added to the charges against me!"

He was so evidently amused by the situation that Phillip asked, surprised, "You are not unduly put out then, sir, by the high-handed behavior of your—er—your comrade in arms?"

"I would scarcely call him that but . . ." the Major shrugged resignedly. "No, I am not put out on my own account, Commander. I'm accustomed to finding myself out-ranked by officers of tender years and greater wealth or influence than, alas, I have ever possessed. Believe it or not, until the outbreak of this war I was a Lieutenant, with twenty-three years' service—most of it active service, in India—and little hope of promotion. So at least I'm better off than I was, for I have my majority but . . ." his smile faded. "I am, as I'm sure I do not need to tell you,

53

anxious for the welfare of my men. All of them were wounded at the battle at the Alma River and they have endured a great deal of suffering. To keep such men, who are barely recovered from sickness and severe wounds, standing to attention for almost an hour, with full packs, is not conducive to their continued physical fitness, is it? Or perhaps you are not aware that this was done before your return aboard?"

"Mr. Fox informed me fully, sir," Phillip answered. "Needless to say, this would not have been done had he been able to prevent it. Now that we are at sea I can make certain that nothing of the kind occurs again—by various means which cannot be construed as interference with military discipline."

"I'm immeasurably relieved. But how?"

"Well, the weather will probably help, Major. All the signs point to the likelihood of a rough passage."

"Capital, my dear fellow!" the Major exclaimed. "And the punishments—can you prevent those being carried out?" He glanced at Martin Fox and then back to Phillip, all trace of amusement gone from his face. "Mr. Fox will have told you that three floggings have been ordered? Ordered for men who aren't fit to receive them, as I need hardly tell you."

Phillip met his gaze steadily. "I'm not one who approves of flogging, sir, save for the gravest of offenses. But I am not sure what power I have to prevent these officially —I shall have to consult a manual of Military Law, if you have one you could lend me? And there's also the matter of your own arrest, is there not?"

"I can dig you up a manual, Commander," Major Leach offered. "But my own arrest does not worry me one jot, since it will simply mean that I shall be compelled to keep to my quarters. And that will suit me very well if the passage is as rough as you predict—I'm a poor sailor, I fear. For the rest, the fact that I shall have no duties to

54

perform will be a relief, so long as I know that the recovered men from Scutari Hospital will not be paraded with unnecessary frequency or punished for their inability to turn out like guardsmen in London. Poor fellows, most of them have only the uniforms they stand up in and few have seen the packs they had to leave behind them at the Alma. Those they have were issued to them in hospital and, like myself, they've had to patch up their coatees as best they could. My own, as you can see, would scarcely pass muster at St. James's." His single hand indicated the numerous but all too obviously repaired rents in the scarlet cloth of his jacket and he added, with a wry twisting of the lips as he touched the patch on his empty sleeve, "This still bears the mark of the Minié ball which shattered my arm but the rest are bayonet thrusts, most of them made long after the battle was over. The Cossacks hacked at us where we lay wounded too, as possibly you heard."

"The Cossacks are inhuman," Martin Fox said and shuddered. "They show no mercy to the wounded."

"No. And it is not only the Cossacks. But. . . ." Major Leach dismissed the subject, as if it were still a painful one for him. He questioned Phillip about the Battle of Balaclava at some length and all three officers discussed the present position of the Allied Armies, Phillip supplying a description of the harbor defenses and those on the right flank of the British Army which lay along the Inkerman Ridge.

"You are extremely well informed, for a sailor," the Major observed.

"I acted as naval liaison officer to Sir Colin Campbell and was with the 93rd when the Russians attempted to break through and recapture Balaclava," Phillips explained. "Officially I am still a member of Admiral Lyons' staff and appointed to the *Agamemnon*. My command of this ship is only a temporary one, due to the illness of her commander, Captain Crawford, and I expect

55

to be relieved of it when we rejoin the Fleet. I came out from England as the *Trojan*'s First Lieutenant——"

"I should not, if I were you, mention this to my present superior officer," Leach put in, his tone faintly derisive. "Or he may decide that he out-ranks even you!" He set down his glass and rose, shaking his grizzled, close-cropped head to the offer of more wine. "I thank you, no, Commander Hazard. I will return to my cabin but I do so with a considerable weight taken from my mind. And, to my own astonishment, with the prayer that you may be proven right in your forecast of bad weather. I'm very pleased indeed to have had this opportunity of meeting my preserver at last. Believe me, Hazard, I thought of you often during my stay in hospital—thought of you and blessed your name because, but for you and your splendid seamen, I should not now be standing here." He waved aside Phillip's embarrassed disclaimer and went on gravely, "Mine are splendid fellows too and if, on their account, I find myself once more in your debt, rest assured that I will repay you, should it ever lie in my power to do so." He wrung Phillip's hand warmly. "Goodnight, Commander . . . and thank you."

Martin Fox went with him to his cabin and returned to Phillip's almost immediately with the information that the glass had fallen still further. "The wind's veered a point, too, Phillip. . . ." he went into technical details and added, frowning, "I don't much like the look of things and nor does Mr. Burnaby."

"And Mr. Cochrane?" Phillip questioned, a faint smile lurking at the corners of his mouth.

The First Lieutenant relaxed a little and echoed his smile. "Oh, Mr. Cochrane asked me if I thought it would be prudent to shorten sail and, in accordance with your instructions, I told him that he should judge for himself, while having regard for standing orders and . . . you hear?" His smile widened as the sound of the pipe reached them, followed by shouted orders and the thud of feet, as the watch on deck went to their stations. "Er ... Mr. Cochrane had men standing by the to'gans'l halliards and the weather braces."

"Fine. You told him to keep the fore-course on her?"

"I didn't need to tell him. *He* told me."

"Excellent!" Phillip approved. "Then we may both rest easy. And you have the Morning Watch, when we can expect to run into some weather, so ..." he laid a hand on the younger man's arm affectionately. "I can sleep off my shoregoing excesses without a qualm, can I not, even if the wind does veer to the nor' west?"

"I hope so, my dear Phillip. I—er...." Fox hesitated. "Have you made up your mind as to the line you intend to take with Durbanville?"

"That will rather depend on what line *he* takes, I think. He's done nothing so far to which I can take official exception, has he?"

"N ... no, I suppose not. But he's a nasty piece of work, believe me." Martin Fox spoke with conviction.

"I do believe you. But don't worry, Martin. If necessary, we'll find a way of keeping him under double-reefed tops'ls, should the weather fail to do it for us," Phillip assured him. He smothered a yawn, feeling suddenly very tired. "Let's sleep on it, shall we?"

"Of course." Fox moved towards the cabin door. Reaching it, he turned, eyeing Phillip thoughtfully. "I did not ask you how you fared in the matter of Miss Moray's passage home, which wasn't for lack of concern but rather because we've had so much else to discuss. But I trust all went well?"

"Reasonably well," Phillip answered. He explained what steps he had taken and added, "I have left her in the care of Lady Stratford de Redcliffe and I gave my brother Graham ten days' sick leave, so that he could arrange her passage and escort her to her ship. There are plenty of transports returning home virtually empty, so that I don't think she will have very long to wait."

He had expected his First Lieutenant to take his leave but, a trifle to his surprise, Fox lingered, concerned eyes still searching his face. "Well?" he demanded at last, when his companion still did not speak. "Do you think I should have done otherwise? I had to inform her grandfather of her whereabouts, let him know that she was safe surely?"

"But of course——"

"Well, then?" Phillip challenged, a hint of impatience in his tone. "What else would you have had me do?"

Martin Fox shifted his feet uncomfortably. "Nothing, I suppose. Although she did express a wish to remain in Constantinople, Phillip . . . in fact, she told me that she intended to offer her services to Miss Nightingale at the Military Hospital and I thought——"

"My dear Martin!" Phillip exploded. "Have you been to the Military Hospital? Have you seen conditions there?" He launched into a brief and bitter description of what he himself had seen. "Ask Major Leach, if you imagine I am exaggerating."

"I don't." Fox shook his head. "But were conditions on the wharf at Balaclava any better? Or in *this* ship, with the wounded crammed cheek by jowl with the dead and dying and the cholera victims? Miss Moray helped to nurse them, did she not, without flinching? And her care of you on the wharf probably saved your life."

"True," Phillip admitted, his momentary anger fading, as he recalled with gratitude all that Catriona Moray had done for him. A Russian rifle butt had all but split his skull during the first attack on the Inkerman Ridge and, if he had been left to lie unconscious on the hospital wharf at Balaclava for a second night, he might well have perished. Catriona had searched and had gone on searching until she had found him, she had brought him help, enabled him to return to his ship and Surgeon Frazer's skilled ministrations. Yet for all that ... he sighed. "Martin, I could not let her go on enduring such a strain. I had to send her back to Scotland, to her home ... it was the only thing to do and, I am convinced, the best for her."

"Did *she* think so?"

"Catriona. ..." Phillip broke off, recalling the manner in which Catriona Moray had bidden him farewell. She had been distant, almost cold as if, submissive to his wishes and agreeing to the plans he had made for her, she yet resented having to fall in with these. Had she imagined that he wanted her to leave, he wondered ... did she suppose that he would not miss her? Dear God, *how* he would miss her! His gaze met that of Martin Fox and he shrugged. "No, perhaps she did not, Martin."

"I did not imagine she would," Fox told him. There was an edge to his normally pleasant, deep voice as he went on, "Phillip, no doubt you'll tell me to mind my own business but ... we've been friends, close friends, for a good many years and for this reason I—well, that is, I ..." he reddened, looking down at his feet now and at pains to avoid Phillip's eyes. "I was aware of the regard you had for our little Grand-Duchess, Mademoiselle Sophie—indeed, I had a high regard for her myself. But I cannot help wondering about Catriona Moray, wondering whether you ... whether you entertain any serious feelings for her?"

Phillip hesitated. This was a question he had been careful not to ask himself and he was still uncertain of the answer. Since Mademoiselle Sophie's marriage to the Prince Narishkin, he had resolutely determined to put all thought of her out of his mind, yet the memory of her remained, enshrined in his heart, refusing to be displaced ... even by Catriona. Yet. ...

"You can tell me to mind my own business if you wish, Phillip," Martin Fox said, when he did not at once reply. "It was only that I——"

Harshly Phillip cut him short. "How can I—how can any of us—entertain serious feelings for any woman in such circumstances as these? We are at war, for heaven's sake! None of us may live through it. In any event I've always believed that a professional naval officer is a fool to allow himself to become seriously entangled, at least until he reaches post-rank. We've discussed it, haven't we, many times . . . and you used to agree with me? To make a successful career in the Navy one can have no divided loyalties, no ties on shore and one is best to wait for marriage until one can afford to live decently on half-pay. Besides——"

"And you still feel this?" Fox put in gravely.

"Certainly I do." Phillip's tone was still impatient and a trifle resentful but, for all his effort to do so, he was aware that he did not sound entirely convincing. Perhaps, he thought wryly, because he himself was not entirely convinced; the few short days he had spent ashore in Catriona's company had been enchanting, a glimpse of a world he had almost forgotten, with dinners and receptions at the British Ambassador's palatial residence, good food and wine, cultured conversation during the course of which the war had hardly been mentioned . . . he expelled his breath in a long-drawn sigh. He had answered Martin Fox's question without giving it sufficient thought, had trotted out the old, well-worn sentiments with which impoverished junior officers defended their enforced decision not to marry, until they attained a rank that would enable them to do so without too many financial worries. And . . . he had sent Catriona away. She had not wanted to go but he had insisted, telling himself as well as her that it was for the best. But what was the real reason? Was it not because he was afraid to let her stay, because he. . . .

"In that case, Phillip," Fox said, with finality, "I'll bother you with no more questions. They weren't prompted by mere curiosity—I honestly wanted to know. And you've

60

told me, so. . . ." he smiled. "I'll bid you goodnight. As you reminded me, I have the Morning Watch."

"Good night, Martin," Phillip acknowledged. It was too late, he realized, to correct the assumption his First Lieutenant had made concerning his feelings—or the lack of them—for Catriona Moray. But there was no harm done and later, when he had had more time to give the matter his full and careful consideration, he could bring up the subject again. Mademoiselle Sophie was a dream, as he had so often told himself, and dreams faded, even if they could never be quite forgotten. He thought of her still, he realized, as he undressed, not as the now tragically widowed Princess Narishkin but as the lovely, unsophisticated girl for whom—as Martin Fox had put it—he had formed a high regard during the voyage out from England and who, when he had been a prisoner-of-war in Odessa, had shown him so much kindness until . . . he sighed. Until her marriage to Prince Andrei Narishkin had raised the final, insuperable barrier between them and that barrier remained, in spite of Narishkin's death. It would always be there.

Phillip sighed again and swung himself into his cot. Within a few minutes he was asleep, undisturbed by the increasingly lively motion of the ship as the wind rose in a sudden, blustering squall. He wakened briefly when, during the early hours of the Morning Watch, Martin Fox wore ship and sent hands aloft to put a second reef in her topsails but, confident of the ability of his second-in-command to cope efficiently with wind and weather, he resisted the instinctive impulse to join him on deck and, instead, forced himself to sleep again. The *Trojan* was snugly battened down, her crew experienced and well disciplined and Fox would, he knew, summon him if he were needed.

2

FOR the next forty-eight hours the wind blew up to fresh gale force from the north-west, lashing the waters of the Black Sea into a desolate grey wilderness of spume crested breakers.

With two good men always at her helm and under double-reefed topsails, the *Trojan* weathered the storm without trouble, but the seamen were weary and chilled to the bone when they came off watch and, below decks, conditions were far from pleasant for the over-crowded soldiers. Phillip had, of necessity, to forbid them the upper deck whilst the gale raged, in order to give his own men room to work the ship. In consequence, apart from his daily inspection of their quarters, he saw little of them and nothing at all of Captain Lord Henry Durbanville. The military commander kept to his cabin and, according to Midshipman O'Hara, who was sent by Martin Fox to enquire how he was faring, he was "disgustingly seasick" and quite incapable of carrying out any of his self-imposed duties.

By the morning of the second day, the wind dropped sufficiently to permit one reef to be shaken out of the topsails and by midday, although there was still a strong swell running and the glass remained low, Phillip was able to accede to a request from Mr. Burnaby, the Master, who had the watch, and order the courses set. He had kept an anxious eye on the foremast—replaced after the bombardment of Sebastopol's sea forts less than a month ago—but a careful inspection convinced him that this had stood up well to the gale and was in no danger of being sprung.

A freak change of wind, just before midnight, had carried away the jib-stay and halliards and two men of Cochrane's watch had suffered slight injuries in their efforts to haul down and furl the sodden, wildly flapping sail. But young Cochrane had ordered the helm put down very smartly and the sail had not split. The gun deck had shipped a good deal of water before, with the aid of a swiftly hoisted fore-topmast staysail, he had brought the ship back on course, but the pumps had done their work well and the carpenter's report of the present level of water in the well had brought a smile of satisfaction to Phillip's lips.

Now, with a watery sun lending pale beauty to the scene, the wind had again shifted to a favourable quarter and the *Trojan* was running before it at a lively ten knots and steadily overhauling two steam transports, sighted half an hour before on the same course and both wallowing sluggishly in the heavy swell, with engines going and very little sail set. The sight of the other ships had a cheering effect on all hands and even the soldiers, Phillip noticed, when he made rounds—despite the prevailing dampness of their surroundings—seemed in better spirits. His announcement that they were once more at liberty to take the air on deck was greeted with subdued cheers but evident relief.

Pacing the weather side of the quarterdeck with Martin Fox, a short while after the first scarlet jacket had made a wary appearance on the forecastle, Phillip observed dryly, "The gale did all we hoped for, did it not, my dear Martin? It may have caused some minor inconvenience but it did, at least, succeed in keeping our youthful Guards Captain below out of harm's way. If old Burnaby's calculations are accurate and provided this wind holds, we ought to be off Balaclava soon after first light."

"Yes." Fox nodded. "But did Mr. Burnaby also tell you

64

that he thinks we're in for more dirty weather? Much worse, he maintains, than anything we have hitherto experienced."

"He mentioned it and he could be right. The glass is still falling."

"If he is right," the First Lieutenant remarked feelingly, "I hope we'll be able to put our passengers ashore before it hits us. However, that should not take long once we berth and——"

"If we are permitted to berth in Balaclava Harbor, Martin," Phillip interrupted. He gestured to the ships they were overhauling. "The *Prince* is carrying a cargo of winter clothing, stores and animal fodder for the Army worth half a million pounds, according to Lieutenant Baynton, who is aboard her as Admiralty agent and whom I met in Constantinople. And the *Resolute* carries munitions, sorely needed, by this time, I imagine, for our gun batteries on the Upland. Both are likely to be given priority over us, if the port commander is still under orders to restrict the number of ships entering harbor. Our troops can be landed by tender."

"But, Phillip"—Fox halted, to stare at him in surprise—"surely those orders will have been cancelled by now?"

"I would not be too certain of that," Phillip returned. "In confidence, Martin, I learnt one thing when I was acting as naval liaison officer to Sir Colin Campbell." He paused and then went on, choosing his words with care, "Had it not been for Admiral Lyons, acting in conjunction with Sir Colin, Balaclava would have been abandoned after the first attack was launched on the 93rd's position at Kadi-Koi. Orders had been issued for the harbor to be evacuated but our Admiral had the *Sanspareil* standing by and I carried *his* orders for her to enter and undertake its defense. The decision that the harbor was to be kept clear, even after the attack had been beaten off, was not made by Captain Dacres. Nor was it made by our Admiral."

"Then by whom was it made?" Martin Fox asked, frowning. "I don't think I understand you, Phillip."

Phillip ceased his pacing and drew his First Lieutenant over to the rail. "It is not easy to understand," he agreed. "Until you realize that what the Admiral once described as 'panic counsels' are, on occasions, heeded at Army Headquarters. That was such an occasion and I should not like to gamble on the supposition that anything has changed. Captain Heath of the *Niger* was, as I feel sure I told you, preparing to relieve Captain Dacres as commander of the port when we left. Dacres was ill and he asked to be relieved."

"Yes, you told me. But surely Captain Heath——"

"Captain Heath," Phillip put in, "will be under the same obligation to keep Balaclava Harbor clear of shipping as Captain Dacres was. For heaven's sake, Martin, Dacres is both a humane and a courageous man! You don't imagine that *he* refused to permit transports to enter, in order to take off the wounded, because he wanted to add to their suffering, do you? He had his orders and he had to obey them and so will Heath, whatever his personal feelings."

"Unless the orders are changed. But. . . ." Fox glanced at him uncertainly. "You evidently don't think they will be changed. Why, Phillip? Are you trying to tell me that the—the panic counsels are still being heeded . . . even by Admiral Lyons?"

Phillip shook his head. "Not by Admiral Lyons but perhaps in spite of him. There is, I was told, a strongly felt opinion amongst the Army High Command that Balaclava can't be held without the constant threat of attack and that the troops employed to defend it ought, instead, to be used in the prosecution of the siege. For which reason they believe that the place should be avacuated and abandoned before the onset of winter. I heard this opinion expressed openly at Lord Stratford de Redcliffe's table, both before and after he received the report of a second attack by the Russians—in great strength—on the Inkerman Ridge position."

"The report gave no details, you said—except that the attack had not succeeded?"

"No, nothing except that." Phillip's brows met, as he recalled his own experiences on the thinly held right flank of the British line, when young Hewett's naval Lancaster had done so much to drive off the enemy. But that day the Russians had not attacked in strength; their sortie had, in all probability, been intended merely to test the British defenses and to ascertain which gun sites on the ridge were armed and manned. He sighed, remembering how few these had been and how precarious the whole position had seemed to him . . . even the so-called Sandbag Battery had contained no guns, although prepared for them. Yet the brief and uninformative report which had reached Lord Stratford de Redcliffe had stated that the second attack—like the first and the earlier one on Balaclava—had been beaten off, with what losses to both sides the report had omitted to mention. Balaclava had already cost the British Light Cavalry Brigade. Since the Inkerman Ridge was a vital part of the port's defensive system, God knew what more it had cost in maimed and slaughtered men. . . .

"We shall find out when we rejoin the Fleet," Martin Fox said, as if in answer to his unspoken thoughts. "When did you say the attack took place?"

"On the fifth. And it *was* repulsed. On this point, at any rate, the report was quite definite. The Ambassador read it aloud to us."

"A victory—and yet you still believe that the port of Balaclava may be abandoned?" Fox pursued, his tone puzzled. "Phillip, I have not the advantage, as you have, of service on shore as a member of Admiral Lyons' staff. But to my simple sailor's mind it seems quite essential that we continue our occupation of Balaclava, if the Army is to be supplied and reinforced. As a harbor, it leaves a great

67

deal to be desired, admittedly, and it is too small but ...
we have to have a port, since all supplies come by sea.
And what other is there? The French have Kamiesch and
Kazatch, the Fleet anchorage at the mouth of the Katcha
is, by reason of its distance, out of the question ... so
what is left, if we do not hold Balaclava? Only Sebastopol
itself and God forbid that we attempt another seaward
assault on Sebastopol!"

Phillip shrugged helplessly. "I don't know, Martin. I'm
simply repeating the opinions I heard expressed in Constantinople. Or, possibly more truthfully, putting my fears
into words." He raised his Dollond to his eye, as a string
of signal pennants fluttered to the masthead of the transport steamer *Prince,* with which they were now closing
rapidly. The sixteen-year-old Midshipman Robin Grey,
who was acting as signals officer, responded alertly to his
summons, forestalling the Chief Yeoman, who was also on
watch. The boy had joined the *Trojan* at Constantinople,
after surviving a severe head wound—sustained while
serving with the Naval Brigade—and two months in the
naval hospital ship *Bombay* at Therapia—and already he
had impressed Phillip with his courage and efficiency. He
was skin and bone and still looked desperately ill but he
never complained and obstinately resisted all well-
intentioned attempts to lighten his duties or relieve him of
watch-keeping chores.

Now as he crossed to the weather side of the deck, eyes
bright and eager in his pale, bony young face, Phillip
found himself admiring the youngster afresh. At an age
when most of his contemporaries were still untried school-
boys, Robin Grey was already an experienced naval
officer, his manhood proven and his gallantry recognized
by no less than three mentions in Captain Lushington's
despatches from Naval Brigade Headquarters. He wondered, as the midshipman and his Chief Yeoman checked
the signal flags in their code book, how Lord Henry
Durbanville would shape up, in comparison to Grey.

There were only a few years between them—Martin Fox, he recalled, had said that the Guards officer was about twenty and Grey was a month or so from his seventeenth birthday although, with his small stature and over-thin body, he did not look much more than twelve or thirteen. Nevertheless, the comparison would be interesting . . . lowering his glass, he met Fox's gaze and guessed that the First Lieutenant's train of thought had followed his own when he said quietly, "That is an exceptionally fine boy, Phillip. I hope we'll be allowed to keep him. He's worth twenty Durbanvilles, in my estimation."

"Sir. . . ." Midshipman Grey was at his side, signal pad in hand. "The *Prince* asks us to arrange immediate berthing for her at Balaclava. She has sprung a leak in her forward hold and her pumps are unable to reduce the level of water."

"Thank you, Mr. Grey," Phillip acknowledged. Again his gaze met that of his First Lieutenant. "In the light of our previous conversation, Martin, this is rather an ironic request, is it not? But. . . ." he shrugged. "Make a signal to the *Prince*, if you please, Mr. Grey. 'Will report your condition immediately on arrival.' Oh, and better ask if we can be of any assistance to her now."

"Aye, aye, sir." Young Grey made for the signal locker, the Chief Yeoman at his heels, an approving smile lighting his weatherbeaten face as he touched his hat to Phillip.

"That's a mighty keen young gentleman, sir. It does my heart good to see him at it."

"You hear?" Martin Fox asked, when the two were out of earshot. "It would be a pity to lose that youngster to the Naval Brigade, don't you agree, sir? If you were to contrive a word in the Admiral's ear, then perhaps we should be permitted to hold on to him. Put him on shore in a gun battery again and his keenness would almost certainly get his head shot off, once and for all next time."

"I'll do my best," Phillip promised and added dryly,

69

"For your sake, Martin . . . and that of the *Trojan*'s next commander."

"Don't speak of it, Phillip. If your promotion's confirmed——"

Phillip shook his head regretfully. "I still shan't rate the *Trojan* and you know that as well as I do." He broke off, as Midshipman Grey again approached him. "Yes, Mr. Grey?"

"Sir, the *Prince* requires no other assistance. She intends to keep the *Resolute* in company. She asks, sir, if her barometer reading is accurate. I can give her ours, sir, which I checked with Mr. Burnaby and I should like to send by semaphore, to give my men the practice."

"And what do you make of the barometer reading, Mr. Grey?" Phillip asked, his tone encouraging.

"It's very low, sir, isn't it?" The boy's face was grave. "I should think it could mean a very severe storm, with gale force winds within . . . well, at a guess, sir, within the next thirty-six hours. And——"

"Well?" Phillip invited.

"I read somewhere, sir—in the *Illustrated London News,* I believe it was, when I was in hospital—that the Black Sea is notorious for its winter gales. These begin about November and are intermittent. They rage for a day or so and then the wind drops, just as it has now, sir. But the glass remains low and the wind gets up again, so that it blows a—a succession of gales, over a period of a week or more. The prevailing wind on the Crimean coast is northly, sir, but in the article I read, it stated that the westerly gales are the worst and, of course, they would be for our Fleet, wouldn't they? They would have little protection at anchor off the mouth of the Katcha. Although in port at Balaclava the high cliffs do offer shelter, don't they, sir?"

They did, Phillip thought glumly, as he dismissed Midshipman Grey. They offered a high measure of protection to shipping berthed below their massive, almost perpendicular, red sandstone walls but the whole anchorage was

70

barely half a mile long, with a maximum width of three hundred feet. Even before the order to clear the harbor had been given, merchant and supply ships had been kept beating about outside—often for days—because there was no space available at the congested, makeshift wharves for them to tie up and discharge their cargoes. In anything like a wind, they ran a grave risk of being driven ashore, on to the cliffs, but . . . he stifled a sigh. Perhaps the *Prince* would be lucky. A leaking hold and a cargo for which the commissariat must anxiously be waiting might swing the scales balance in her favor—even if his grim forebodings were right and the decision to abandon Balaclava had been reached, it surely could not be implemented immediately. The troops on shore needed the winter clothing which the *Prince* carried for them, as much as the siege batteries needed the *Resolute*'s powder and besides, if there had been an engagement on the Inkerman Ridge on 5th, then undoubtedly there would be more wounded to be evacuated to the hospital at Scutari. Probably the *Trojan* would again be one of the ships called in to load them from the hospital wharf. He hoped, if this proved to be the case, that he would be able to put back to sea before one of Midshipman Grey's intermittent gales returned to plague him. In the open sea, with room to maneuver, a storm held fewer terrors for him than one which might strike when his ship was lying at anchor off the Balaclava cliffs. He. . . .

"Are you ready to dine, sir?" Martin Fox's voice broke into his thoughts and Phillip glanced up, to see his steward hovering in the lee of the quarterdeck hatchway. He nodded. "Yes, indeed. I hadn't realized what time it was."

He did not, as Captain North had always done, dine in the solitary seclusion of the captain's cabin, but ate in the gunroom* with the rest of his officers, feeling more at home there. Occasionally, more for their sakes than his own, he entertained a few of them in the day cabin and he

* served as wardroom in a frigate

71

took his breakfast there, often with one or two of the midshipmen as his guests . . . the nearest he had come, he reflected wryly, to playing the rôle of *Trojan*'s Captain. But now, on impulse, he decided to do so and called his steward over.

"Serve dinner in my cabin, if you please, Smith. For three . . . no, for four. My compliments to Major Leach and Captain Lord Durbanville and ask them if they would care to join me."

"Aye, aye, sir." The steward departed on his errand and Phillip turned to Martin Fox. "You, too, Martin, if you will."

The First Lieutenant's raised brows betrayed his surprise. "Of course, sir, if you wish," he acceded dutifully. "But——"

"But what, my dear fellow? Remember this may well be my last opportunity to entertain you aboard this ship."

"We'll meet that hurdle when we come to it, shall we? But I was thinking . . . if your aim is to encourage Major Leach and Durbanville to bury the hatchet before they land——".

"Which it is," Phillip agreed. "Carry on."

"Well, why not invite young Grey in my place?" Fox suggested. "His age and his record might . . . well, let's say they might put Durbanville in *his* place."

It was a good suggestion, Phillip decided, and he nodded appreciatively. "They've both recovered from their—er—temporary indisposition—Leach and Durbanville, I mean?"

"The Major has, although he's still keeping to his cabin. I don't know about Durbanville. I haven't set eyes on him since we sailed from Constantinople. Shall I arrange a relief for our Mr. Grey and send him to you in ten minutes?"

"Thanks, if you would. It will be an interesting experiment." Phillip smiled. "Don't you want to watch it yourself? Smith can easily set an extra chair for you and——"

"To be frank," Fox put in apologetically, "I'd rather not, Phillip, if you'll forgive me. I should not eat with the smallest enjoyment in Durbanville's company. I had as much of him as I could stomach the day we sailed." He followed Phillip to the companionway. "You don't mind, do you?"

"No, not in the least." Phillip clapped a friendly hand on his shoulder. "I've no wish to spoil your appetite, my dear Martin . . . though I confess to a certain curiosity concerning the man who can do so!"

They separated, Fox to go in search of Midshipman Grey and Phillip to return to his day cabin where his steward, busy setting covers on the table, told him that both Army officers had accepted his invitation to dine there.

Lord Henry Durbanville was the first to arrive. He entered the cabin, still somewhat white of face but freshly shaven and dressed in an impeccably tailored uniform, his sword buckled on and his bearskin carried, very correctly, in the crook of his arm, as if he were about to parade for guard mounting at Windsor Castle, rather than share a midday meal with his naval host.

"Captain Hazard?" Both tone and bow were formal and both contrived somehow to seem faintly condescending.

"Commander Hazard," Phillip amended. Hospitably he waved the new arrival to a chair. "This is quite an informal gathering and my other guests should not be long. Sit down, will you not, and let me pour you a glass of Madeira?"

"I thank you no, sir." Pale, almost lashless blue eyes met Phillip's in a hostile stare. "There are certain matters which, in my view, should be attended to at once." Still standing to attention, the young Guards officer waited. He was not a particularly prepossessing young man, Phillip thought, returning the stare. His face was inclined to a puffy plumpness, the skin sallow and disfigured by what appeared to be a German duelling scar, running down-

73

wards in a livid line from the left cheekbone to the corner of his small and now tightly compressed mouth. For all the stiffness of his stance, his bearing was curiously unmilitary and his body, like his face, looked unhealthily flabby. Even the expertly cut scarlet coatee, with its new, untarnished rank badges and glittering braid, could not entirely conceal the paunchy corpulence it covered nor disguise its wearer's lack of height.

But perhaps he was prejudiced, Phillip reminded himself, perhaps he was allowing Fox's forcibly expressed opinion to cloud his judgment. "There's no need to stand on ceremony," he suggested mildly and, to add emphasis to his words, resumed his own seat. "I shall, of course, attend to any matter you consider urgent but at least let my steward relieve you of your sword and headgear, so that we may talk in comfort."

"Thank you, I prefer to remain as I am," Durbanville returned uncompromisingly. "You will not find what I have to say to you pleasant."

"Very well." Phillip gave up all attempt to placate his guest. He had liked most of the Army officers he had met, with one or two exceptions, but this young man was, he decided, definitely one of the exceptions. He shrugged and helped himself to a glass of Jack Lyons' excellent Madeira, signaling to his steward to leave them. "If I cannot persuade you to drink or to sit down with me, then perhaps we had better dispose of whatever business you have before our meal is served. I trust that it won't take very long? Er—your name is Durbanville, I believe—Lord Henry Durbanville?"

"It is. My father is the Marquis of Leyton—a close friend of your Commander-in-Chief—and I hold a captain's commission in Her Majesty's Foot Guards." There was no alteration in the studied arrogance of the boy's tone as he went on, "I have a number of complaints that I must bring to your attention, Commander Hazard, con-

74

cerning certain of your officers and the treatment I have received since I boarded this ship."

"Then state them, if you please," Phillip invited coldly. Henry Durbanville had seemed to him at first to cut a figure more likely to inspire merriment or derision than any stronger emotion, but now he was not so sure, becoming himself aware of a far stronger and more primitive emotion than either of these. He must, he knew, keep a tight rein on his temper, whatever the provocation offered, since he could not—as Major Leach had so wisely decided to do—retire to his own quarters, in order to avoid being provoked. And Durbanville, as he started to list his complaints, appeared maliciously eager to provoke him.

The complaints included several slighting references to Martin Fox, whom he accused of incivility and incompetence and who, he insisted, had deliberately deprived him of his two horses and his sergeant, and he dwelt at some length on the discomfort of the quarters allotted to him. Midshipman O'Hara had, he claimed, insulted him; the Surgeon had refused him medical treatment, despite the fact that he had felt unwell when he came on board, and Lieutenant Cochrane had ordered him below when he had sought fresh air on the quarterdeck.

"This morning, when I informed your Officer of the Watch that I wished to parade my men, he told me that—on *your* instructions, Commander—they could not be permitted to muster on deck."

"These are normal instructions when the weather makes it necessary." Patiently, Phillip explained the reason for the instructions he had issued. "I gave permission for your men to come on deck as soon as the weather improved. If you look, you'll see that a number of them are on the fo'c'sle now."

"And not before time," the young Guards officer retorted waspishly. "They have been confined in the most appalling conditions in the bowels of your ship which, I may tell you, is an apt description of its filthy and insanitary

75

state. Indeed, Commander Hazard, I would go so far as to say that I consider this ship a disgrace to the British Navy and I intend, at the first opportunity, to make the fact known to your commanding Admiral who, as I mentioned, is a very close friend of my father's."

Phillip stared at him, shocked into momentary speechlessness by such effrontery. Was this boy quite sane, he wondered, could he possibly be? The threat he had uttered did not worry him unduly—young Durbanville would not find it as easy as he imagined to gain the ear of Admiral Dundas, whatever terms the latter might be on with the Marquis of Leyton. But the malice underlying both threat and complaints appalled him, the more so because it came from one who was little more than a schoolboy. . . .

"You are, I am given to understand"—the insolent voice broke abruptly into his thoughts—"only temporarily in command of this ship? And, indeed, the holder only of the acting rank of Commander?"

"You understand correctly," Phillip confirmed, his voice dangerously quiet. "Is that all you have to say?"

"No, it is not. I wish deck space to be provided, so that I may parade and inspect the men under my command. It is my duty to ensure that they land in good order and I will thank you not to interfere with me in the execution of my duty."

"I have no desire to do so. You are at liberty to muster your men for the purpose of inspecting them, Captain Durbanville, so long as the weather does not worsen."

"Is it likely to worsen?" the boy sneered. "Or don't you know?"

Phillip could feel his temper rising. But it was absurd, he chided himself sternly, to allow this little—what had Martin Fox called him, that first evening?—this little upstart to get under his skin. By tomorrow, he would be gone and it would be left to his own Commanding Officer to put him firmly in his place—which, no doubt, he would do, with very little loss of time.

76

"The glass is falling," he replied, careful to speak without heat. "It seems not unlikely that we shall meet with another gale."

"In that case, I shall order a parade at once," Durbanville told him. "But there is one other matter, before I go ... the matter of the officer I placed under arrest, Major Leach of the 7th Fusiliers."

"Pray continue," Phillip bade him. But before this invitation could be accepted, there was a tap on the cabin door. The Marine sentry threw it open and Major Leach came in, followed by Midshipman Grey. Both were smiling, evidently over some jest they had shared on their way to his quarters, and both were bare-headed, Leach in his faded coatee with its patched bullet holes, the empty sleeve hanging limply at his side. Phillip rose to welcome him but Durbanville, his sallow face suddenly suffused with angry color, moved to place himself in the Major's path.

"I have just had occasion to remind Commander Hazard that I placed you under arrest," he said waspishly. "Is it necessary to remind you, sir—who profess to have so much more service than I—that an officer under close arrest is in honor bound to remain in his own quarters, until released? And I do not recall having released you."

Leach's smile faded. For an instant, he looked surprised but then, recovering himself, he answered indifferently, "As you wish. I might point out that I could escape no more easily from the Captain's quarters than from my own but ... I will return there, if you insist." He turned to Phillip apologetically. "I ask your indulgence, Commander Hazard."

Phillip went with him to the passage-way. Out of earshot of his tormentor, the Fusilier officer said dryly, "His attack of *mal de mer*—which I believe was severe—has not sweetened his temper, has it?"

"It has not," Phillip agreed, with feeling. "He has described my ship as a disgrace to the British Navy and

77

threatened to make its filthy and insanitary state known to my Commander-in-Chief!"

"Not seriously?"

"Well, he seems to *be* serious. I console myself with the thought of what his own C.O. will do to him, when he joins his regiment." Phillip smiled and saw the Major echo his smile.

"Yes, indeed, that is a consoling thought. A strange young man, is he not? Thank God there are not too many like him in the British Army ... or in the Navy, come to that. I am sorry about the meal. I had looked forward to dining with you and indulging my newly returned appetite."

"I can countermand the boy's orders, if you wish," Phillip offered but the older man shook his head.

"No, no, don't bother. I'll eat in my cabin. We shall both be rid of him by tomorrow, shall we not?"

"It's to be hoped we shall!" Phillip said emphatically. On his return to his day cabin, he found Midshipman Grey facing their guest in constrained silence. Durbanville bowed to him stiffly and took his leave without apology. When he had gone, Phillip motioned the boy to seat himself at the table, calling to his steward that they were ready for their meal.

"Only for two, sir?" the man questioned, puzzled. "I understood you to say that the two military gentlemen were going to join you ... and I gave them both your message, sir. The Major——"

"See that the Major is served in his cabin," Phillip ordered. "Mr. Grey and I will dine here."

Young Grey said nothing, until the steward had served their first course and they were alone. Then, his voice oddly shaken, he said, "I know Durbanville, sir—I was at school with him. Not for long, of course, because I left to go to the Royal Naval College and I was three years younger, so I did not know him well. And I doubt if I'd

78

have recognized him ... I mean, it's a long time ago, and he's put on quite a lot of weight."

Phillip eyed him thoughtfully. "You hadn't seen him since he came aboard then?"

"No, sir. That is, not to speak to—I saw him when he joined, in the Ambassador's *caique*. We all did, it caused quite a stir. And, of course, we all ragged Paddy O'Hara about that, because *he* reported to Mr. Laidlaw that His Excellency was on his way out to us, and turned up the side party *and* a guard of honor!" The midshipman grinned, obviously still savoring the joke. "O'Hara was furious, sir, but we didn't allow him to forget it."

Phillip, with vivid recollections of what the humorists of the midshipmen's berth could make of such an incident, was hard put to it to suppress a smile. "It was an understandable mistake," he suggested.

"Oh, yes, sir, I know. Any of us might have made it." Tucking in manfully to the enormous helping of roast mutton the steward had given him, young Grey observed appreciatively, "I say, sir, this is awfully good."

"I'm glad to see you're doing justice to it."

"Oh, yes, indeed, sir. I doubt if Durbanville would have, though. O'Hara paid a visit to him in his cabin yesterday—the First Lieutenant sent him to find out how he and Major Leach were getting along—and he said that Durbanville was in a shocking bad way."

"Disgustingly seasick was O'Hara's verdict, I believe," Phillip supplied.

"Not only that, sir." Robin Grey's ingenuous blue eyes met his with sudden gravity. "Paddy—Mr. O'Hara, sir— said the fellow was in tears. In tears, sir, can you imagine that?"

Oddly enough, Phillip thought, he could and found himself wondering anew about Henry Durbanville. Did the clue to his strangely unpleasant and contradictory character lie, perhaps, in his schooldays? Had his behav-

79

iour then given any hint of the sort of young man he was to become?

"What was he like at school, Mr. Grey?" he asked curiously. "Can you remember?"

Midshipman Grey pushed his empty plate aside with a satisfied sigh. The steward served their second course and he waited, fair brows puckered in concentration, until the man withdrew. "Yes, sir," he answered, "I do remember. Durbanville was a bit of a swine. Not to me personally, but to some of the other fellows . . . especially the new ones. When I was there, he wasn't senior enough to have a servant, only the prefects and Sixth Formers had them but he . . . well, he bent the rules rather and made some of them do his chores for him. If they objected, he beat them. I can remember that very well, because one poor little devil was brought into the san., and I was there, with a billious attack. Durbanville had laid it on too thick, sir, in this boy's case. He cut him about the face with his cane and there were weals all over him, not only on his posterior, which he couldn't hide."

"Didn't Durbanville get into trouble over that?" Phillip enquired.

Grey shook his head. "No. The kid was a well-plucked 'un, he didn't give him away. But he told *me* who had beaten him and I wasn't altogether surprised—surprised that it was Durbanville, I mean, sir."

"Why not?"

"Well, sir, he was known as 'Bully' Durbanville and some of the chaps used to call him 'Hateful Harry.' No one liked him much, not even the fellows in his own House—in fact, I don't think he had a really close friend, not at school, anyway." The boy hesitated, looking down at his piled plate and then, a trifle uncertainly, at Phillip. "He was always throwing his weight about and boasting about his father's importance and influence, the people he knew and his money. At the time, sir, his father hadn't a title, he was just plain Mr. Durbanville . . . that was why I didn't realize that Lord Henry Durbanville was the fellow I was at school with. Although I suppose I should have done ... it's an unusual name and I can recall his saying once that his father would eventually inherit a title from a cousin. But none of us took him seriously then—I mean, he was always making the most extraordinary claims, which we knew couldn't be true, so we didn't believe that one. The only one we *did* believe was the story about his Pater having money, because Durbanville never seemed to go short. He had a purseful of sovereigns on him usually and he spent them pretty freely. He seemed to think that money could buy anything."

"But you don't think it can?" Phillip suggested.

Young Grey shook his head. "Not *anything,* sir. Oh, it can buy a lot, I know but not the kind of things that Durbanville tried to buy. Things like ..." he reddened. "Well, things like friendship and popularity, which have to be merited. I think he wanted people to like him but somehow they didn't and so he put the best face he could on it and tried to pretend he didn't care. He was rude to everyone and insolent to the masters and he used to talk awfully big, sir, in the hope that it'd impress people. I—er—" the boy's color deepened and spread. "I overheard part of what he was saying to you, sir, when Major Leach and I were waiting outside in the passageway, and to tell you the truth, sir, Durbanville sounded just like he used to at school. And you noticed the scar on his face, didn't you, sir?"

"I did, yes. I imagine it's a duelling scar, of the kind they inflict on each other at German universities, isn't it? Did he go to a German university?"

The midshipman nodded. "Yes, I believe he did, sir, and I don't suppose that improved him. I mean, in Germany the officer class behave like little tin gods, don't they, sir? The Army officers, that is ... and Durbanville hasn't been in the Army for very long, so possibly he imagines this is the manner in which he's expected to behave, if you see what I mean, sir."

Out of the mouths of babes and sucklings, Phillip reflected. This particular babe had shed a good deal of light on the complex character of Lord Henry Durbanville and now he was able to regard the arrogant young Guardsman, if not with liking, at least with a measure of understanding. If Grey was right, he was the product of an over-indulgent and wealthy father who, no doubt, had purchased him his captain's commission—in one of the most expensive regiments in the British Army—for the purpose of family aggrandizement. And he had come out here, with no previous experience of soldiering at all, intent on proving his right to the rank he held and yet, probably, with the secret fear that others might dispute it. That he was in for a rude awakening seemed inevitable . . . but perhaps he would learn, as other men had learned amid the harsh realities of war, that there was more to soldiering than strutting round in a resplendent uniform and giving orders to men of the caliber of Major Leach. It might be the making of him, if he survived and, in the meantime, Phillip supposed, Henry Durbanville would have to be tolerated, but he hoped fervently that there would be no delay in putting the young man ashore. In a way, it was a pity that the weather had improved since, alone in his cabin suffering the pangs of *mal de mer,* he had caused no trouble. But now. . . .

"Do you think I'm right, sir?" Midshipman Grey had demolished the contents of his plate and he looked up expectantly to meet Phillip's gaze.

"About Durbanville? Well, it's an interesting theory and I shall bear it in mind, youngster. I'd be obliged, though, if you did not repeat this conversation to your messmates. We'll keep it to ourselves, shall we?"

"Yes, of course, sir," the boy assented readily enough but he looked a trifle crestfallen and Phillip smiled at him.

"Would you like a second helping of that duff, Mr. Grey?" he invited.

The promptings of a healthy appetite fought a losing battle against Midshipman Grey's reluctance to abandon his newly-acquired rôle of amateur psychologist and adviser to the Captain. "Indeed I would, sir," he admitted truthfully. "If I may, sir."

The steward, summoned to replenish his plate, did so with a lavish hand. There would not, Phillip thought, amused, be very much left of the meal which had originally been ordered for four. But, throughout the British Fleet, the midshipmen's messes were notoriously ill-supplied, their rations meager and their mess bills severely limited. It was therefore hardly surprising that when invited to dine with their seniors, the "young gentlemen" took full advantage of the opportunity to eat their fill of wardroom fare and, spooning large quantities of the sticky but sustaining plum duff into his eager mouth, young Robin Grey slipped easily back into the more familiar rôle of ever-hungry mid. By the time coffee had been served—steaming hot and in large cups—his bony young face was wearing a sleepy and very contented smile. He would, Phillip felt reasonably certain, be more inclined to regale his messmates with an exaggerated account of the hospitality he had enjoyed in the Captain's day cabin than to repeat what he had seen or heard there—or even to mention what he had himself contributed to the conversation. The subject of food, in any case, was of more interest to his listeners than that of Henry Durbanville since, with the exception of O'Hara, none of the midshipmen had had any contact with him.

And until Durbanville left the ship it would be better so, Phillip decided, as he dismissed Durbanville's schoolfellow with the friendly suggestion that he had better "cut along and sleep it off." He wanted no more trouble between his officers and their awkward passenger and, on the passenger's part, no further cause for complaint,

83

whether or not his complaints ever reached Admiral Dundas. Relations between the two services were on the whole very good, with seamen and soldiers serving side by side in the gun batteries on the Upland, sharing in their defense and, on occasions, mounting combined attacks or supporting each other's sorties. Apart from the Naval Brigade of over 1,700 officers and men, 1,500 Marines and Marine artillerymen had been landed to take part in the siege and, in addition, much of the military transport was undertaken by ships of war and, on this account, it was of some importance to preserve mutual respect and cordiality between Navy and Army, as Phillip was well aware. While the presence of passengers, with the inevitable overcrowding and loss of efficiency this caused, was never wholeheartedly welcome aboard any naval vessel, so far as his own ship was concerned he hoped that nothing would occur to change the pattern.

Had Major Leach been in command, he would have had few worries, but with Captain Lord Henry Durbanville . . . his brows met in a pensive frown. Durbanville's lack of military experience was the danger but, by this time tomorrow, God willing, the fellow would be gone. Until then . . . Phillip sighed. He could only hope that, by exercising forbearance, no untoward incident would occur which might lead to trouble.

3

PHILLIP'S hopes were, however, rudely shattered. Ascending to the quarterdeck in response to an urgent summons from Lieutenant Laidlaw, who was on watch, he saw that Durbanville had paraded his men, lining them up to form three sides of a square, with himself, two ensigns and half a dozen senior N.C.Os forming the fourth. They occupied every available foot of the forward part of the upper deck, each man in parade order, with the exception of three who, clad only in shirts and blue overalls, stood under guard in the center of the square. Their appearance made Durbanville's intentions self-evident and Phillip swore softly under his breath.

"I thought I had better call you, sir," Lieutenant Laidlaw explained. "Although Captain Durbanville assured me that you had given your consent to his parading his men."

"I gave him permission to parade them for inspection, Mr. Laidlaw," Phillip answered, tight lipped. "But not for this, as I need hardly tell you." He felt a sudden cold anger well up inside him, felt the sour taste of it in his mouth. *"Did* he inspect them?"

"Yes, indeed, sir," Laidlaw said with distaste. "It took him something over an hour and. . . ." He was interrupted by the arrival of Martin Fox, who had just time to warn him that Major Leach was on his way when the Major himself came striding across the quarterdeck to join them.

"Commander Hazard"—his face was white and beaded

with perspiration but he spoke with controlled calm—"the men whom that unspeakable little pup is proposing to flog are all *my* men, they're all of the Seventh. Two of them received severe wounds at the Alma and the other has only lately recovered from the cholera. He could kill them, if he only lays on half the number of lashes he's ordered! I cannot stand by and see it happen, although I have put up with the farce of my arrest with cynical tolerance until now, in the belief that I might thereby spare you unpleasantness. That was a mistake, of course, and I'm ready to accept the blame for my error of judgement. But now, in God's name, sir, I must beg you, as Captain of this ship, to use your authority to put a stop to what is going on."

Phillip drew in his breath sharply. He had not wanted it to come to this, had not wanted a trial of strength between himself and the military command, as represented—however temporarily—by Durbanville. But the arrogant young fool had now made this impossible to avoid and, in the interests of justice and humanity, his own course was plain. He could not permit men, only recently discharged from hospital, to be flogged for no more serious a crime than failure to pass a kit inspection—but his authority, as the *Trojan*'s commander was unhappily much less plain. He knew that he could not forbid the punishment but he could surely demand an explanation or even, if necessary, try to reason with Durbanville? The boy could refuse, of course but . . . he hesitated only momentarily, having an alarming vision of what might afterwards be made of his action and then, turning to Martin Fox, he said formally, "Mr. Fox, be good enough to present my compliments to Captain Lord Durbanville and ask him to step aft to the quarterdeck so that I may have a word with him."

"Aye, aye, sir," Fox acknowledged, an understanding gleam lighting his eyes as they met Phillip's. For the sake of discipline, even Durbanville must not be humiliated in the sight and hearing of his men but Fox would deliver his message correctly, Phillip knew, phrasing it as a request and thus affording the young Guards officer the opportunity to withdraw without loss of dignity. It also offered him a chance *not* to withdraw, he realized, but that chance would have to be taken. He could not order an Army officer to attend him on the quarterdeck without good and sufficient reason and the fact that he did not approve of the manner in which that officer chose to discipline the men under his command was not anything approaching a sufficient reason. He nodded to Midshipman O'Hara who, as Midshipman of the Watch, was standing alertly by.

"Accompany the First Lieutenant, Mr. O'Hara."

O'Hara obeyed with alacrity, unable to suppress a delighted grin as he sped after Fox. From beside him, Phillip heard Major Leach give vent to a sigh of relief. "Thank you, Commander." His voice was low. "I am indeed sorry to have placed you in so invidious a position but rest assured that I shall back you up to the hilt in any action you may deem it necessary to take. This unfortunate affair is entirely my fault—I should not have let that obnoxious young man supercede me in command."

"No, Major. The blame for it is equally mine," Phillip told him ruefully. "*I* shouldn't have given permission for the parade to be held. I'm afraid I gave it because I was in danger of losing my temper with Durbanville and, at the time, it seemed the easiest way to get rid of him. I was a fool—I should have known better!"

"I overheard the manner in which he sought your permission," Leach confessed. "And, in your place, Hazard, I'd have done as you did. Or worse still, lost my temper with him."

His admission was consoling but Phillip, watching Martin Fox, apparently engaged in an argument with Durbanville, was conscious of a gnawing anxiety. He had based his hopes on the belief that even Durbanville would not refuse his First Lieutenant's courteously worded request but this, it seemed, was precisely what he was about to do. As if to confirm his assumption, he saw Midshipman O'Hara break away from the square of scarlet-jacketed soldiers to head towards him at the double.

"Sir!" The youngster was pink cheeked with indignation and obviously shocked by the implications of the message he had been charged to deliver. "He—that is Captain Durbanville, sir—told the First Lieutenant that he could not interrupt the—the performance of his military duty in order to comply with your request, sir, but that he would be pleased to do so, *after* he has dismissed the parade. He said he craved your indulgence, sir. But . . ." O'Hara swallowed hard and lapsed into his own, more normal vocabulary as he went on breathlessly, "That's just eyewash, I think, sir. He has the gratings rigged at the gangway and a man standing by with the cat and, when we got there, sir, he was reading from the—the Articles of War. I don't believe he has any intention of reporting to you until the floggings have been carried out, sir, and I heard one of the soldiers say that he——"

Phillip silenced him with a crisp, "Thank you, Mr. O'Hara. You may carry on." But the youngster did not move, continuing to regard him with stunned astonishment. In the whole of his brief naval career Midshipman O'Hara had never heard an order questioned, in this ship or any other, least of all an order issued by his Captain, however it was phrased, so that his astonishment was, perhaps, understandable. And under Captain North's command . . . Phillip's mouth hardened. In a situation like this, would North have worried about regulations or doubted either his right or his power to flout them?"

"Sir," O'Hara ventured apprehensively, with a swift glance over his shoulder, "Surely this—this is mutiny, isn't it, sir?"

"No, Mr. O'Hara," Phillip said curtly. Technically it was not, he reminded himself, if his interpretation of the manual of military law lent him by Major Leach was correct. It seemed reasonable to suppose that Durbanville knew it was not, since no doubt he had also studied his manual and would therefore be aware that, when on board one of Her Majesty's ships—even in time of war— the officer commanding troops on passage was responsible for the good order and discipline of his men. The regulations did not provide for the ship's Captain to overrule an order given by the military commander to his own men, unless its execution were likely to endanger or interfere with the efficient working of his ship which, in effect, meant that . . . Phillip's hands clenched at his sides, as he saw Martin Fox walking aft to rejoin him. His First Lieutenant's step was slow and measured, his tall body ramrod stiff—unmistakable signs of a sorely tried temper.

"Commander Hazard. . . ." Major Leach's voice in his ear was low and urgent. "You have, in my view, done all you officially can in this unfortunate affair. I fancy it is now up to me, so with your permission, sir I——"

"What do you propose to do, Major?" Phillip demanded bluntly. "*You* are officially still under arrest, as I need hardly remind you."

"No, you need not," Leach returned with feeling. "But—" he gestured to where one of his fusiliers, stripped to the waist, was being secured by his wrists to a grating, which stood on one end and had been lashed in position at an angle to the gangway. "That infernal young sadist is quite determined to have his own way, as you can see. I cannot, in all conscience, stand by and watch him flog a good soldier to within an inch of his life . . . and a man of my own regiment at that. I cannot, Hazard, and to hell with the consequences! I propose to ignore the fact of my arrest—or ask you, as Captain of this ship, to release me. Damn it, I don't care how we get round the difficulty! I am going to take over that parade and order those men released . . . and I shall be obeyed, never fear. The Seventh form the bulk of the contingent. They'll accept my authority and gladly."

"I don't doubt that, Major," Phillip conceded. Leach started to move but he laid a detaining hand on the older man's arm, as Martin Fox approached them. "The consequences to you could be disastrous, sir. However little we may like it, Durbanville is within his rights, you know."

"And he's only too well aware of it, Major," Fox put in, his voice shaking with controlled fury. "I've had every damned regulation he can think of quoted at me and even the Articles of War have been flung in my face! He's either mad or . . . God knows what he is! But as Commander Hazard says, sir, according to the letter of the law, he *is* within his rights, as senior ranking military officer. And he has an Army surgeon present, who will stop the punishment if necessary. I managed to obtain his assurance on that point, at least." He lowered his voice. "Believe me, sir, I could cheerfully murder the damned young swine and I hold no brief for what he's doing but—if you attempt to intervene, he'd have a strong enough case against you to have you broken. He as good as told me so just now and I honestly think it's what he *wants* you to do—or any one of us, come to that—so I beg you to have a care, sir."

From the gratings came a high pitched agonized cry and they could hear, quite clearly, the hissing swish of the cat being expertly laid on. Leach, almost beside himself, turned a white, tormented face to the two naval officers. "If I don't intervene, Mr. Fox, who is going to? A divine providence, perhaps? I'm sorry but I no longer believe in miracles, I——" Phillip cut him short.

"Wait, Major, please." His brain was suddenly clear and ice cold, as an idea came to him and he spoke with elation, his gaze on the sky to windward, from whence the

90

idea had come. "Providence is about to intervene, if we can offer some assistance and I fancy we can. Martin, do you see what I see?"

Martin Fox followed the direction of his gaze, his expression blank at first and then a smile of understanding spread slowly across his face as he, too, glimpsed the ominous, scudding clouds. "A miracle indeed!" he agreed, with heartfelt relief. "And not before time . . . shall I warn Laidlaw?"

Lieutenant Laidlaw, however, on the lee side of the quarterdeck, had also seen the approaching squall. In obedience to standing orders and because this was the usual procedure in squally weather, he prepared to shorten sail and pay the ship's head off, allowing himself plenty of time in order to have the topmen safely back on deck and the rest of the men ready to go below, out of the rain, before the squall struck. It looked a heavy squall but he decided that he would have between five and ten minutes to make the ship ready to meet it and, aware that his commander and the First Lieutenant were crossing the deck towards him, he called out an order to the man at the helm before turning to the senior boatswain's mate.

"Pipe hands to stations for shortening sail, Bo'sun's Mate. In spanker and upper sails, down jib. And I'll have the lower yards braced. Man lee sheets and braces and——"

"Belay that, Mr. Laidlaw," Phillip told him and, to the helmsman, "Steady, Quartermaster! Very well thus."

"Sir?" Laidlaw exclaimed, scarcely able to believe the evidence of his own ears. He gestured in the direction of the racing clouds, pregnant with the dark threat of rain. "Sir, there's——"

"I want two men on the helm, if you please, Mr. Laidlaw—two good men," Phillip returned crisply. "I'm going to luff her into that squall."

"*Luff* her, sir? But——" Young Duncan Laidlaw stared

91

at him, his jaw dropping in ludicrous bewilderment. According to his training and experience, to luff a square-rigged vessel in these conditions could only result in the sails being taken aback and the ship becoming unmanageable. He seemed about to offer a diffident warning but hurriedly changed his mind when Martin Fox put in curtly, "You heard what the Captain said, Mr. Laidlaw."

"Aye, aye, sir," Laidlaw acknowledged. His face was a study as he glanced from one to the other of his two seniors, as if fearing that both had taken sudden and inexplicable leave of their senses. He had, of course, witnessed the punishment parade but, occupied with his watchkeeping duties and—since serving under Captain North—averse to the barbarity of the spectacle, had deliberately paid less attention than they had to what was going on. In consequence, he failed to see any connection between the orders he had just been given and the fact that, as he had expected, when he had first reported the nature of the parade, a soldier was receiving a brutal flogging. But he was too well trained to ask for an explanation and Phillip, at that moment, was too busy to supply him with one as, his glass on the sky to windward, he sought to assess the strength and speed of the squall and con his ship to meet it.

Duncan Laidlaw, accepting his authority without another word, waited at his elbow and, whilst the two boatswain's mates stood by expectantly, he relayed his commander's orders and, when required, acted upon them with faultless efficiency. Once or twice, when the watch had still not been piped to stations for shortening sail, he glanced up at the looming storm clouds and frowned, apprehensively aware of the press of sail the ship was carrying and of the increasing strength of the wind in his face. But his faith in Phillip Hazard's seamanship had stood the test of time; so, too, had his loyalty and, he reminded himself, the responsibility was no longer his. When the

Captain had assumed command, his duty as Officer of the Watch was simply to do as he was told and it was, in any case, becoming evident to him that—far from taking leave of their senses—his two seniors knew exactly what they were about and were acting in concert.

He saw the First Lieutenant go forward, heard him shout something which sounded like a warning to the red-jacketed square of soldiers but not a man moved and Fox returned, moments later, gravely shaking his head.

"No use, sir," Laidlaw heard him say. "He's affecting deafness."

"Well, he's been given a chance," Phillip answered, his voice clipped. "It's going to be a close-run thing, Martin, and I don't want to take any more risks than I have to . . . I think we'll turn up both watches. She's likely to ship quite a lot of water when the time comes and the topmen will have to work fast, because our margin of error may well be too small for comfort. Those soldiers have *got* to go below—we can't have them cluttering up the deck for very much longer."

"They're not too happy now, sir," Fox told him, "I don't give them much longer once this sea gets up."

In the center of his closely packed square, Henry Durbanville did not, at first, sense the growing uneasiness of the men grouped about him and, intent only on the completion of the task he had set himself, he had taken in very little of what the First Lieutenant had endeavored to tell him. The fellow had bawled at him through some sort of speaking trumpet that distorted his voice, he thought indignantly. In any case, Fox had already demanded his presence on the quarterdeck once before which—quite rightly—he had answered with a firm refusal. He knew from whom the demand had really come . . . Major Leach, of course, had prompted it in his wholly unjustifiable anxiety to spare his indolent, slovenly fusiliers from the punishment which their filthy turn-out had earned them. They needed to be disciplined, the whole unruly horde of so-called heroes of the Alma, and not pampered, as Leach appeared to believe.

He despised Leach, both for his softness with the men he was supposed to command and for the fact that he was so palpably not a gentleman. True he held a Queen's commission but it was well known that professional officers, in regiments of the line, were *not* gentlemen in the accepted sense, since they were dependent on their pay and could not afford to purchase promotion. A gentleman, with proper pride in his regiment, would never have permitted his men to parade for inspection in the state in which Leach's fusiliers had appeared—he would have paid for new uniforms for them, out of his own pocket if need be. He. . . .

"Captain Durbanville . . ." the surgeon was beside him looking agitated. "In my opinion as medical officer, the prisoner cannot stand further punishment. I should be obliged if you would order his release at once."

Henry Durbanville, not liking his peremptory tone, was tempted to reject his request but a glance at the semiconscious figure, hanging limply by the ropes which secured his wrists to the top of the grating, brought a swift change of mind. The man's back was reduced to a bleeding pulp, he saw, and was astonished for, after his first scream of pain when the lash had bitten into his flesh, he had borne his punishment in stoical silence.

"How many lashes has he had?" he enquired, having lost count when Lieutenant Fox had been yelling at him.

"A dozen and a half. But he——"

"I ordered him two dozen. Oh, all right, cut him down if you think he's had enough. Surgery's your trade, not mine." There were still two more of Leach's fusiliers to be disciplined, Henry Durbanville reminded himself. He hoped they would be made of sterner stuff than the first fellow and also that Leach was still skulking about on

94

deck, where he could see them, even if it did mean that he had broken his arrest ... he sighed, as he watched the sagging body slither down from the grating. Even the bucket of salt water with which it was doused failed to bring any reaction .. Durbanville passed his tongue over his lips, feeling them oddly dry.

He had never witnessed a flogging before and, although he had, of course, read every detail of the procedure and heard the scene described by various brother officers, until now he had not realized what a dramatic spectacle it all made. The solemn roll of a single drum, the reading of the requisite extract from the Articles of War and of the sentence, the glum expressions of the men and, in particular, the sick terror in the eyes of the prisoner as he was led to the gratings ... he sighed again.

It had been quite a novel experience and had had a much greater emotional effect on him than the illicit cockfighting he had watched, as a boy, in one of his father's barns. And to be in command, wielding almost the power of life and death, with every man's eyes on him—a few rebellious but most of them awed and all of them, standing there silent and motionless, because he had ordered them to do so. They would not move now, until he dismissed them. He had even—quite correctly, in the circumstances—defied the ship's acting Captain and, Durbanville told himself, he would continue to defy him, as well as ignore the messengers he sent, until his duty was done. He would teach them to respect him, from the Captain to the deck-hands, from Leach to the youngest drummer boy ... he felt the ship lurch and became uneasily conscious that the deck beneath his feet was no longer as steady as it had been. There had been a certain amount of motion but he had believed that his stomach had overcome its earlier queasiness. Now, as a wave of nausea swept over him, he was not so sure.

God, if it was rough again, as damnably, miserably

95

rough as it had been during the past few days! He had always been a poor sailor, hating the sea but he could not, he must not disgrace himself in front of these men, just when he had got their measure and taught them the sharp lesson they had all needed . . . dear God, he must not do that! Impatiently he brushed aside the objections the surgeon was attempting to make in regard to the second prisoner, having scarcely bothered to listen to them. The wretched fellow was a soldier, was he not? Well, then . . . the ship seemed to have steadied a little and he read out the sentence, conscious of a sense of extraordinary elation, which banished his nausea, as the prisoner looked up with mutely pleading eyes to meet his own stern gaze.

He was an elderly man, with a pale, thin face and greying hair and, as he was stripped of his shirt, an imperfectly healed scar could be seen, running in a livid line from one side of his bony chest to the other.

"What the devil's wrong with him?" Durbanville asked the surgeon, shocked in spite of himself by the sight of the hideous wound.

"This man was sabered by the Russians and left for dead, Captain Durbanville, as I've tried to explain to you. He was also commended for gallantry by his commanding officer." The surgeon was young and he was rapidly losing patience with the arrogant Guards officer who, although even younger than himself, was—for the time being, at least—his military superior. Unlike Durbanville, he had heard the First Officer's warning of an approaching squall and was worried lest, by delaying for too long on deck in order to complete these infamous punishments, any of the men should suffer injury. In bad weather, their place—as passengers—was below and, encouraged by Durbanville's silence, he pointed this out in no uncertain terms, the ship's renewed pitching and a flurry of rain adding emphasis to his words. He had expected to provoke an

96

outburst but, somewhat to his surprise, Durbanville nodded.

"Damn the weather," he said, quite mildly. "I'm not concerned with that and these infernal sailors make rules to suit themselves. However, if this man is not fit to take two dozen lashes, you may release him. What about the other fellow?"

The ship was now pitching violently and the wind, like a devil released, drove the rain savagely into his face. His treacherous stomach started to heave and he had to swallow the bile that flooded into his mouth but he managed somehow to remain on his feet, although the men about him were experiencing difficulty in keeping to their ranks.

"Well?" Durbanville glared at the surgeon, willing him to suggest some face-saving reason which would enable him to pardon the third of Leach's fusiliers but, to his chagrin, the surgeon simply shrugged.

"Fusilier Denton is fit to receive punishment, sir," he stated flatly and added, making no attempt to hide his distaste for the whole proceedings, "If you insist on carrying out your sentence, which I consider both unjust and undeserved . . . and at the present time also dangerous."

In other circumstances, Henry Durbanville would have known how to deal with his insubordination but now, he realized with sick dismay, he was caught in a trap of his own making. He would have to order the sentence carried out or yield to the surgeon's insolent defiance of his authority, with Leach and Hazard and his officers no doubt looking on . . . but, dear heaven, he hoped that, once he had given the order, they would hurry and get the thing over. He gave it, in a strained, high-pitched voice and, having done so, instantly regretted his decision. The fools were taking as long as they could, staggering this way and that as the ship rolled, stumbling into each other and breaking ranks. Even the hefty drummer holding the cat joined in the absurd pantomime, Durbanville saw with impotent fury, as the man first cannoned into his relief and then let the whip fall from his grasp and roll into the scuppers.

"Damn them, damn them!" he swore aloud, not caring who heard him. He had been counting on the emotional impact of the flogging to take his mind off his growing nausea but, although the prisoner was eventually secured to the grating, the lash was never laid on. A stentorian bellow from close at hand ordered his men below and, as they hesitated in their broken, swaying ranks for him to endorse this order, the shrilling of the boatswain's mates' pipes sounded above the roar of the wind. And suddenly Leach was beside him, calm and purposeful and authoritative amidst the confusion as he gave the command to dismiss, which was instantly obeyed by all save the two drummers, who—again on Leach's orders—paused to release Fusilier Denton from the gratings.

"Come on, Durbanville," the hated voice urged, "I'll assist you to your cabin." Leach had him by the arm, holding him upright, urging him towards the companionway but again the waves of nausea were flooding over him, irrepressible now. He could not avoid the final humiliation. Dragging his rescuer with him, he lurched to the rails, as the ship began to plunge like a mad thing and his stomach churned uncontrollably. He could not speak and tried to free himself from the grasp of Leach's single arm but the Major held on, standing over him when they reached the ship's side and a swarm of seamen made a rush for the shrouds in response to the insane yelling of their petty officers.

"All right, boy, take your time," Leach bade him, with unexpected gentleness. The topmen vanished into the rigging above their heads but, a few yards away, more seamen were hauling on the braces and he remained where he was, his arm about Durbanville's heaving shoul-

98

ders, hiding him from their view. "You'll feel better in a minute."

"Damn you," Durbanville retorted thickly. "Damn your eyes, leave me alone." Leach ignored his plea and when, at long last, the young Guardsman was able to stumble away from the rail, he helped him to negotiate the slippery companionway and led him to his cabin.

"Brandy is what you need, my lad," he stated with conviction. "I have a bottle in my quarters. I'll fetch it and we'll share a glass or two, shall we? I'm feeling nearly as seasick as you are and I find it's the only thing that does me any good."

Slumped on his cot, Henry Durbanville avoided his eye. "Thank you, Major," he muttered shamefacedly. "I— I'm grateful."

"Curiously enough, so am I," Major Leach admitted. "Although not to you, on this occasion. But you've taught me a few things about myself that I didn't know. I fancy it's about time I returned the compliment." He went out, the door of the cabin slamming shut behind him with the force of the ship's motion, and Durbanville lay with closed eyes, sunk in misery. . . .

On the quarterdeck, Phillip watched with relief as the topmen regained the safety of the deck. The upper sails and jib had been lowered and furled without incident and now, maneuvering with fore and main courses and the rudder, he had brought the ship's head round. Laidlaw's watch had been due for relief in less than twenty minutes, so that the men of the watch below, already out of their hammocks, had answered the call almost as speedily as those on deck. And both watches—the Starboard on the starboard side, Port on the port side—had done their work quickly and well, almost if not quite compensating for his deliberate delay in shortening sail. So far as Durbanville and his soldiers were concerned, his improvised plan had succeeded . . . there was now not a soldier in

99

sight, save for two who were clinging to the lee rail, evidently overcome by seasickness and, as he watched them, they staggered across to the companionway together and vanished below.

At his side, Martin Fox said, having to shout to make himself heard above the shrieking of the wind, "Did you recognize those two, sir? I believe it was Leach and Durbanville!"

"Impossible," Phillip objected.

"Indeed it was, sir," Laidlaw confirmed. He had, by this time, understood the reason for the oddly contradictory orders his commander had given him when the squall had first been sighted, and he looked at Phillip now with renewed respect. "Durbanville was overcome by *mal de mer*, sir, and Major Leach went to his assistance. I saw him, saw the whole thing, sir. He was standing beside me and he suddenly let out a yell—something about the young imbecile falling overboard—and then he legged it across the deck after him, sir."

Wonders, Phillip reflected a trifle cynically, would never cease but he doubted whether, in Leach's place, he would have risked crossing the heaving, rain-swept deck to succour any man who had behaved as Durbanville had behaved to him. Still less would he have remained there, he told himself, in infinite danger of being flung overboard or knocked down by the seamen of the augmented watch, as they doubled to their stations but . . . . he shrugged. There was no doubt that Major Francis Aloysius Leach, of Her Majesty's Seventh Royal Fusiliers, was a remarkable officer—and a Christian gentleman, if ever there was one. Indeed he . . . the ship was wallowing in the trough of a mountainous swell, he realized, and jerked his thoughts back to the task in hand. It was time to take the mainsail off her and time, too, to permit Laidlaw's watch to go below. They had done enough and were due for relief;

Mr. Burnaby, he saw, like the good man he was, was standing by.

"All right, relieve the watch," he said and, meeting Burnaby's faded blue eyes, nodded in confirmation of his unspoken question. "Brace in the mainyard, if you please, Mr. Burnaby, and haul taut the rolling tackle. Send your maintopmen aloft when the yard's secured. We'll have the main course off her now." He gave his orders with the confident certainty of long experience, knowing that the risk he had taken was virtually over and that, if he were ever called upon to justify his actions, he could do so.

The rain lashed down, soaking him despite the oilskin his servant had brought him, and a deluge of water broke over the forecastle, momentarily hiding the fore part of the ship from his sight. The *Trojan* heeled over, shipping water fore and aft and Phillip shouted to the quartermaster to ease the helm down. Burnaby had the mainyard secured and his topmen aloft and, when she was relieved of her main course, the ship righted herself, her bows rising buoyantly as she responded to her helm. The gusty wind shifted and the watch were fully occupied, trimming and shortening sail but within another half hour, the squall had blown itself out and, leaving the deck to the experienced old Master, Phillip went below with Martin Fox to change into dry clothing.

4

JUST after seven bells of the Morning Watch, the red sandstone cliffs of Balaclava were sighted and Phillip stared about him in dismay as these drew nearer and he saw the number of ships at anchor or beating to and fro off the entrance to the port. There were twice, if not three times as many now as there had been when he had sailed for Constantinople with his cargo of wounded. Most were supply ships and troop transports, at least two of which, he was certain, had been at anchor off the port when he left. There was no sign of the *Agamemnon,* Admiral Lyons' flagship, but he recognized the steam frigates *Retribution, Niger, Vulcan* and *Vesuvius* lying close inshore. He made his number and, as he had feared, after some delay received instructions from the signal station at the cliff head to remain outside the harbor with the rest. His signal concerning the *Prince* was acknowledged, again after some delay, and when he made *"Where to anchor?"* was given no more precise instructions than *"Where convenient."*

The wind had dropped considerably since the previous evening but was gusty and shifting and, not liking the haphazard manner in which the majority of the motley fleet appeared to have distributed themselves, Phillip told Martin Fox, as they ran in, "I think we'll be best off lying at a single anchor, for the present. If it should come on to blow, I don't much fancy mooring too close inshore, do you?"

Fox looked up at the towering cliffs and shook his head.

"Indeed I do not .. and the glass is still too low for comfort." He gestured ahead. "I see the *Niger* is still outside—didn't you tell me that Captain Heath was to succeed Captain Dacres, as port commander?"

Phillip shrugged. "So I was told and poor Dacres was certainly very ill the last time I saw him on board the *Sanspareil*. But no doubt we shall find out in due course. In any case, if Captain Heath is port commander, he'll have been appointed to the *Sanspareil* and *Niger* will have a new commander. Bring up two cables' length from the *Niger*'s port quarter and perhaps we shall find out."

The *Trojan* had scarcely dropped anchor when a boat put off from the *Niger*, bringing an invitation to Phillip to take breakfast with her Captain. He found Leopold Heath awaiting him on board the 14-gun steam frigate and, as they ate, Heath confirmed most of his suppositions.

"Poor Dacres is still officially in command of the port but he's a very sick man, Hazard, and I am doing most of the work for him. My promotion has come through but"— as Phillip started to speak—"don't congratulate me, for I'm to succeed him and it is not an appointment I am at all eager to accept." He sighed, his dark eyes frankly worried. "You'll have observed the fleet of, as yet, not unloaded supply ships we have at this perilous anchorage, I imagine?"

"I have, sir. And I share your opinion of the perils of this anchorage," Phillip said. Captain Heath was an old friend and he knew that, to him, he could speak freely. "Why are all these ships here, sir? Why are they not permitted to enter the harbor to discharge their cargoes?"

Leopold Heath's expression was glum. "Captain Dacres

has his orders and, strictly between ourselves, Hazard, the reason he is remaining in command of the port is because he is anxious to spare me the odium that attaches to his enforcement of those orders, which he likes as little as I do. Decent, kindly fellow that he is, he is aware that I shall have a better chance if, when I succeed him, I am able to reverse his orders. And I do not, I feel sure, need to tell you by whom or, indeed, for what reason we have been instructed to keep Balaclava Harbor clear of shipping."

Admiral Lyons, Phillip thought, as he nodded his understanding of this cryptic statement, would also have small liking for the orders he had been compelled to issue.

"Is the port to be abandoned then?" he asked.

"This would seem to be the Army commanders' considered wish," Captain Heath admitted reluctantly. "Since the battle on the Inkerman Ridge on the fifth, I gather most of them feel strongly that to defend Balaclava is—if not impossible—likely to prove too great a drain upon the land forces available to be strategically wise. You've heard about the battle, I suppose?"

"I heard no details, sir. Only that it had taken place and that the Russians were beaten off."

"More by the sheer heroism and fighting qualities of the regiments involved than by the strategic wisdom of the generals who directed the battle," Heath told him bitterly. He launched into a brief and scathing description of the action. "Her Majesty's Foot Guards fought magnificently, I am told ... but now, like the Light Cavalry Brigade, they scarcely exist as a fighting force, poor devils. Their Divisional Commander, the Duke of Cambridge, has repaired on board the *Retribution*—heartbroken, Captain Drummond says. I believe that, though I haven't seen His Royal Highness. Sir George Cathcart was killed and poor old Brigadier Strangeways, Goldie and Torrens too. Sir George Brown was severely wounded and John Campbell is said to be dying on board the *Agamemnon*, at the Fleet anchorage off the Katcha—both may be already dead, for all I know. Men of their caliber can ill be spared, Hazard . . ." his voice charged with emotion, the *Niger*'s commander listed some of the killed and wounded who were known to them both and Phillip listened in stunned dismay.

"How did the enemy fare?" he asked when, at last, Captain Heath was silent.

"Well, I cannot vouch for the accuracy of the figures but I've heard that they lost five thousand dead, in addition to three times that number wounded and taken prisoner. But the Russians do not mind sacrificing their unfortunate soldiers. They're said to have attacked with upwards of sixty thousand and they've plenty more to use as cannon fodder. We, alas, have not and we lost something like two thousand five hundred in killed, wounded and missing, I believe. The Inkerman ridge was a shambles for days after the battle, with dead still unburied . . . enemy dead. The Russians left us to inter them."

"And the French, sir?" Phillip questioned. "Did they take part in the battle?"

"Oh, yes—but too late and there were too few of them, which I fear is all too often the case." Heath's resentment was in his voice. "Bosquet's division was sent to our aid but the remainder of their forces were kept in reserve. They had suffered a feint attack earlier on and Canrobert refused for a long time to believe that the main attack was against our Second Division and he would risk no more, until he'd come to see for himself. Nevertheless, Bosquet is a brave man and his Zouaves, as always, fought with zest and courage. Their losses are put at less than half ours—a fact that speaks for itself, does it not?"

Phillip supposed that it did. Captain Heath gave him scraps of other news, adding that Sir Edmund Lyons was well but seemed in poor spirits. "He was here two days ago. The *Vulcan* brought him and then he shifted his flag to the *Miranda* and Jack Lyons conveyed him back to the

Fleet anchorage. He was, of course, delighted to see his son . . . I believe you saw him also, did you not, in Constantinople on his way here?"

"Yes, sir, I did."

"Let's hope he's able to cheer the Admiral up . . . more coffee, Hazard?"

"No, thank you, sir."

"Well, I'm going to have some more. Tell me—how were things in Constantinople?" Captain Heath poured himself a second cup of coffee and, as he drank it, Phillip gave him an account of what he had seen and heard during his short stay in the Turkish capital.

"One, at least, of our officers emerged with great credit from the Inkerman engagement," the Captain said suddenly. "I almost forgot to tell you, although heaven knows, it's an event in this war when the British Navy is allowed any chance for its officers and men to distinguish themselves! But William Peel, the *Diamond*'s Captain, managed to do so—as an infantryman. He and his A.D.C., a midshipman named Daniel, who's serving with him in the Naval Brigade, chanced to be visiting the ridge when the Russians launched their attack. From what I hear, they both joined in the action and were largely responsible for saving one of the Guards' regimental Colors. The Duke commended them and I understand they've both been mentioned in one of Lord Raglan's despatches." His blunt featured, be-whiskered face relaxed a little. "He's a remarkably fine fellow, Peel, and should go a long way in the service if he survives this campaign. You've met him, of course?"

"Yes, indeed I have, sir," Phillip replied. "Also his mid., young St. John Daniel, who always seems to be in the thick of it whenever I've come across him." He liked and admired William Peel, second-in-command of the Naval Brigade under Captain Lushington, and the youngest officer in the Black Sea Fleet to hold post rank and, remembering what Midshipman Daniel had told him about his Chief, he smiled. With his record, Captain Peel should indeed go far, as the *Niger*'s commander had said ... if he lived long enough. According to his young aide-de-camp, he paid very little heed to his own safety and only recently had picked up an unexploded 42-pounder Russian shell, which had fallen into one of the naval gun batteries, and very coolly rolled it over the parapet, where it exploded harmlessly.

"You smile?" Captain Heath observed. "Well, I'm glad you still have it in you to smile, Hazard. I very much doubt if you will after a week or so lying at anchor here."

"I have troops on board, sir," Phillip reminded him.

"They'll be landed by tender, my boy. *You* will not be allowed inside the harbor, no matter what reasons you may advance. Some of these supply ships have been here for over a fortnight, a few even longer. And don't tell me their cargoes are badly needed—I *know* they are! Captain Dacres is being driven nearly mad by the pleas of their commanders to let them unload and go ... but there is nothing he can possibly do, poor fellow, if Lord Raglan decides that Balaclava can't be defended."

"What is the alternative, sir?" Phillip's smile faded. "To share Kamiesch with the French or take over Kazatch? We must have a port, surely——"

Leopold Heath's face looked suddenly old and careworn. "Lord Raglan is, I fear, the only man who can answer your questions, Hazard—I cannot. And by the same token, your message regarding the *Prince* should have been directed to his lordship, not to those in nominal command of this harbor. She may be leaking like a sieve but that won't get her inside and God help her if we get any bad weather ... judging by the glass, it appears on the cards that we may. But"—he relented—"go ashore in your gig or in the steam tender with your passengers, if you wish, and have a word with Captain Dacres, on behalf of the *Prince*. I've heard that the Army commissariat is anxiously looking for her arrival. You'll find General de Lacy Evans on board the *Sanspareil,* incidentally."

"Wounded, sir?"

"No, Hazard—like poor Dacres, he's sick, and was so when his Division was attacked on the Inkerman Ridge. He was there but he left the tactical command to General Pennefather, his second-in-command. Talking of seconds-in-command, my young friend"—Captain Heath smiled faintly—"for how much longer do *you* expect to have the *Trojan?"*

Phillip spread his hands. "I don't know, sir. I had hoped that perhaps you might be in a position to tell me."

Captain Heath pushed a box of cigars across the table to him. "No," he answered, "I can't. All I can tell you is that Captain Crawford went with General Bentinck and other wounded officers to Constantinople in the *Caradoc—* and Bentinck, I know, is for home. But your Captain may convalesce there and return to his command." He lit his cigar and puffed at it, a thoughtful frown bringing his dark brows together. "I have received no instructions concerning either you or your ship, so presumably you'll remain in command for the time being. And consider yourself lucky, my lad—a thirty-gun steam-screw, at your age, is quite a prize."

"I know that only too well, sir," Phillip assured him.

The older man's smile widened. "If you'll take my advice," he offered, "you'll keep away from the Fleet anchorage and the Commander-in-Chief. You——" there was a tap on the cabin door and a midshipman appeared, cap in hand. "Yes, Mr. Race, what is it?"

"Message for Commander Hazard, if you please, sir," the youngster replied. "You are requested to report to Captain Dacres on board the *Sanspareil* at once, sir," he added, addressing Phillip. "Your gig's alongside, sir."

Was this the summons he had been dreading, Phillip wondered, as he took his leave of the hospitable Captain Heath. Would he find himself relieved of his temporary command and, if so, would Admiral Lyons again employ him as a member of his staff? His gig was waiting for him, with Midshipman O'Hara in charge, and he sat in the sternsheets as her crew began the long pull into the harbor, lost in his own thoughts.

The *Sanspareil* was moored in her old berth inside the harbor, dwarfing the ships about her of which, apart from the *Diamond*—denuded of her guns and most of her crew and in use as a naval hospital ship—most were small transports engaged in loading wounded. And there were not many of them, Phillip noticed; the harbor was less crowded than he could remember seeing it, although Lord Cardigan's private yacht still occupied her privileged position at the head of the harbor, presumably with her owner and his French chef on board. The hospital wharf was the only one where any signs of activity could be seen; on the rest, a few soldiers lounged, waiting for stores in a straggling line, and the stench of putrefying vegetables rose, as always, from the filthy waters of the inlet.

Phillip's interview with Captain Dacres was brief. The port commander greeted him kindly but he was, as Captain Heath had said, obviously a very sick man. He asked about the *Prince,* seeming more interested in Phillip's opinion of her seaworthiness and her crew's ability to deal with her leaking hold than in the cargo she carried. He said, with resigned bitterness, "I cannot permit her to enter this port, Hazard . . . I wish to heaven I could. But I have my orders and have no choice but to adhere to them, without fear or favor."

"I breakfasted with Captain Heath, sir, aboard the *Niger,*" Phillip told him, anxious to spare the sick man an unnecessary explanation.

Captain Dacres looked relieved. "Ah, then I do not have to justify myself to you, Mr. Hazard."

"No, sir."

The Captain shifted in his chair, closing his fever-bright eyes for a moment and Phillip waited, fearing what was to come as, opening his eyes again, the older man started to search among the papers on his desk. "I have orders for you from the Admiral, who was here a couple of days ago to meet his son . . . you remember Jack Lyons, of course. In fact, I believe you served under him at one time, did you not? Ah, yes, here are your instructions, Mr. Hazard." He looked up unexpectedly to meet Phillip's gaze and smiled in sympathetic understanding. "Oh, don't worry, you are not being relieved of your command as yet. There is a strong probability that Captain Crawford will soon be fit enough to resume it but, until he is, you are to remain in acting command and you are to take your ship to Eupatoria at once."

"Very good, sir." Phillip could not hide his elation. He listened to the rest of his instructions and said diffidently, "I can sail as soon as we have landed the troops we are carrying, sir. I understand they will require to be taken ashore by tender and——"

The port commander cut him short. "No, Mr. Hazard— you are to take the troops with you. They are needed to reinforce the garrison at Eupatoria. The place has been attacked several times recently and, due to sickness, it is undermanned. So you can sail immediately and you will remain under Lord George Paulet's command for as long as necessary in order to meet the present emergency. I don't anticipate that you will be there for very long because your frigate will be needed here and Lord George has, in any case, his own *Bellerophon,* in addition to several small steamers and, I understand, the French three-decker *Henri Quatre* has been sent there. Captain Brock's anxiety, as garrison commander, is natural—he had to

111

dispatch nearly four hundred Marines from the garrison to meet a request from Lord Raglan, so that his strength on shore is greatly depleted."

"Yes, sir"—Phillip had listened with interest—"I understand. Will that be all, sir?"

"It is, Mr. Hazard. Good luck to you!"

"And to you, sir. I hope you may soon enjoy improved health and also Sir George Brown, whom Captain Heath told me was severely wounded and——"

Again Captain Dacres cut him short. "Your good wishes are appreciated and I shall convey them to the General. As for myself I shall not, I fear, know any improvement in my health until I leave Balaclava and I pray God that may be soon!" He sighed. "Good-bye, Hazard—when you return I trust you will find Captain Heath in this cabin."

Phillip left him and returned to his gig. On board the *Trojan* once more, he acquainted Martin Fox with their change of destination and instructed him to get under way as soon as possible, sending a midshipman below to impart this information to Major Leach and Durbanville.

"Well," Fox said wryly, "I think I prefer Eupatoria to our present berth although it means, alas, that we are not yet rid of Lord Henry Durbanville. Which is a pity!"

"I don't fancy it will please Durbanville over much," Phillip returned. "He will not enjoy being at Eupatoria away from all contact with his father's influential friends . . . and unable even to report the filthy state of this ship to the Commander-in-Chief!" They both laughed and Fox said, still smiling, "But our young hero may see some action which, I feel sure, he is anxious to do."

"Are you, Martin? I confess I don't share your conviction. But so far as we're concerned, I hope we may find an opportunity to exercise our guns . . . well, pass the word for Mr. Burnaby, will you please? And then pipe hands to stations—I'll be in the chartroom if you want me."

"Aye, aye, sir. And needless to tell you, I'm glad that you are still in command of this ship."

"And so, my dear Martin, am I," Phillip confessed.

He was in the chartroom, with the Master, when Henry Durbanville made his appearance, looking upset. But he spoke politely enough, addressing Phillip as "sir" and phrasing his request to be put ashore before sailing in an almost humble tone.

"My Division is here, sir, not at this Eupatoria place and I'm under orders to join my regiment, so that if you could spare me a boat, I should be most grateful."

"But you are in command of this contingent," Phillip pointed out, careful to avoid Mr. Burnaby's eye.

"I can hand over command to Major Leach, sir," the young Guards officer volunteered eagerly. "He is a most competent officer and, in any case, most of the men are his Seventh Fusiliers. I only have my servant—my sergeant, as you will recall, was left . . . er, that is inadvertently left behind in Constantinople. I sent him to———"

"I do recall the circumstances," Phillip assured him unsmilingly. "But I, too, have my orders and these are to get under way immediately. I cannot therefore spare you a boat, since to do so would delay our sailing. But"—he relented—"I will, if you wish, make a signal concerning you to the shore station and if a boat can be sent out for you, I'll delay until it's alongside."

"I'm uncommonly grateful, Commander Hazard," Durbanville responded. "Er—I . . . perhaps I had better hand over command to Major Leach now and———"

"Major Leach is under arrest," Phillip reminded him coldly.

"Oh, but I'll withdraw the charges I made against him." Durbanville reddened. "Not that I ever intended to press them, you understand, Commander. It was simply that I—that he . . ." he shuffled his feet, obviously embar-

113

rassed. "I—er—excuse me, if you please. I'll find Major Leach and explain the situation to him."

"Very well," Phillip agreed. "I trust you are ready to go ashore, if required?"

"Oh, yes, indeed, sir. My kit is packed. I shall not keep the boat waiting or delay you an instant longer than I must, if you would be good enough to send that signal for me."

Phillip and Burnaby exchanged glances as he hurried off in search of Major Leach and the Master's faded blue eyes held an amused glint as he asked, *"Will* you make the signal, sir?"

"I'll make it, Mr. Burnaby," Phillip assured him. "But whether or not I receive a favorable answer is, I fear, another matter."

The signal was duly made and acknowledged. But, although Durbanville, attended by his servant and surrounded by his baggage, stood hopefully by the entry port, no boat was sighted and the signal station, after some delay, eventually answered with an uninformative, *"Shore to Trojan: proceed to sea."* Captain Durbanville's services did not appear to be urgently required on shore and Midshipman Grey, with undisguised satisfaction, made this fact known to the discomfited young Guards officer, in a rapid interpretation of the semaphore signal. He approached Phillip, grave faced but a suspicious gleam in his eyes, to ask, on Durbanville's behalf, if he might be transferred to one of the other warships remaining at anchor and the gravity vanished when Phillip shook his head.

"I have no orders to transfer Captain Durbanville."

"Aye, aye, sir. May I tell him so, sir?"

"Yes, Mr. Grey. But"—Phillip eyed him sternly—"don't rub it in too hard, will you?"

"No, indeed, sir. No harder than I have to, sir," Grey promised, grinning openly now and clearly enjoying his errand. "Thank you, sir."

The *Trojan* weighed anchor and, with a gusty and constantly shifting wind which necessitated much work for the duty watch, weathered Cape Kherson and set course for the ancient Ottoman town of Eupatoria. The small town, with its mixed population of Tartars, Cossacks, Greeks, Armenians and Germans, had surrendered to the Allies on 13th September, when the two Fleets had been on their way to Calamita Bay to land the invasion forces, and a garrison of Marines, under Captain Saumarez Brock, had been put ashore to hold it. Situated about ten miles from the landing place, Phillip remembered it as a pleasant looking little town, with white painted stone or wooden houses, red tiled roofs and unexpectedly friendly inhabitants who, far from opposing the British landing, had appeared to welcome it. Its position was of some strategic importance which, he supposed, was the reason why the town was under such frequent attack. The road to Perekop ran northwards across a flat plain, on the edge of which the town was built and a second road, winding through a low range of hills to the south, led to Simpheropol, where Prince Menschikoff, the Russian Commander-in-Chief, had established his field headquarters. Most of the reinforcements from Odessa had come via Perekop, he recalled his brother Graham telling him, in a series of overland marches which the Allied sea blockade had been powerless to prevent and the Russians, presumably, either feared a land attack on their supply route from Eupatoria or else wanted to deny the ships of the Fleet the port facilities it afforded. Whatever the reason, Eupatoria was well guarded by the British three-decker *Bellerophon* and the *Henri IV*, the finest first-rate the French possessed, built only five years ago and mounting a hundred guns.

Phillip spent most of the night on deck. He was anxious about the weather, which was becoming steadily worse. An easterly wind, which rose to gale force at times, lashed the

115

sea to fury and, rather than beat against wind and sea, he ordered steam up and set his course away from the treacherous, cliffbound coastline. By five a.m., the *Trojan* was proceeding under her engines, with only her treble-reefed topsails set. Even so, she shipped a good deal of water and the pumps had to be kept going throughout the night. He had hoped to make port by first light but, fearful of being driven on shore in darkness, prudently stood off at a safe distance from the rocky shore, aware that his charts were not always accurate and remembering all too vividly how the *Tiger* had been wrecked on this coast when on her way to Odessa. Then it had been fog which had led to her undoing but this strong, shifting wind was even more dangerous, he knew.

Mr. Burnaby shared his apprehension. The white-haired old Master had grown old in the Service and Phillip had learned to respect his instinctive ability to read and assess the weather portends. When Martin Fox came on watch at 4 a.m., Burnaby came with him, to spend twenty minutes or so on deck engaged in what one of the midshipmen had once irreverently described as "sniffing the wind like a bloodhound." He welcomed Phillip's decision to order the screw lowered and when, toward the end of the Morning Watch, he again made his appearance on the quarterdeck, he was looking frankly worried. But he said nothing until he had studied his charts and checked their position and then, after his usual ten minutes "sniffing the air", he crossed over to where Phillip was standing, with Martin Fox, both holding themselves upright with some difficulty, and said bluntly, "Commander Hazard sir, I don't like this—I don't like it at all."

"It's blowing," Phillip agreed ruefully, having to shout to make himself heard.

"And it will blow a great deal harder," the Master stated positively. "The wind has shifted to south by west and the glass . . ." he shrugged, raising his eyes to the

116

heavens. "In all my experience, Mr. Hazard, I've never known the glass so low. I fear we are in for a hurricane, sir."

"A hurricane, Mr. Burnaby?" Phillip exchanged an anxious glance with his second-in-command. "When do you anticipate it will strike?"

"Within the hour, sir." There was the same conviction in the old man's voice. He added grimly, "As I see the situation, you have two possible alternatives."

"And what are they?"

"I think you know as well as I do, sir."

"You mean try to make port at Eupatoria or give up the attempt to do so, and ride it out, with the help of our engines, well away from shore?" Phillip suggested.

The Master nodded his grizzled head. "Aye, sir. Both courses have their dangers, as again you know."

He did, Phillip reflected grimly, conscious that a decision would have to be made, one way or the other, and that it would be his—and his alone—to make. Leaving Fox and Burnaby together, he started to pace up and down by himself, considering every aspect of the problem with which he was faced.

The Bay of Eupatoria offered shelter and, under engines, would be easy enough to enter but it was open to southerly winds, which blew right through, making it—although good holding ground—none too safe an anchorage. The wind was south by west now. With so many ships at anchor in the bay already, there was always the added danger of anchors dragging or chains snapping and ships running foul of each other, if they were not driven on shore.

The *Trojan* was tightly battened down, her guns secured with extra lashings, her upper yards sent down and no trouble had been reported from the engine room. If he stood out to sea, there was no risk of being driven ashore or of being fouled by a three-decker and the question of

117

dragging his anchors would not arise—all he would have to do would be to keep his ship's head to wind, under bare poles, if necessary, and wait until the gale abated. On the other hand, he was carrying reinforcements for the garrison, which was under strength and which might also be under attack, and his orders were to land them as soon as possible. But was it possible? If he ran ashore, of what use would his passengers be to the garrison? Being driven ashore, on this coast, meant the loss of any ship unfortunate enough to suffer such a fate; in addition, this was an enemy coast, offering no hope of succor to the shipwrecked. Rather men who did manage to escape the wreck were liable to find themselves under fire from wandering Cossack bands and the ship herself might be captured, as the *Tiger* had been . . . Phillip drew in his breath sharply, as he remembered the Russian guns, firing redhot shot into the *Tiger*'s defenseless decks, setting her ablaze.

It was this thought that finally decided him. To run any risk of losing the *Trojan* was a prospect he could not contemplate. He had been entrusted with her command and, he told himself, her safety and the safety of her passengers and crew must be his first concern. But, as he crossed the quarterdeck to rejoin his First Lieutenant and the Master, he was very conscious of the loneliness of command and of the isolated position he occupied—and must continue to occupy, until the danger was over.

He made his decision known and, seeing the relief in old Burnaby's face and the approval in Martin Fox's smile, felt better in his own mind. Neither said more than the formal, "Aye, aye, sir," but he sensed that both had been afraid that he might decide to adhere strictly to his orders as . . . a grim little smile twisted his lips. As Captain North would, undoubtedly, have done—rightly, perhaps. But, right or wrong, he had decided and events would prove which of the two alternatives open to him was the one he should have taken. . . .

5

I⊤ was a long and nerve-straining day, mentally and physically one of the most exhausting Phillip had ever spent in his life. As the Master had predicted, the wind rose to hurricane force soon after six in the morning and this continued without ceasing throughout the hours of daylight. A tremendously heavy sea got up, crashing over the ship and sending hundreds of tons of water streaming across her from stem to stern so that, at times, she seemed to be buried beneath the deluge and her exposed upper deck became a place of extreme peril.

Even with two men at the wheel, who were relieved every hour, Phillip experienced the greatest difficulty in keeping the ship's head to the wind and there were moments when, despite the aid of her engines, she did not respond to the helm but lay like a log, her lee channels awash. He himself remained on the quarterdeck all day. He lashed himself to the mainmast backstay and clung there, wet and chilled to the bone for hour after anxious hour, scarcely knowing whether it was night or day, so intense was the gloom of the wintery sky and so slowly did the time pass. Any sort of conversation was impossible. His orders, when he had to issue any, were shouted into the ear of a seaman and relayed from man to man, until they reached the officer for whom they were intended.

It was seldom necessary to give an order, for there was

119

little that anyone could do, and Phillip had taken every precaution possible before the storm broke. He had had the upper yards sent down before he had made his decision to ride out the gale at sea and, stripped of all save a single storm staysail, the *Trojan* was alone in a waste of angry grey water, bobbing about like a cork, now rising to the crest of a mountainous wave, now sliding down from a dizzy height into its heaving trough. The wind screeched and sang eerily in the rigging, sounding as if some monstrous musician were plucking at her shrouds and stays with giant fingers, to draw from them an insane and infinitely depressing dirge, with which to mourn her impending doom.

But she remained afloat almost, it seemed to Phillip, by a miracle, although many times during that endless day he came close to despair, certain now that the choice he had made had been the wrong one. He dared not think of what his hapless passengers were enduring in their confined quarters below deck. His own men were, for the most part, also below and only when one of the quarter-deck guns broke loose did he summon part of the duty watch on deck. He had the gun bundled unceremoniously over the side, preferring to lose it rather than risk injury to the seamen who were struggling vainly to secure its 95 cwt. of menacing metal. Then, as he watched the 68-pounder vanish into the seething blackness astern, he found himself once again doubting the wisdom of his decision ... but he would have to stand by it, he knew, just as he would by his other, more important decision to put to sea instead of seeking the shelter of Eupatoria Bay. In any event, he had no doubt that the loss of a gun mattered a good deal less to him than the loss of a single one of his seamen but, to salve his conscience, he ordered double breechings rove on the remaining 68-pounder and sent Lieutenant Sutherland, the gunnery officer, with a working party, to make a careful check of the gundeck, to ensure that the accident did not reccur.

There were, inevitably, other accidents. Two stokers were badly scalded, when a steam pipe cracked, another burned both hands when he was flung against the door of the furnace he was endeavouring to replenish and a soldier, falling down a hatch-ladder, suffered head injuries and a broken leg. Able-Seaman O'Leary, who had acted as Phillip's orderly when he had been attached to Sir Colin Campbell's brigade at Kadi-Koi, was one of three men carried below after an heroic but somewhat foolhardy attempt to prevent the quarterdeck gun from breaking loose but none of the three, Phillip was thankful to learn, was seriously hurt. O'Leary, the Surgeon told him, had a crushed foot but was cheerful enough once this had been dressed and splinted.

By 4 p.m. when the watch changed, the wind had veered again to the north and moderated a little and, although the sea was still pounding the *Trojan*'s wooden walls with unabated violence, the glass had—at long last—started to rise. Mr. Burnaby, when Phillip dragged himself with difficulty to the chartroom, half an hour later, expressed the cautious opinion that the worst of the gale was over. Inevitably, the ship had been blown off course and was now many miles south-west of her destination, according to his reckoning.

"If the delay in landing the troops at Eupatoria is causing you concern, sir," the Master added, his shrewd old eyes sympathetically on Phillip's white, exhausted face, dark with stubble, "I believe that we might soon venture into the bay with the assistance of the screw and, of course, exercising due care."

The possibility that he might attempt to complete his mission had already been in Phillip's mind and, encouraged by the fact that his supply of coal was not as depleted as he had feared it would be, he called for a report of

121

damage sustained and ordered the well sounded. Both reports, when he received them, were as encouraging as that from the Engineer Warrant Officer had been. Most of the damage could be repaired; the *Trojan*'s only serious loss remained the quarterdeck gun and, although she had shipped a good deal of water, the pumps were slowly clearing it and the level was not alarming. All her masts were intact, no boilers were leaking and the rudder had apparently stood up to the stresses and strains put upon it during the storm.

"We've been fortunate," Martin Fox observed, blowing on his blue fingers in an effort to warm them. "I was afraid, more than once, that we were going to lose the foremast. And when the bowsprit shroud carried away and that sixty-eight pounder broke loose ..." he shuddered. "It's a miracle more hands weren't injured. O'Leary did well—he sang out just in time and most of the men were able to jump clear. He's a good man in a tight spot, O'Leary—if he hadn't waited to warn the others he wouldn't have got his foot trapped."

With vivid memories of just how good a man O'Leary had proved himself during their service on shore together, Phillip agreed emphatically with his second-in-command's assessment. "But as you say," he added, "we have been fortunate, Martin—exceptionally fortunate. To be honest I've wondered many times today whether I was right in deciding to put to sea, instead of trying to make port at Eupatoria."

"I'm quite sure you were right, Phillip." Martin Fox looked up, a smile lighting his weary face. "Much of our good fortune was due to the fact that the *Trojan* had you as her commander, because no one could have handled her better than you did. I mean that with all my heart and I know there's not an officer or a seaman who'd disagree with me." He laid a hand on Phillip's arm. "Is it any use my suggesting that you entrust the ship to me for an hour,

122

while you go below for a meal and a change of clothing? You've not left the quarterdeck all day and I don't doubt you'll want to be here when we sight the coast again but, since that won't be for at least a couple of hours, why not rest while you have the chance?"

Phillip thanked him and agreed. "Let's hope our luck holds," he said when, after consultation with the Master, he had ordered the necessary change of course. "Have the Paymaster issue an extra gill of grog to all hands, would you please, Martin? They've earned it, heaven knows, and they will need it to keep out the cold. And a hot meal as well, as soon as it's possible for the cooks to get to work. Meantime see that each man on watch gets a mess-can of cocoa, even if the meal has to be delayed ... and let them go below to drink it, in relays, if necessary. The engine room can probably produce sufficient steam-heated water for the cocoa with that distilling apparatus they're so proud of, if the galley cannot—the tank was full yesterday and Ross complaining that no one would drink the stuff."

Fox made a grimace. "It tastes quite foul. But flavored with cocoa, perhaps it will be drinkable."

"I don't think the men will object to it now," Phillip said dryly. Swaying a little, as the ship rolled, he consulted his pocket watch. "I'd like the watch below to take their meal before they relieve the deck and then, if we do run into trouble, they'll have some food inside them at least. The galley fire can be doused again before we attempt to enter the bay, if necessary. How are the soldiers getting on?"

Fox shrugged his broad shoulders. "A few seem to have found their sea-legs sufficiently to bear a hand in mopping up but most of them are pretty miserable, I fear. And that includes the officers! I've only seen one ensign on his feet, although Major Leach did manage to pay them a brief visit during the Afternoon Watch. Poor fellow, he was as white as a sheet and could scarcely be described as 'on his feet.' But it was a gallant effort on his part, I must say. Durbanville, on the other hand, was conspicuous by his absence."

They discussed one or two other matters and then left the charthouse together. Phillip, after an anxious look about him, braced himself against the still considerable force of the wind and, choosing his moment, crossed to the companionway and descended to his cabin. He changed into dry clothes, after towelling himself briskly to restore the circulation to his numb body, shaved as well as he could and then, having gulped down the mug of scalding coffee his steward brought him, went to pay a call on the injured men. He found all of them in good heart, including O'Leary, who displayed his heavily bandaged foot with a certain wry pride and who did not now appear to be in very much discomfort. His breath exuded a strong smell of spirits and he gave Phillip a gap-toothed grin.

"Medical comforts, the Surgeon was sayin' to me, sor. But when he gave me the glass and I smelt the strength of me tot, I was frightened near to death, for I thought he was plannin' to take me foot off. I drank it down and then talked him out of *that* idea—and 'twas as well I did, sor, for now I'm feelin' the benefit of it and not a twinge of pain at all."

Phillip laughed. It was, he thought typical of O'Leary and of other men of his kind. In peace time, a great many of them were labelled "Queen's hard bargains," but in war—and in action—none could compare with them.

"You did a fine thing this afternoon, O'Leary," he told the big Irishman. "When that foot heals, I'll have a word with the Gunnery Officer about having you rated Gunner's Mate. And if I'm not here, I'll see to it that whoever is appointed to command is informed of your behavior."

"That's good of you, sor. But"—the seaman's grin vanished—"I thought *you* were to be in command? Sure

124

they're not going to bring anyone in over your head, are they?"

"That remains to be seen," Phillip evaded, conscious of the familiar ache in his throat as he visualized the possibility. O'Leary sat up belligerently, obviously intending to argue the point and, to avoid upsetting him, Phillip excused himself and went in search of Surgeon Fraser, whom he found ministering to Durbanville's servant, a tall, fair-haired young guardsman who had suffered a fall.

He asked, when the soldier was dismissed, about O'Leary and saw Angus Fraser's expression change. "I should have taken his foot off—it's an appalling mess—but like a damned fool, I let him persuade me not to. If gangrene sets in . . ." the doctor spread his small, neat hands in a despairing gesture. "Well, it'll have to come off and probably his leg with it. But he's quite a lad, that one, and he has his own cure in which he, at any rate, firmly believes. He asked for a second tot of whisky, when I had tidied the mess up a bit and, thinking he was in rather a deal of pain, I let him have his tot. And what do you suppose he did with it?"

"Well, knowing O'Leary, I imagine his action was original." Phillip was smiling. "What did he do—pour it over the wound?"

The Surgeon inclined his balding head. "Aye, that's precisely what he did, sir. And I'm fearing it will prove a waste of good whisky. Ah, well . . ." he sighed and turned to subject his visitor to a keen, professionally searching scrutiny. "How's that leg of yours bearing up? You'll have put quite a strain on it today, I'm thinking."

"Don't worry, Doctor—I've not felt it at all."

"No doubt because you were numb with the cold," Angus Fraser said tartly. "I'll take a wee look, shall I, since you're here?" He suited his action to his words, deaf to Phillip's protestations that he felt perfectly fit, and was not satisfied until he had examined the old wound and

125

applied a firm bandage to the leg. "There, that'll be better, Commander Hazard. You'll be wise not to neglect that leg, for if yon wound opens up again I will not be answerable for the consequences. How do you feel in yourself?"

"A trifle weary," Phillip admitted. "As you must be too, Doctor—and hungry, now that I come to think about it. I'm going to the gunroom in the hope that the steward has been able to procure something for us to eat—are you coming?"

"Aye, I am." The doctor rose, flexing his tired muscles. "What a day and what a gale! I cannot remember one like it, can you? Not for the first time, I've been asking myself why I was ever fool enough to come back to sea . . . and I had no answer. Is there any sign of that wind abating?"

"Mr. Burnaby forecasts that it will moderate very soon and, as you know, he's a fairly reliable weather prophet, so I'm praying that he's right." The two men made their way aft to the gunroom which, in a frigate, provided messing accommodation for officers of wardroom rank. "I'd like to seek the shelter of Eupatoria Bay tonight, if I can," Phillip went on. "The wind is veering to the nor' nor' west and the glass has risen a fraction, so we may be better off there."

"And you'll be able to set the passengers ashore, will you not, sir?" Angus Fraser stood aside, holding open the gunroom door for Phillip to procede him, a gleam of something that was not amusement in his eyes. "Including the delectable Lord Durbanville?"

"After you, Doctor." Phillip waved him to the door. "Yes, there's that," he agreed. "And also the fact that, if we have another night under engines, our supply of coal will run dangerously low. As a sailing ship man, I hate to have to admit this but"—he shrugged—"our engines saved us today and I was very grateful that we had them. Entering the bay with our screw to assist us will not, I pray, prove to be too difficult—even if the wind shifts again to the sou' west."

126

of the ship's straining timbers, there came the un-
...able sound of gunfire.

...llip tensed, his glass again to his eye, as Lieutenant
...rane yelled an excited warning. "Guns, sir, cannon, I
—firing from the shore!"

...es," Phillip confirmed grimly, catching a glimpse of
...annon flash in the darkness ahead. "Indeed, yes, Mr.
...rane. Well, we need look no further for our ship in
...ess. I fear she's aground and the Russians are trying
...ke her."

...istory, it seemed, was about to repeat itself. Phillip's
...t sank, as he remembered the brief and bloody battle
...ad fought beside the crew of the ill-starred *Tiger,*
...arly stranded on the enemy shore in thick fog. The
...sians had sent a gun battery galloping up, to unlimber
... fire from the cliff top on to the defenseless frigate
...w them—a ship whose own guns had not sufficient
...ration to reply to the murderous hail of grape and
...hot shot which had rained down on her. They had set
...ablaze and her seamen and Marines had fought the
...ze with despairing gallantry, refusing to haul down her
...ors until, to avoid useless loss of life, her dying Cap-
...had ordered them to do so. His own leg had been
...ttered by an exploding shell, Phillip recalled, conscious
...t the old wound was paining him as, from the cliff top
...econd gun opened up.

...He swung himself up the mainmast shrouds, glass in
...d, hoping to get a better view. The two guns on the
...mit of the cliff were firing rapidly now and it was
...ssible to pinpoint their position, although that of the
...anded ship was less clear. It became clearer as the
...ance between the *Trojan* and the shore diminished and
...ally all too clear, when a fire was started on her deck
...idships—the result, as nearly as Phillip could judge
...m its explosive nature and rapid spread, of a lucky hit
...some ammunition brought up for the unhappy vessel's

"Then I'll join my prayers to yours, Commander," the Surgeon said, with mock piety. "For my patients' sake and for my own. And now to eat—if we're lucky!" He went into the gunroom and Phillip followed him.

They had, however, consumed only their first course when Midshipman Grey presented himself apologetically, cap under arm, with a message from Martin Fox.

"If you please, sir," he said, addressing Phillip. "The First Lieutenant sent me to inform you that he has sighted what appear to be distress rockets, sir. They are a long way off on our port bow but he thought you would wish to know, sir."

"Thank you, Mr. Grey. Tell the First Lieutenant that I'll join him right away." Phillip was frowning. Distress rockets meant a ship in trouble and, with the Allied Navies supreme in the Black Sea, the ship would, in all probability, be either British or French. The coastal block-ade deterred other merchant ships from venturing into these waters and . . .

"Begging your pardon, sir," young Grey went on polite-ly, "The First Lieutenant instructed me to ask that you finish your meal before coming on deck, sir. He will keep the flares under observation and report when he has been able to ascertain their origin and cause, sir."

But Fox had been able to ascertain little more by the time Phillip rejoined him on the quarterdeck. He indicated from whence the flares appeared to have come and, from a study of the chart, it seemed probable that they had originated from a ship which had either been driven ashore or was in danger of going aground on the rocky coast fifteen or twenty miles west of Eupatoria Bay.

"There have been no more rockets sent up since I informed you of the sighting, sir," the First Lieutenant said gravely. "Which could mean that she's making for the bay—or that she's foundered."

"All the same," Phillip decided, "I think we should

investigate, don't you? If she's . . ." he broke off as, from a little further west than Fox had first seen the flares, a rocket rose to cleave a brightly lit path across the darkening sky. It was closely followed by a second and, his mind now firmly made up, he ordered a change of course. "Whoever she is, she's still afloat and it would seem that she's in need of assistance, so we had better get to her as fast as we can. Pipe hands aloft to make sail, if you please, Mr. Fox. We'll run in on the starboard tack under as much sail as she's able to carry and then wear and approach her under engines."

"Aye, aye, sir. Bo'sun's Mate . . ." Martin Fox passed on the order and, as the pipe sounded, Phillip said, "When Mr. Cochrane relieves you, Martin, go below and have your meal. I shall be here and I'll send for you if necessary. It will take us a good hour to come up to her, even on this wind and I daren't risk too much canvas . . ." he looked up at the towering masthead with narrowing eyes, before giving his instructions for sail to be set. "We shall have to watch that bowsprit . . . ease her a spoke or two when she sends, Quartermaster. And, Martin"—he turned again to his second-in-command—"you have at least an hour. Make the best use you can of it, understand?"

"Aye, aye, sir." Fox permitted himself a brief smile. "Thank you, sir. I'm anxious to try the cocoa, I must confess!"

It was quite dark when Anthony Cochrane relieved him and Phillip, as he explained the situation to the young watchkeeper, began to wonder how, in the inky blackness, it would be possible to locate the unknown ship which had sent up the distress rockets. And in the heavy sea that was still running, to put off boats to her, if he had to, would be a difficult and dangerous undertaking. Nevertheless, he knew that he could not ignore her call for help. If need be he could stand by her during the hours of darkness, keeping a safe distance off shore . . . again he

128

glanced anxiously aloft, at the close reefe[d]
the ship heel and shudder beneath his
Cochrane ordered the yards trimmed but
saw, was anxious. The wind had lost some
on this tack, there was no risk of being
but occasional gusts still gave considerable
cern and when it became necessary to we[ar]
ered, only partly from cold.

There was ample coal in the bunkers, he
the Trojan into Eupatoria Bay but a night
beating back and forth in order to keep
distance of the stranded vessel, could not b[e]
out the help of the screw. Better, perhaps,
boats and endeavor to take off her crew—
darkness, on a hostile coast guarded by ro[ving]
Cossacks, this, too, would carry a high risk. P
to pace the deck, wrestling with his problem
again heeled violently and he was compelled
the weather hammock netting to keep himself u[p]

Half an hour passed, then three quarters of a
the wind, to his intense relief, unexpectedly
and a wan moon made its appearance from
scudding clouds. He rapped an order to the
helm and raised his night glass, searching for so
the unknown ship but, beyond glimpsing a line
breakers a long way ahead, he could see nothin[g]
not sent up any more flares, he thought. Could
that she had, after all, managed to weather the
make for Eupatoria Bay? Or had her crew been
abandon her or, worse still, had she foundered
down, taking some or all of them with her? The[re]
means of knowing but he could not set the Troja[n]
for the bay until he had found an answer to the
he had asked himself—could not and would not.
suddenly, rising above the low moan of the wind

129

own upper-deck guns. That she could not use them with any effect became evident for, like the *Tiger,* she was lying close under the cliff and could not elevate any of her guns sufficiently to find their target. She tried but the few shots she managed to get off either buried themselves harmlessly in the overhang of the cliff face or ricochetted high above the heads of the Russian gunners. After this puny display of defianse, her crew were all engaged in fighting the fire on deck and their guns were—temporarily, at any rate—abandoned.

The Russians, satisfied that they were secure in their vantage point, lit a bonfire—for the purpose, Phillip could only suppose, of making the service of their field-pieces easier—and soon both guns and gunners could be seen, dark shapes silhouetted against the red glow of the brush-wood blaze. Evidently they had not, as yet, seen or heard the *Trojan*'s approach. The roar of their own guns and the pounding of the breakers on the rocks beneath them would, no doubt, drown the sound of her engines when he called for them, and probably the Russians were concentrating too intently on their helpless victim to observe the navigating lights of a ship at sea.

The *Trojan* was out of their range, of course and they, for that matter, were out of hers, Phillip decided regretfully. To have a chance of hitting them with his main-deck guns, he would have to come dangerously close inshore and, even then, in a heavy swell and at extreme elevation, it was doubtful whether even the *Trojan*'s well-practiced guns' crews could do more than force the enemy to withdraw temporarily. Whilst this might give the crew of the stranded ship a welcome respite, it would not, in the long run, save her, since he could not remain in position for very long and dared not attempt to anchor in deep water, lest *Trojan* suffer the same fate as the vessel she was endeavoring to assist. The darkness was an added hazard, as the fog had been when the *Tiger* was driven on

131

shore—accurate ranging on so small a target would be far from easy.

He descended to the deck and glanced at the 68-pounder mounted just forward of where he stood. Its range was greater than that of his main deck guns and positioned as it was, perhaps he could harry the enemy into retreat for long enough to send boats to take off the shipwrecked crew. If boats could be launched and if they could survive in this sea . . . he turned to Cochrane.

"Pass the word for the First Lieutenant and the Gunnery Officer, if you please, Mr. Cochrane. And then pipe hands to stations to wear ship. I'm coming about and——" he was interrupted by a voice urgently calling his name.

"Commander. . . ." It was Major Leach, pale and evidently still far from well but gamely determined as, with his single arm to aid him, he staggered awkwardly from the companionway. Anthony Cochrane went to him and assisted him to Phillip's side. "I heard gunfire," the Fusilier officer began and broke off, as he saw and slowly took in what was happening. With a murmured apology, he crossed to the starboard rail and stood there, clinging to it and staring across the heaving expanse of black water to the scene on the cliff top.

"Give the Major this, Mr. Cochrane," Phillip said, offering his glass and, as the Officer of the Watch took it from him, Martin Fox emerged from below. His gaze, too, went to the Russian gunners grouped around their bonfire and he winced as the twelve-pounders spoke again.

"So that's it!" His voice was low and shaken and, after a swift study of the scene, he turned to glance enquiringly at Phillip. "I don't recognize her, do you? But I don't believe she's one of ours although, in this infernal murk, it's hard to tell and I can't see her colors, if she has any hoisted. What are we going to do, Phillip? What in heaven's name *can* we do?"

Phillip was silent. The men of the duty watch were

132

assembling at their stations in obedience to the pipe and he nodded to Cochrane to carry on and then, brows knit in a frown, gave all his attention to the attempt to find an answer to the question his First Lieutenant had asked him. He considered one plan, only to discard it as impossible, thought of another but was compelled to discard that also, as being equally impossible. Finally, he said, "She's lying stern-on, Martin, and I fancy she's a transport—French, probably, although, as you say, it's hard to tell. From the little I can see of her, she doesn't appear to be badly damaged and her stern's afloat—though God alone knows what she's suffered for'ard."

"Perhaps not a lot," Fox suggested. "If her stern's clear, she can't have grounded too hard."

"Quite," Phillip agreed. "I'd like to tow her off, if I could. But we should have to close her to get a tow rope aboard and, even if we fire one across by rocket, we could still run a hell of a chance of joining her on shore ourselves. Failing a tow, perhaps we could send boats across and take her people off. I know it's a risk, in this sea but at least it would be the lesser risk. Whatever we attempt, we've got to drive those enemy gunners off for long enough to enable us to do it."

"The quarterdeck guns?" Martin Fox queried.

"The quarterdeck *gun*," Phillip amended. "We——" young Sutherland, the Gunnery Officer, was standing breathlessly at his side.

"You sent for me, sir?"

"I did, Mr. Sutherland." Briefly Phillip told him what he wanted done. "Pick your best crew and man the sixty-eight pounder. I'm going to wear and close the shore . . . go aloft and get the best sight you can on those field pieces. You won't have long on target and the range will be extreme . . ." he added a few technical instructions and dismissed the young Gunnery Officer, turning again to Martin Fox. "That's the best we can do, for the present,

133

I'm afraid. At least it will give them a breathing space and a chance to get their pumps to work and hose down that fire. Sutherland will distract the enemy's attention, for a time, anyway, though his chances of hitting them are pretty slim, I fear."

Fox inclined his head in thoughtful agreement.

"Shall I volunteer a boat's crew and have them standing by?"

"If you will, yes. And lend me your glass, Martin, for a moment . . . the Major has mine." Phillip gave the shoreline a careful and anxious scrutiny, and when, on Cochrane's shouted orders, the ship came about, he crossed the deck to continue his study of its rocky, dimly seen contours, marked here and there by a line of foaming breakers, lighter than the dark water from which they had emerged. With the *Trojan* close reaching on the port tack, he lowered the glass and, seeing that Sutherland and his gun's crew were waiting alertly by their gun, he called the Midshipman of the Watch over to him.

"Sir?" It was O'Hara, eager as always, his voice high-pitched with excitement.

"Stand by to pass on my orders to the gun's crew, Mr. O'Hara," Phillip bade him and again swung himself up into the mainmast shrouds. From there, his visibility was only a little better than from the deck and he silently cursed the dark murkiness of the night and the storm-driven clouds which had, once more, blotted out the faint light of the moon.

He knew now, as he clung to the shrouds, the night-glass to his eye, how helpless the crews of the other ships of the *Tiger's* squadron must have felt when she had been under attack. Fog had obscured their vision, as the darkness was obscuring his . . . they had heard the guns but had been unable to see them or even to make out exactly where the stricken frigate had been lying. He, at least, thank God, could catch occasional glimpses of his target and the Russians' bonfire, glowing through the darkness, enabled him to keep them in sight. He called down an order to the man at the helm, which O'Hara efficiently passed on at the pitch of his powerful young lungs, his voice under control now and then, as the light of the bonfire steadied and came abeam, he gave the order to open fire.

Sutherland's men worked well, maintaining a creditably rapid fire but, as Phillip had feared, with the best will in the world, it was not accurate. During the few minutes that he was able to allow them, they strove tirelessly to correct their errors but their last few shots fell short and, alarmed lest they should hit the grounded ship, he ordered them to cease fire. Twice more he came about and ran past, closing the range as much as he dared and, on the third tack, an exultant cheer from the men announced a near miss which sent the enemy gunners running for cover. But the *Trojan* was now perilously close inshore and he was forced to haul off. They had, however, achieved their first objective by scattering the Russian gunners, and the bonfire, starved of fuel, was reduced to a tiny red glow.

"That has bought the poor devils on the transport a little time," Martin Fox observed, when Phillip descended to the quarterdeck. "Let us hope they may use it to good purpose. They . . ." he gave a smothered exclamation, as from the deck of the transport, a flare zig-zagged skywards, momentarily bathing the whole area in a golden light. Phillip saw the boat pulling desperately towards the *Trojan* an instant before the maintop look-out yelled out a warning of her approach. In the brief glimpse he had, his mind registered the fact that the boat was a small gig, with only two men at the oars and two others, apparently baling in a frantic effort to keep their frail craft afloat. Then the light from the flare died away and he was left, peering blindly into the darkness, uncertain whether or

135

not he had really seen a boat but ... the look-out had reported one and Martin Fox, when he turned in mute question, nodded emphatically.

"It was a boat all right, sir. Shall we try to pick her up?"

"We must try," Phillip told him, wondering how, in that wilderness of tossing water, they would manage to do so. He issued his orders with a confidence he was far from feeling but, to his own thankful surprise, when the *Trojan* brought-to, a second flare from the stranded transport revealed a gig less than twenty yards from her. Two seamen, with scant regard for their own safety, assisted her crew to secure her to the frigate's chains and, aided by others leaning dangerously from the entry port, the four shipwrecked men were brought on board.

6

THE four rescued men proved to be French, as Phillip had surmised, one of them the transport's Second Mate, who gave his name as Gaspard and introduced his fellow oarsman as Lieutenant Lejeune, of the Chasseurs d'Afrique.

Leaving Martin Fox in charge of the deck, and the Gunnery Officer with instructions to return the enemy's fire whenever the opportunity arose, Phillip sent the French seamen below and escorted the two officers to his own cabin. He despatched his steward for hot coffee and, in the meantime, poured Gaspard and Lejeune liberal tots of rum. Wrapped in blankets and gratefully sipping their rum, they gave him a brief and moving account of what they had endured since the gale had driven their ship on to the rocky shore. The ship, the *Rapide*, was a small steam transport, schooner-rigged, Gaspard told him, carrying two Army surgeons, two Sisters of Mercy and medical supplies—all destined for the French base hospital at Kamiesch—and, in addition, fifteen cavalrymen and their horses. The *Rapide* had been making for Eupatoria in the hope of finding shelter there at the start of the gale but her rudder had been damaged and the mountainous seas had flooded her engine-room, and she had drifted helplessly until driven aground some three hours before the first of her distress rockets had been sighted by the *Trojan*.

"We sent them up," Gaspard explained, in tolerably

good English, "in the faint hope that someone might see them and come to our aid. They brought you, Monsieur, praise be to God ... but alas, we were already under enemy attack, for they also brought the Russians. Their guns would, it is certain, have destroyed or set us ablaze had you not driven them off with your shells. You gave us time to extinguish the fire they had started on our forecastle."

Phillip questioned him about damage and learned that the engine-room had been pumped dry, temporary repairs made to the rudder and—apart from whatever harm the fire had caused—as far as Gaspard knew, his ship was seaworthy.

"Our cargo is sorely needed by the hospital at Kamiesch," the Second Mate added. "Also the surgeons and the two brave women we carry, *les deux religeuses* ... I—my *capitaine* sent me out to you to beg that you will assist us, if you can, to get our ship off the rocks. Had you, perhaps, thought that it might be possible to tow us off, Monsieur?"

"Yes," Phillip assured him. "I have given it much thought. But, before I can attempt to get a tow-rope aboard you, those Russian gunners must be forced to withdraw. I can only bring one quarterdeck gun to bear on them, Monsieur Gaspard and, as you will have observed, at night and with this sea running, accurate fire is virtually impossible. But, if I am to attempt to tow you off, our best chance will be before daylight, there is no doubt and——"

"But you have surely more than one gun?" the Chasseur lieutenant put in, his tone puzzled. "Is this not an English frigate of"—he spread his hands—"at least twenty guns?"

"My ship has thirty-one," Phillip answered wryly, "or to be strictly accurate, thirty—we lost our second sixty-eight pounder in the storm. But without running the risk

138

of joining your ship on the rocks, I cannot use my main-deck guns. You will understand . . ." he was explaining the reason for this to the mystified young cavalryman when Major Leach requested his permission to join them.

"I have a suggestion to put to you, Commander Hazard. That is why I have ventured to intrude on you, I——"

"You are not intruding, Major," Phillip assured him. He made the necessary introductions, hearing as he did so, the renewed thunder of guns from on shore. Guessing his thoughts, Major Leach observed gravely, "Yes, they are again firing on the *Rapide* and now they've brought up a full battery of four guns—I suspect with the intention of holding off your ship, Commander. The guns are well spread out, to make them an even more difficult target than they were before . . . which is the reason behind my suggestion, if you will hear it."

"Of course, sir." Time was passing, Phillip thought uneasily, aware that if he were to have even a slim chance of rescuing the passengers and crew of the wrecked transport, he must do so while darkness hid the approach of the *Trojan*'s boats. Or, indeed, of the *Trojan* herself, if he attempted a tow for, with daylight, the Russians could bring up still more guns and blow her out of the water if she came within their range. . . .

Again uncannily as if he had spoken his thoughts aloud, Leach said, "Mr. Fox tells me that you would endeavor to tow off the *Rapide* if there were any way of silencing the enemy battery—is that so?" Phillip nodded and the soldier went on, turning briefly to the young Chasseur officer, "One of your men informed me that you found a path leading to the cliff top and that you led a party up there, *mon lieutenant,* intending to try to pick off the enemy gunners with muskets?" The cavalryman looked blank until Leach repeated himself in excellent

French, upon which, beaming, he replied with a torrent of excited words in the same language.

"He says, Hazard, that the cliff path is only about fifty yards from their ship," Leach translated. "And that, at the summit, he found a place among the rocks which offered excellent protection for a party of, perhaps, up to a dozen men. I'd like to volunteer to lead a party of eight of *my* men, all good shots, up that path . . . if you can put us ashore. Once in position, I would guarantee to occupy the attention of the enemy gunners for long enough to enable you to tow off the French ship. Or, if that should prove impossible, then to take off her passengers and crew. Will you consider my suggestion?"

It was almost the only practical suggestion he *could* consider, Phillip thought, but he hesitated, frowning. "Why did Lieutenant Lejeune fail when he made the attempt?" he asked.

Gaspard answered him with a resigned shrug of the shoulders. "They had capsized the boat in which they went to the foot of the path, Monsieur, and their powder, as well as their carbines, became wet. They were unable to open fire when they reached the summit of the cliff and therefore returned to the ship for fresh ammunition. They were not seen, ascending or descending, and would have gone back without hesitation, had we not sighted your frigate. Lejeune will, I am certain, volunteer to guide your party to the path or even back to the summit—*n'est pas, mon lieutenant?*"

"Of course," Lejeune assented readily.

"Good," Phillip said. His mind busy with the various courses now open to him, he consulted his pocket watch. "How long do you think it would take you to get your party into position on the cliff top, Major?" he asked Leach.

"It took the Frenchmen thirty-five minutes—with Lejeune to guide us, let us say twenty-five to thirty, once we

140

are ashore." The Major's tone was confident and he added quietly, "And I can relieve you of one small problem, which may be on your mind, Commander—you need not concern yourself with the question of how we are to get back to the ship. Eupatoria is only about fourteen miles distant as the crow flies, according to my map, and perhaps twenty by the post road ... which, of course, we should avoid and——"

"But we cannot abandon you in enemy-held territory," Phillip objected. "The boat in which you land will stay to take you off."

"You may require all your boats for rescue work, Hazard, if you're unable to take the *Rapide* in tow," the Major pointed out, with irrefutable logic. "I am quite confident, I assure you, that with eight well-trained soldiers and an adequate supply of ammunition, I can make my way to the town. Please"—as Phillip opened his mouth to voice another protest—"permit me to know best in what is, you will agree, a purely military problem. In matters of seamanship I yield to *your* judgement, Hazard, but in this. . . ." He rose, smiling. "And now, I think, if you will excuse me, I will go and choose my men and make sure that their firearms are protected against a possible ducking."

Phillip let him go, with some reluctance. When he saw him again, the *Trojan* was closing the shore and his boats' crews standing by to lower the first boat. Leach had mustered his small party by the entry port, each man with his musket carefully wrapped in oilskin and each wearing a borrowed naval watch coat over his scarlet jacket. Phillip recognized the young French officer, Lejeune, similarly equipped and then, to his stunned astonishment, noticed that Lord Henry Durbanville stood with them, also with a shrouded musket but wearing a grey Guards overcoat, his servant with him.

He offered no comment but his surprise must have

141

registered for, as he halted by the little group, Durbanville said, with a hint of defiance, "I am a good shot, Commander. I have won medals for my shooting and, in any case, as I told Major Leach, I can stand no more of your ship's infernal rolling and pitching—I shall be very much more comfortable on dry land. I—er—" he held out his hand. "I bid you good-bye, sir."

Phillip accepted the proffered hand, feeling, for the first time in their brief acquaintance, some liking for the boy. Arrogant and unpleasant in manner he might be, but at least he did not lack courage. "I see," he said. "Then au revoir, Captain Durbanville—and I wish you every success in your mission."

"Thank you, Commander Hazard. I have no doubt that it will be successful. As"—the addition was made with studied insolence—"I trust yours may be." He drew himself up and saluted. "Perhaps we shall meet again."

"Perhaps," Phillip acknowledged stiffly. His farewell to Major Leach and Lieutenant Lejeune was more cordial and Leach, after expressing his thanks for all that had been done for him, wrung Phillip's hand warmly.

"I have a letter here, if I might prevail upon you to take charge of it, Hazard—to my wife, you understand. Should my military judgement prove, after all, to be at fault, I should be deeply obliged if you would consign it to her. Good-bye, my friend—and good luck!"

"Good luck to *you*, sir," Phillip answered with sincerity. "The boat will wait for Lejeune, so that if you change your mind about not rejoining us, you'll have that much longer in which to do so."

He returned to the deck to watch the launching of the boat which, under Martin Fox's careful supervision, was accomplished without a hitch. The men of Major Leach's party were assisted into it and, under the command of Lieutenant Laidlaw, the boat put off and was lost to sight in the darkness as the *Trojan* again got under way. From

142

the shore, the Russian guns kept up their merciless attack on the French transport and, with time to spare while Leach and his party were rowed to the foot of the cliffs, Phillip decided to make a final attempt to silence them with the 68-pounder. Like all the rest, the first few shots were unsuccessful but, with his next, Sutherland scored a hit on a carelessly positioned limber containing what could only have been the battery's reserve of powder. The weary gun's crew cheered themselves hoarse as they watched the resulting blaze shoot skywards and saw the enemy gunners scatter in panic as first the limber and then a number of shells exploded in a series of dull roars.

"Well done, Mr. Sutherland!" Phillip shouted above the din, and the Gunnery Officer turned a smoke-grimed face towards him, beaming with pride. To Martin Fox, who stood beside him, Phillip observed with satisfaction, "And it was also well timed, I think. The boat should be almost at the foot of the path now, if they've kept afloat. You haven't seen their signal yet, have you?"

Watching intently with his glass, Fox shook his head but corrected himself a moment later. "That's it, that's the lantern signal now! They've made the shore, sir." His tone was exultant. "As you say, the hit was well timed. And if that *was* their reserve powder, those gunners may find themselves running short, which will be all to the good. What now, sir?"

"Well, we have to allow twenty-five to thirty-five minutes for Leach to ascend the cliff and take up his position," Phillip responded, conscious that, for all the icy chill of the wind, his brow and the palms of his hands were damp with perspiration. "One more run for Sutherland's gun, I think, to distract the enemy's attention and then we'll go in under engines, Martin." He gestured towards the shore. "They've ceased fire, do you hear? If they have to send for more ammunition, it will gain another respite for which, I am sure, our Frenchmen will be

143

thankful. The *Rapide* has two women on board—nuns of a nursing order—did you know?"

"No, I didn't." Martin Fox lowered his glass, turning to stare across at Phillip in horrified surprise. "Poor souls, what they must be enduring!" He passed on the necessary orders to Cochrane and Sutherland and returned to his post, his glass once more trained on the shore. Over his shoulder he said, "I wish it was not quite so infernally dark! Have you decided how we shall get the tow-rope across?"

"Not yet," Phillip admitted. "It rather depends on circumstances and how much we can see, when we close the *Rapide*. But by rocket, if Leach *is* able to hold those gunners. It will be the quickest way, don't you agree?"

"Yes. But if he's not able to hold them?"

"Then by boat, I suppose. We shall have to send boats to take off her passengers in any event—the two nuns and the Army surgeons and any wounded she may have. Because even if we get a tow-rope to her, we may not be able to haul her off." This was as far as he had gone in his plan of action but now, Phillip knew, he would have to work out, in detail, what they would need to do. Of necessity his plans had to be flexible—so many things could go wrong at the last minute and there was no way in which he could guard against every possible eventuality. But if he put Martin Fox in charge of the boats and left all decisions to him, including the direction of an armed landing party, which would cover the evacuation of the passengers and any wounded who could be moved, then the flexibility he wanted could be achieved. His First Lieutenant would, in this case, have to decide on the spot whether an attempt to tow the *Rapide* off was—or was not—feasible. He was an experienced and completely reliable officer, capable of making such a decision . . . there need be no anxiety on that account and, if the French ship could not, in Fox's opinion, be refloated, then he would

144

have to supervise the loading of passengers and crew into the boats. Should this be necessary . . . Phillip sighed. The boats might have to make two or even three trips, unless the *Rapide*'s own boats were able to help. He would have to keep the *Trojan* as close inshore as he could, so as to cut down the distance they had to row and he would have to have at least one boat standing by, in case any of the others were swamped in the heavy swell or ran into any other kind of trouble.

If, on the other hand, Fox decided that it was worth while trying to tow off the French ship, then one boat—O'Hara's—would suffice to bring off the four passengers and the wounded could stay on board their own ship. An armed landing party might be required to give Major Leach support . . . Phillip frowned. He wished he had more Marines but, in common with most of the ships in the British Fleet, two-thirds of the *Trojan*'s normal complement of Marines were serving as part of the Balaclava defense force, under their Captain, Alex Murray. The men who remained were commanded by young Lieutenant Smithson, who had little experience of active service conditions but . . . Phillip's frown relaxed. Cochrane could take charge of the landing party, augmented by some tried and trusted seamen, with a boat standing by to take them off as soon as possible after the *Rapide* was refloated. Should anything go wrong, both landing party and boat's crew would have a chance of boarding the French ship. A system of signals would have to be worked out—Midshipman Grey could attend to that—and now all he had to decide was exactly how he could ensure the safety of his own ship and how best he could handle her throughout the operation.

"Martin . . ." as briefly as possible, Phillip explained what he proposed to do and was relieved when his second-in-command nodded approvingly.

"I'll send young Grey to you, shall I, and then make a

start by assembling the boats' crews and landing party?"

"Yes, if you would, please. Grey can devise a signal to cover each stage of the operation, using a lantern to show negative or affirmative. In case of emergency or to signal a change of plan, the landing party had better take some distress rockets with them. And Smithson is to remain on board."

"Aye, aye, sir. Is that all?"

"Yes. Carry on, will you, Martin? I want to have a word with Mr. Burnaby." Phillip entered the chartroom as the quarterdeck gun once again opened fire. He listened, tense and anxious, as he and the Master pored over charts but this time there were no triumphant cheers from the gun's crew. Young Grey reported just after the 68-pounder ceased fire and, his quick, intelligent mind grasping at once what was required, he settled himself at a corner of the chart table with signal pad and pencil.

"You'll wish me to take over the deck, sir?" Burnaby asked.

Phillip nodded. "Yes, if you please, Mr. Burnaby. I'm putting Mr. Cochrane in charge of the landing party, under the First Lieutenant. Have two good hands on the lead . . . these charts are not too accurate."

"Aye, aye, sir. Just one more point—when we bring the ship inshore, are you intending that the enemy should see her or are we to endeavor to slip in, without attracting their attention?"

This was a question that had been in Phillip's thoughts for some time and he hesitated, still undecided. There were obvious advantages to the second alternative since, if the enemy did not suspect his intentions until the last possible moment, he would have a much better chance of carrying them out successfully. On the other hand, if he doused the *Trojan*'s deck and navigating lights, the boats would find it hard to locate her and, heavily laden as they might be and with a strong sea running, it was essential that he pick them up with the minimum delay. They would have to depend on sighting the ship in order to rendezvous with her, since he could not forecast her position at any given time and, indeed, might have to change both plan and position without warning should circumstances demand it. Grey's signals could be used, to inform the boats' crews and the landing party of any such change but ... Phillip sighed. A great deal *had* to be left to chance and, whatever he did in an effort to hide the *Trojan*'s approach, the enemy might still see her and, as easily, guess her intention when they realized that she was closing the shore.

He looked at old Burnaby, aware that the Master was still waiting for a reply to his question and was tempted to ask his opinion. Captain North had never invited any of his officers to express an opinion, he reminded himself, he had never sought advice, never explained any order he gave or considered that he ought to justify it. As commander, his must be the final decision, he knew but ... Burnaby had had a great many more years at sea than he had. He was a fine seaman and a wise old man, who never offered advice but, when he was asked, he gave it freely and it was usually good.

Phillip broke the silence. "In my place, Mr. Burnaby, what would you do?"

"I've been wondering," the Master confessed. "Ever since we sighted that Frenchman. In your place, Mr. Hazard, I believe I'd try to tow her off, if I could manage it without risking the *loss* of my own ship." His deliberate emphasis on the word "loss" brought a brief, appreciative smile from Phillip. It implied that, like himself, Burnaby was prepared to risk damage to the *Trojan* but no more and he was conscious of a feeling of relief. "The least risk to this ship," Burnaby went on, "is to slip her inshore without being seen, is it not?"

"Yes, obviously," Phillip confirmed. "Carry on, Mr. Burnaby."

"Well, sir, as I see the situation, the *Trojan* is safe enough while she's out of range of those shore guns and under her engines, she's not likely to be driven ashore. So that another run past and a few more shots from the quarterdeck gun would, I fancy, aid the boats to get safely across to the Frenchman, because the Russians will be watching us and not the boats . . . which I take it is what you are aiming at." Burnaby, too, was smiling now. "After that, sir," he added, "I'd employ a little deception, I think."

"Deception, Mr. Burnaby?"

The old man inclined his grizzled head. "Aye, sir. I'd try to mislead them—make them think we're on one course when, in fact, we're proceeding in the opposite direction. It could be done, sir."

"Could it?" Phillip was interested. "How?"

The Master's smile widened. "There was a little trick we tried on the Chinese in '42 which might work, sir. Those gunners can't see much but, if they can see anything at all, it will be our navigating lights and, of course, the gun flashes. Well, sir, suppose we make another run past, with our navigating lights reversed—green showing to port and red to starboard—and then douse all lights and close the shore? We should bring-to where they weren't expecting us, which might give us a useful few minutes in hand, so to speak, sir."

Young Grey, who had been listening to the Master's suggestion with as much interest as Phillip, could not suppress an excited exclamation.

"Beg pardon, sir, it isn't for me to speak, I know, sir but . . . it's a capital idea and I believe it would work. And I could make some signals too, sir—confusing ones, purporting to be to another of our Fleet—so that we could fox them properly, sir."

148

"Restrain yourself, Mr. Grey," Phillip bade him, but without rancor, "you will have more than enough to do maintaining communication between the boats and ourselves. Have you worked out your signals yet?"

"Yes, sir." Grey offered his pad for inspection.

"Good." Phillip studied it and then returned the pad to him. "Find the First Lieutenant and Mr. Cochrane and make sure that these signals are made clear to them. Instruct your Chief Yeoman to issue signal lanterns and to make sure that each boat has a supply of rockets. And Mr. Grey——"

"Sir?" All eagerness, the boy waited.

"One more signal to add to yours—a green rocket or, in an emergency, a series of long and short blasts on our steam whistle is to recall all boats and to be obeyed immediately. Clear?"

"Aye, aye, sir." Young Robin Grey sped off on his errand and Phillip turned again to the grey-haired old Master.

"As our young gentleman rightly observed, yours is a capital idea, Mr. Burnaby, for which I am grateful. Relieve Mr. Cochrane of the deck now, if you please, and take in all sail. We'll proceed under engines and, as soon as you've seen the boats away, start putting your plan into operation. Those Russian gunners may not know port from starboard but . . . it's worth trying."

"Aye, sir, I think it is," the Master agreed.

With no lights showing, the *Trojan* slowly closed the shore, propelled by her screw. Burnaby brought her to and the boats were lowered, not without difficulty but, to Phillip's heartfelt relief, without mishap. There was still no signal from Major Leach's party but, Phillip realized with astonishment, only thirty minutes had passed since the first boat had grounded at the foot of the cliff. Warning young Grey to keep a keen look out, he saw the reversed navigating lamps placed in position and rekindled and heard Burnaby order their change of course.

On this, which would, he hoped, be their final run, Sutherland's crew—with the range considerably shortened—gave the 68-pounder its maximum elevation and maintained a rapid fire which was returned from the cliff top. The dismaying news that the gun had jammed was, to a certain extent, offset by a report from Grey that Major Leach's signal had at last been made. Sutherland and his Chief Gunner's Mate were working on the 68-pounder, confident that they could have it back in operation within ten or fifteen minutes, and Phillip knew that, if it were humanly possible, their promise would be kept. The gun was, in any case, the least of his worries now, he thought and, when Martin Fox's first boat flashed intelligence of the landing party's arrival across the expanse of heaving dark water which lay between them, Phillip gave the order to douse all lights and again close the shore.

There was no means of knowing whether or not Burnaby's ruse had deceived the watchers on the cliff top and it seemed to take an interminable time to bring the ship in under her screw. Phillip stood with the Master, glass to his eye, listening to the monotonous chant of the leadsman in the main chains. There was an adequate depth of water but this began alarmingly to lessen as the minutes passed and he was compelled to order the engines to "Dead Slow."

On board the *Rapide,* as they neared her, lights could be seen, coming from her lower deck. The fire on her upper deck had, seemingly, been put out and, although he could see nothing, Phillip guessed, from the sounds carrying across the water, that her crew were at work heaving guns and other heavy gear overboard, in an effort to lighten her. This could only mean that Martin Fox had reached her with the information that the *Trojan* would attempt to take her in tow . . . he turned to Burnaby and the Master nodded his understanding, as from the cliff top high above their heads, first one and then another of the Russian guns again opened up. They were firing on the luckless *Rapide* but a few shots, wildly off target, spattered the narrowing gap between the two ships. Burnaby's ruse had succeeded, Phillip's mind registered, but for how long they could conceal the *Trojan's* presence was a matter of conjecture, and the most difficult part of the maneuver had yet to be attempted. He had to bring his ship about and ease her, stern first, close enough to the French ship to be able to take her in tow . . . and the tow-rope must be got across to her. He expelled his breath in a long sigh, listening tensely to the leadsman's monotonous chant.

There was a crackle of musketry, almost drowned by the echoing roar of the Russian guns, but Phillip knew that Major Leach and his party were now firing on the enemy gunners. That their fire was effective very soon became apparent, since that directed on the French ship grew suddenly less and then ceased altogether. He blessed Leach and blessed him still more warmly when O'Hara's boat hailed them and, a few minutes later, secured to the starboard chains. The first of the *Rapide's* passengers were in it and they included the two nuns, shivering in the tarpaulin sheets in which O'Hara's men had wrapped them but, mercifully, unhurt and unafraid. . . .

It took a further seemingly interminable thirty minutes to work the *Trojan* into position and get the tow-rope aboard the stranded *Rapide*. Aware that, at times, he had little more than a fathom of water under his keel, Phillip— although outwardly calm—felt almost sick with apprehension. Both wind and swell had moderated considerably but his anxiety did not lessen until he was able, at last, to take his ship into deeper water. Even then, he waited anxiously for the Russian guns to open fire on her, unable to believe that they were still in ignorance of her presence

151

or that Leach and Durbanville and their tiny party could have held the enemy at bay so consistently and for so long. But, apparently, they had. The sound of musketry still reached him faintly, coming from several different parts of the cliff top but the wind distorted the sound and he could not tell whether only Leach's fusiliers were firing or whether the Russians were answering their challenge.

Towing the *Rapide* off the stony beach was, to his surprised relief, the easiest part of the whole operation. She slid off, as if eager to return to her accustomed element and only for a short time was there any undue strain on the *Trojan*'s 300-horse-power engine. Then she was afloat, stern on and with a distinct list to starboard, but with no other visible sign of damage and Phillip let out his breath in a deep sigh of thankfulness.

By reason of her list and the crashing breakers which sought constantly to cast her back from whence she had come, she was an awkward tow and only became more manageable when Phillip increased the *Trojan*'s engine speed and her own screw started to turn. The Russian gunners, as if suddenly wakening to the realization that their prey was about to escape them, blazed away at both ships in a frenzy of activity. Their aim, however, was hurried and the range rapidly lengthening, so that most of their shots fell short. Three or four half-spent round shot thudded against the *Trojan*'s quarter, as she came about, and then fell harmlessly into the sea. Only when two of the guns loaded with chain shot did they cause either ship any trouble and then it was of short duration, the *Rapide* coming off worst in the encounter.

Sutherland's 68-pounder, once more operational, returned the cannonade from the shore and a series of small flashes from the head of the cliff path revealed that Leach's party was still a force to be reckoned with. Regretting now that he had not insisted on leaving a boat to take the soldiers off, Phillip called out to Midshipman Grey to fire the recall signal for his remaining boats, and the *Trojan* brought-up, well out of range of the enemy guns, to await their return. As she did so, the *Rapide*'s captain hailed Phillip with the news that he could proceed under his own power.

"I will cast off your tow-rope, Monsieur, with my deepest thanks for your so timely assistance." He added, in his strongly accented English, that his ship was leaking fairly badly but that her pumps were holding their own and he would make for the anchorage in Eupatoria Bay.

Phillip wished him well and the *Rapide,* leaving her passengers on board the *Trojan,* dropped astern and was soon lost to sight in the darkness. From the shore a fierce cannonading could be heard and Phillip began to worry about the safety of his boats and the two landing parties. To aid them, he ordered that a second recall rocket should be fired and, almost immediately, two boats made their appearance in the brief light of the rocket. First to return was Laidlaw's and then, a few minutes later, Martin Fox's came alongside, two men assisting the First Lieutenant from the sternsheets. Phillip met him at the entry port and saw that his head was roughly bandaged and his right cheek dark with congealed blood.

"It's nothing, sir—a splinter from the *Rapide*'s deck, which looks worse than it is." He forestalled Phillip's question, and then posed one of his own, "I'd like permission to return to shore, sir, if you've no objection."

"In your present state, I have every reason to refuse you permission but"—Phillip drew his second-in-command to one side—"why do you want to go back, Martin? Is Cochrane in trouble?"

Fox inclined his bandaged head, wincing involuntarily as he did so. "Yes, I'm afraid he is. I sent him to support Major Leach's party but the Russians caught him on his way up the cliff path and he's suffered a number of casualties. We brought three of his men back"—he gestured to where, from the boat he had just left, three injured seamen were being assisted on board the *Trojan*—"Wilks, Strachan and Mackay, sir. But there are others, from his party and Leach's, although Laidlaw took off two of the fusiliers ... all men who were able to walk, with assistance. The rest will have to be carried."

"I see." Phillip's heart sank. "Exactly what is the situation, as briefly as possible?"

"Well, sir, the Russians have four guns, twelve-pounders mounted in battery and apparently they've been joined by a mounted Cossack patrol. When Leach's fusiliers started their sharpshooting, all four guns were ranged on the *Rapide*. The attack from the head of the cliff path obviously took them by surprise and must have been fairly successful. All four guns ceased fire, a wounded fusilier told me, and the gunners ran for cover. But ..." Fox sighed. "The Cossacks took a hand and must have reported how few men Leach actually had. The next thing we heard, just after you took the *Rapide* in tow, was a terrific cannonading. We realized they had boused two guns round in order to range them on Leach's party and, although I gather from Lejeune that the position they're holding is quite a strong one, behind a natural barricade of rocks, it's hardly proof against cannon. And Leach can't hope to make his way to Eupatoria overland, because those infernal Cossacks are there to cut him off. Also he has wounded. I think they'll have to be taken off by boat, Phillip, there's no other way. Which is why I——"

Phillip cut him short, his gaze on two more wounded men, both unconscious, now being handed up from Laidlaw's boat. Two of the *Rapide*'s seamen, he decided, as Surgeon Fraser gave each man a cursory examination and then ordered them to be carried below. "What of Cochrane, Martin?" he asked. "Do you know where he is? Did he join Leach or what?"

"That was his intention," Martin Fox confirmed. "Or,

alternatively, he said he would try to work his way round behind Leach, in order to create a diversion and enable Leach to withdraw down the cliff. But I'm afraid he must have been spotted—by the Cossacks, probably—before he could get his party under cover. Wilks and Strachan were wounded before they were halfway up the cliff path. That's why I want to go back. You see——"

"No." Again Phillip interrupted him. "I'm sorry, Martin, you're in no fit state to go back. Carrying wounded down that cliff is a task for fit men. You and your boat's crew are wet and exhausted and Laidlaw's too. You——"

"But, Phillip, I can volunteer a fresh boat's crew and——"

"I shall go myself," Phillip told him. "You will please take command of this ship in my absence."

"Sir, is it not my prerogative, as First Lieutenant, to take command of boat and landing parties?" Fox objected. "Besides I——"

"Mr. Fox, I have given you an order." Phillip's tone was one that brooked no further argument. "Is it not my prerogative, as commander, to have my orders obeyed without question?"

"Yes, of course, sir. But . . ." Martin Fox abandoned formality and added, his tone pleading, "Phillip, I beg you to permit me to go. I'm perfectly fit and I let young Cochrane in for the trouble he's met with, so that I——"

"We are wasting time," Phillip pointed out. He called the Master over and gave his orders with crisp decision, before turning once more to his discomfited First Lieutenant. "Mr. Sutherland can continue to give support with the sixty-eight pounder. Have that wound of yours attended to, Mr. Fox, and then take command of the ship. We will employ the same system of signals but with one addition—a red followed by a white rocket will be the signal for you to close the shore, but remain out of range of the enemy's guns. You understand?"

155

"Aye, aye, sir," Martin Fox acknowledged resignedly. He gripped Phillip's arm. "Good luck."

"Thanks, Martin. And I'd be obliged if you would have that head wound of yours attended to at once. Mr. Burnaby"—the old Master was at his side. "Volunteer fresh crews for both boats, if you please. There are wounded to be taken off. I shall be in command of Mr. Fox's boat and I'd like Mr. Smithson to divide his Marines between the two boats. And we shall need stretcher parties and a medical officer."

"Aye, aye, sir." Burnaby's shrewd old eyes met his with an unvoiced question in them but, when Phillip did not answer it, he went silently to carry out his orders. Burnaby, it was evident, did not wholly approve of his decision to leave the ship but . . . Laidlaw was soaked to the skin and exhausted and, as he had told Martin Fox, this was a task for fresh men. He *had* to go, the men on shore were his responsibility, as well as the ship, Phillip told himself, as he crossed to the entry port. His gig's crew, with the addition of three others, had now manned Fox's boat, and Laidlaw's, secured astern of it, was in the process of taking aboard a fresh crew, under the command of Midshipman Grey. Lieutenant Smithson was in his own boat, a Marine Sergeant in the other, their men's muskets protected against immersion. Grey's boat cast off and his own came to the foot of the accommodation ladder. A small figure, smothered in oilskins, sat in the sternsheets but it was not until Phillip took his place beside the boy that he realized it was O'Hara.

"Mr. O'Hara," he said sternly, "I gave instructions that fresh crews were to be volunteered. You've already been ashore with a boat, have you not?"

"Yes, sir," the boy admitted. "But I'm your gig's midshipman, sir, and these are my men. Let me come, sir, please. I'm perfectly fresh, sir, I promise you I am."

There was no time to waste and Phillip gave in. "Very

156

well, Mr. O'Hara, you may come. But you'll stay in the boat. Carry on."

"Aye, aye, sir," O'Hara acknowledged happily. "Cast off forrard," he shouted to the bowman and, as the boat left the shelter of *Trojan*'s stout wooden side and felt the full force of wind and swell, "Give way together—come on, my lads, put your backs into it! Pull!" The boat's crew pulled with a will but it was a long, hard pull and they were all exhausted and breathless by the time the boat grounded on the rocky beach. The boat which still waited for the return of Laidlaw's party was only a few yards off and the midshipman sent the two men who were waiting with him to assist in hauling Phillip's boat on to the shingle.

"Bale her out, while you're waiting, Mr. O'Hara," Phillip instructed his young boat commander. "And signal the shore party, as soon as you can, to let them know we're coming. Also I think you'd better post a look-out at the first bend in the path. As wounded are brought down to the beach, load them into Mr. Malcolm's boat, and then into Mr. Grey's and each is to put back to the ship as soon as his boat is fully loaded. On no account are any of the boat commanders to leave their boats, is that understood?" Both midshipmen assured him that it was. "You know the signal for recall, Mr. Malcolm?"

"Yes, sir." The boy repeated it.

"Right. Keep a watch on the cliffs. A red and white rocket will be my signal for the *Trojan* to close the shore but, if that is followed by a second red, you are to put off to the ship as soon as you see it—without waiting for anyone else to rejoin you. Clear, Mr. O'Hara?"

"Aye, aye, sir. But——" O'Hara hesitated. "When you say *anyone* else, sir, are you including yourself?"

Phillip smiled at him. "I am, Mr. O'Hara. One has to be prepared for every possible contingency and I want no heroics from you or your boats' crews, either of you. Tell

157

Mr. Grey the same. You are here to take off wounded. If you are fired on by the enemy, take cover close under the cliff. If necessary, drag the boats up with you."

"I understand, sir." Shyly O'Hara held out his hand. "Good luck, sir. It—it's like the *Tiger,* isn't it, in a way?"

It was, Phillip reflected ruefully, remembering that O'Hara had been in command of the boat which had taken him out to the ill-starred frigate. He wrung the outstretched hand.

"Don't worry, youngster—I'll make a point of coming back this time!" He smiled again at both youngsters and followed the rest of his small party to the beach.

The darkness was not quite so intense now and the gun flashes from the cliff top gave him his direction. Head bent against the wind, he led his party to the foot of the path, finding this without much difficulty. Smithson, the Marine Lieutenant, gestured above their heads to where the crackle of musket fire could faintly be heard and observed gravely, "They're not firing quite so rapidly now, sir, are they? I wonder how many of them are left?"

Phillip had also been wondering much the same thing and, as they ascended the path in single file—the Marines in advance of the seamen with stretchers—he was listening intently and with growing apprehension to the sporadic firing. There were some of the landing party left, obviously but ... *how* many? And were they Leach's men or Cochrane's?

After a steady ten minutes' climb, a faint voice hailed them—an English voice—and, rounding a curve in the steep path, they found four seamen of Cochrane's party, all wounded, sheltering beneath an outcrop of rock. The man who had hailed them told Phillip that the rest of his party had, as far as he knew, joined up with Major Leach's men.

"They caught us a bit higher up the path, sir," the seaman said. "Cossacks, I think they were, firing down on

158

us with muskets and pistols ... we walked right into them. Mr. Cochrane returned their fire and drove them off—our shooting was better than theirs, sir. Then he had us carried down here and he said we was to wait until he could get back to us ... not that there was much else we could do. Then he went on up, sir, with the others, and we've not seen him since. The Bo'sun's Mate, Cleary, sir, he's hurt pretty bad. I did what I could for him but he's bled a lot, sir."

"Good man," Phillip told him warmly. "We'll have you down to the boats as soon as we can." He left the young military surgeon, who had volunteered to accompany him, to care for the injured men and detailed two of his stretcher parties to get them back to the beach. With his now depleted party, he continued to climb, after cautioning all of them to move as quietly as possible and to maintain strict silence. They met no one—the enemy apparently not having seen the approach of the two boats or else not expecting that an attempt at rescue would be made. From above them, the sound of firing continued but now it was almost exclusively small arms fire, with an occasional roar from a single cannon. Lieutenant Smithson said, his voice low but holding a note of suppressed excitement, "They obviously don't think the opposition merits the use of their guns, sir."

Or more probably, Phillip thought, the Russian commander believed that the *Trojan,* having accomplished her purpose and towed the French transport safely out of his clutches, had abandoned the shore parties, leaving them to fend for themselves. In which supposition, he would imagine that there was no reason for undue haste. Lack of ammunition, food and sleep must eventually compel the survivors to surrender, so that, by his reckoning, the expenditure of his own ammunition would be wasteful. He had only to wait, employing a few of his men to pin down the British party and prevent their escape,

159

either back by the way they had come or overland to Eupatoria . . . climbing steadily upwards, Phillip frowned. The sky, he realized, was lighter than it had been. Dawn was not far off and with daylight, the danger to his own party would increase. His resources were limited, those of the Russians were not and, at present, all he had in his favor was the element of surprise—an advantage of which the dawning of day would rob him, unless he could make effective use of it. But how? They were nearing the head of the path and he paused to get his bearings, a hand on Smithson's shoulder to bring him to a halt. To his right, judging by the sound of desultory musket fire, Leach was entrenched, with Cochrane and the rest of their two parties. He could not see them, but could glimpse a massive outcrop of rock in dark silhouette against the now greying sky, which appeared to answer the description Lejeune had supplied.

"Shall I make a reconaissance, sir?" Smithson offered but Phillip shook his head.

"No. I'll have a look round myself. You wait here." Careful to make no noise, he moved on and upwards, aware that the *Trojan* had ceased her supporting fire, which had until now come at regular and almost predictable intervals. That could, of course, mean that the 68-pounder had again jammed or . . . cautiously he raised his head. It could mean that the Russian gun battery had withdrawn or was about to withdraw, leaving the Cossacks to await the surrender of the British landing party. And if that were so . . . Phillip inched his way forward, his eyes straining into the darkness. He heard the clink of metal on metal, a shouted order and then the thudding of horses' hooves on the iron-hard ground and, abandoning caution, moved swiftly forward, the wind knifing through him as he emerged from the shelter of the cliff path. One gun, at any rate, *was* withdrawing—however limited his vision, the sounds were unmistakable. He waited, his heart thudding as if it were echoing the hoofbeats, and heard a second gun limber up and canter past him.

The odds were, at least, more even now, he thought, although a sudden fusilade from his left warned him that the Cossacks were still attacking the men entrenched behind their barricade of rock to his right, from whom a few sporadic shots came in answer. As they had before, his mind registered, suggesting either that they were running short of ammunition or that their numbers had been seriously depleted. Then, with a suddenness that took him completely by surprise, a series of shots—evidently fired by one or, at most, two riflemen—came from a new direction, to his right front and a high-pitched scream of pain testified to their effectiveness. A shouted order, in Russian, brought Phillip to a standstill, again searching the grey dimness and, at the same moment as he heard the sound of marching men, he glimpsed a moving shadow, dark against the skyline, coming towards him.

A party of Cossacks, he decided who, as nearly as he could judge, were making for the cliff path, presumably with the intention of outflanking Leach's position and cutting off his retreat. He doubled back, to be met by Smithson with the information that Leach and Cochrane had started to evacuate their wounded, of whom two had already begun the descent to the beach, with the assistance of his own stretcher parties.

"Walking wounded are coming out now, sir," the Marine Lieutenant told him. "Mr. Cochrane is——"

"Form your men up," Phillip interrupted urgently. "We're about to be attacked ourselves on our front." His warning was just in time and the Marines, taking what cover they could, were waiting as the first shadowy form reached the head of the path. The Cossacks came casually, not expecting to meet with any opposition and a single volley, at point-blank range, sent them reeling back in confusion, leaving several of their number—dead or

161

wounded—behind them. A second volley, as Smithson's Marines charged after them, put the whole party to panic-stricken flight. The solitary marksman Phillip had located to his right front again fired on the fleeing Cossacks and, attacked on two flanks, as they evidently imagined, their rout was completed.

There was no need for silence now and leaving two of Smithson's Marines to keep watch on the path, Phillip led the rest of his party to the rear of the rocky escarpment, the men, at his behest, raising a lusty cheer as they scrambled over the rocks. As he had feared, the defenders had suffered heavy casualties, in proportion to their numbers, due mainly to the fact that their barricade had been insufficient to protect them from the heavy cannon balls the Russians had hurled at them. Miraculously only one of Leach's fusiliers had been killed, but three others were wounded and, of Cochrane's seamen and Marines, only four had escaped unscathed, including Cochrane himself.

"Most of the damage was done in the past half-hour," Anthony Cochrane explained wryly. "We saw your signal from the beach and were starting to withdraw when they turned all four guns on us at devilish close range, and forced us to hang on. The Major"—he gestured to where Leach leaned against a rock, supporting himself with his single arm—"was hit by a rock splinter, which half-blinded him. But I don't think he's too badly hurt and he and his fellows have done a magnificent job. They——"

"They have indeed," Phillip put in, with an anxious glance at the rapidly lightening sky. "I'll hear the whole story when we're back on board the *Trojan* but now you had better start withdrawing your party—wounded first, and as quickly as you can, Mr. Cochrane. The Army surgeon should be on his way up, with a supporting party of Marines landed by Mr. Grey, and you'll meet them before you've gone very far, I hope."

"Aye, aye, sir. And you?" Cochrane hesitated. "Do you suppose the enemy will attack again?"

"It's to be hoped not. But Smithson and his Marines will cover your withdrawal and I'll stay with them," Phillip answered. "There are three boats waiting near the foot of the path and, as soon as you are clear, I will signal the *Trojan* to close the shore. We picked up your four wounded seamen and sent them down—they should be safely in one of the boats by now." He crossed over to Major Leach, whose orderly was assisting him to his feet. "How are you, Major?"

"Hazard?" Leach turned a bruised and swollen face to his, both eyes tightly closed. "Your arrival was, to say the least of it, most timely. Thank you for coming back for us—I'm afraid I was wrong, we should never have been able to reach Eupatoria overland. Those infernal guns of theirs and the Cossacks . . ." he expelled his breath in a frustrated sigh. "We were all right until they turned two of their twelve-pounders on us."

"They've withdrawn the whole battery now," Phillip told him.

"Have they, by Jove? Well, I shall never know why—they had us at their mercy. Did you get the French ship off?"

"We did—largely thanks to you, sir. You made it easy for us and——"

"Don't thank me, my dear fellow," the Major protested. "I got half the cliff in my face soon after we established ourselves here and since then I haven't even been able to see the gun flashes, much less use a musket. If thanks are due to anyone, they're due to our friend Durbanville, who directed our defence with great efficiency. His shooting was worthy of the medals he told us he'd won for it, too—is that not so, Jones?" The orderly confirmed his claim. "Oh, yes, sir. He's a fine shot, sir."

Phillip endeavored to hide his astonishment. He peered

round, wondering where the young Guards officer was and puzzled by his absence. Cochrane and his party had gone and, in the grey light of dawn only Smithson and his Marines could be seen, muskets at the ready, standing alertly by the barricade. "Where *is* Durbanville?" he asked. "I can see no sign of him."

"Up there, somewhere." Major Leach pointed vaguely. "He said he would have a better field of fire from some spot he had picked over to our front, from which he told me he could cover our withdrawal. He went off—oh, about twenty minutes ago, I think, with his servant and two Minié rifles. But I've no idea when he came back ... I'm a bit dazed, I fear, and not being able to see out of either of my eyes, I honestly cannot tell you where he is. Perhaps he went down with the wounded."

"An example you should follow yourself, sir," Phillip advised. "I'll look for Durbanville." He turned to Leach's orderly, "Take the Major down to the boats, Jones, will you please? If you need any help from my people, just ask for it."

"I misjudged young Durbanville," Leach said, as the orderly put an arm about him. "He's a good soldier and a braver one than I'll ever be. Tell him that, when you find him, Hazard, there's a good fellow. I wish I'd told him myself."

"Don't worry, I'll tell him," Phillip promised, guessing now who the solitary marksman had been. When Leach and his orderly were clear of the barricade, he ordered the agreed signal to be made to the *Trojan* but, as the rockets hissed skywards he saw, by their eerie light, that some of the Cossacks had re-formed, evidently with the intention of launching another attack. Smithson saw them also and, without waiting for orders, yelled out to his men to open fire. They did so effectively and the lone marksman added his quota, the flashes from his rifle revealing his position.

7

As the Cossacks again withdrew in confusion, Smithson glanced questioningly at Phillip. "Isn't that Captain Durbanville up there, sir, in those rocks, doing the fancy shooting?"

Phillip nodded. "Yes, I think it is. I'm going up to him now. Hold on here until you're quite certain that the wounded have been given a fair margin of safety—say for another fifteen to twenty minutes—and then start your withdrawal."

"Without waiting for you and Durbanville, sir?" Lieutenant Smithson sounded worried but Phillip laid a reassuring hand on his shoulder. "We'll join you. Give me a hail when you're ready to go."

He made his way to Durbanville's lonely fastness, not without difficulty, for the way up to it was steep and strewn with loose boulders. But it was, he saw, an extremely well chosen position, affording its occupant a much wider field of fire and vision than the barricade behind which Major Leach and his party had taken shelter. Henry Durbanville lay in a deep crevice in the rock, his greatcoat covering the lower part of his body, a rifle in front of him ready to his hand and a second, which he had just loaded with deft speed, at his side. His servant, to whom the task of loading had previously been delegated, was lying dead a few yards from him—the victim, Phillip could only suppose, of a random musket ball, which had caught him off guard, since the crevice appeared to offer adequate protection to anyone lying inside it.

Durbanville raised a languid hand in greeting as Phillip dragged himself up the last few precipitous yards and, skirting the body of the unfortunate guardsman, slithered in beside him. "Well, Commander Hazard, good of you to come!" His greeting was cheerful. "Although there was really no need, you know. I'm not doing too badly on my own and I've been on my own since Leeston was hit ten minutes ago."

"He's dead—" Phillip began but his companion interrupted him, not turning round. "Yes, I'm afraid he is, poor chap. He was a mite too eager to spot for me and lifted his head at the wrong moment . . . pity, he was an excellent servant and I shall miss him. He . . . oh, no you don't!" His last remark was addressed to a shadowy figure Phillip had scarcely noticed and, taking careful aim, he gently squeezed the trigger of the Minié rifle he had picked up. The shadow emitted a shrill cry of pain and Durbanville shrugged apologetically, "Oh, dear, I only winged that one, didn't I? But better luck next time, perhaps." He reached for the rifle at his side and laid it on the flat surface of the ledge of rock in front of him, gesturing to Phillip to possess himself of the weapon he had just fired. "If you would not mind re-loading for me, since you're here, Commander, I can continue to keep my eye on those infernally slippery customers down there."

Phillip complied with his request. "Slippery customers, are they?" he repeated, amused in spite of himself.

"Yes, indeed," Durbanville told him gravely. "They keep trying to work their way round to the rear of Major Leach's position in the hope of cutting off his retreat to the cliff path. But the light is improving. In another ten minutes or so, I'll show you some real shooting. I really did win a number of medals for my shooting, you know, and I am quite good at it. To be honest"—his tone was unexpectedly deprecating—"it's about the only thing I *am* good at. I always was. I have excellent eyesight, even at night, you see. Er—you're proposing to stay here for a while, I take it? Because if you are, you might as well make yourself useful with that second rifle."

"No, I am not proposing anything of the kind," Phillip answered, amazed by the boy's coolness as much as by his sheer effrontery. But Henry Durbanville *was* only a boy, he thought—a schoolboy, playing at war with a schoolboy's light-hearted exuberance. He explained the situation briefly and added, "I came up here to inform you that we are about to withdraw and to advise you to join us. The wounded have been evacuated and are on their way back to the beach, where I have boats waiting to take them out to the ship. Major Leach has gone with them and the Marines, who are at present holding his position, have orders to follow them almost immediately, so I think we had better make our way down at once."

"You are perfectly free to go whenever you wish, Commander," Durbanville said loftily. "But I shall stay here."

"There is no point in your staying," Phillip returned. "As I told you, we've towed off the French ship and the enemy have withdrawn their gun battery. The operation has been successful, thanks in no small measure to you, Major Leach informed me. He——"

"The Cossacks have *not* withdrawn," the young Guards officer observed. "And there seem to be quite a number of them, do there not? Do you imagine they will simply stand by and watch you withdraw your Marines? My dear fellow, they will come after you!"

"I expect they will," Phillip agreed. "But we ought to be able to hold them off without too much trouble. The path is narrow, the Marines will make a fighting withdrawal and a second party is on its way up to our support."

"*I* can hold them off without any trouble at all," Henry

167

Durbanville pointed out, with conscious pride. "In daylight, I give you my word, not a single Cossack will reach the path so long as I am here. Why risk the lives of your Marines?" He tensed and the rifle in his hands spat flame, to be followed an instant later by an unearthly shriek, as a dark figure disengaged itself from the rock face twenty yards from them and fell heavily, not to rise again. "You see?" His tone was exultant. "I could hold off a whole army, if I had to, so what are a few Cossacks?"

Phillip lost patience with him. "I cannot leave you here, Durbanville. You would be risking certain death. The Cossacks aren't noted for their humane treatment of prisoners and in addition they——"

"I'm sorry, Commander Hazard, but I'm not coming with you. Before you go, would you mind re-loading that Minié rifle for me, like a good fellow? You understand, I——"

"I am giving you an order, Captain Durbanville," Phillip put in, an edge to his voice. He ignored the proffered rifle, hearing Smithson hail him from below. "The Marines are ready to commence their withdrawal, so I must insist that you accompany me to join them immediately."

"To my infinite regret, my dear sir, I cannot do as you wish." Henry Durbanville spoke quietly, without bravado. "I had not meant you to know but ... look and you will see that I am incapable of obeying your order." He drew back the greatcoat which covered his legs and, in the dim light, Phillip saw that his left leg had been almost severed below the knee. "The excellent Leeston put on a tourniquet just before he got himself killed. It stopped the bleeding and, curiously enough, I feel very little pain."

"But——" Phillip stared at him with new respect. "When did this happen?"

"Oh, I don't know, I've lost count of time. About thirty minutes ago, as far as I can recollect. It was a round shot from one of their infernal twelve-pounders and the irony

168

of it is that it was never intended for me. Their gunnery is wildly inaccurate and this was a ricochet, if you please!" The young Guards officer shrugged helplessly. "The one thing I did not bargain for, when I selected this position. But, as I trust I have proved to your satisfaction, sir, I cannot obey your order. I can't walk."

"I can carry you, Durbanville," Phillip assured him. "And we'll send for a stretcher party." Smithson, he saw, craning forward to look, was still waiting and he called out to him to delay the retreat to the beach for a few more minutes. Turning again to the wounded boy, he urged gently, "Come on, lad—I'll take you on my back."

Durbanville smiled at him. "Thanks but I should bleed to death before you could carry me as far as the head of the path. Don't you realize, my dear fellow, the rock is all that is keeping my leg in place now? I beg you—load that second rifle for me and then leave me here where, at least, I can be of some use."

"The military surgeon is with my second party of Marines"—Phillip started to tell him but the boy shook his head, shuddering.

"For pity's sake, Commander, don't let any sawbones touch me! That would be more than I could endure." His tone changed, becoming authoritative, "We're wasting valuable time, you know—it's almost daylight. Leave me, Commander Hazard . . . you have the responsibility for getting your men back to the ship. Just load the rifle for me and permit *me* to accept responsibility for ensuring that your rearguard makes an unmolested withdrawal. I may be rather an amateur soldier and a tyro at war but even I can see that this is quite a favorable exchange— my life for yours and that of—how many trained Marines? Ten—twelve . . . any one worth more than I am, if you're honest, surely? In any event, how many poor wretches survive the amputation of a leg?"

He was right, Phillip was unwillingly forced to admit.

169

He loaded the rifle and placed it close to Durbanville's side and then laid a hand on his shoulder.

"I had a message for you, from Major Leach," he said. "He asked me to tell you that he misjudged you and to add that, in his view, you were a good soldier and—in his words—'a braver one than I'll ever be.' I should like to associate myself with that message, Captain Durbanville . . . and to wish you luck. As to the Cossacks——"

Durbanville did not let him complete the warning he was about to utter. "Don't worry, Commander—I shall keep the last shot for myself. And permit me to wish you Godspeed."

It had been a curiously moving yet melodramatic scene, Phillip reflected, conscious of a tightness about his throat as he slithered awkwardly down to rejoin Smithson. But then, Henry Durbanville was a curiously melodramatic young man, who had been acting a variety of parts ever since he had boarded the *Trojan,* apparently intent on dramatizing everything he did. By an odd quirk of Fate, the final act had afforded him an opportunity to play the heroic rôle in which, no doubt, he had always seen himself—and he had played it with admirable courage and coolness, as well as a certain cynical enjoyment.

It went very much against the grain to leave him there, alone in his small stronghold but . . . Phillip sighed. The boy had been right, of course—he had his own responsibilities, there was nothing else he could do but leave him there. Although perhaps, when he had seen the last boat safely away from the beach, he could return, if only to salve his own conscience.

"Captain Durbanville isn't with you, sir?" Smithson said, sounding puzzled. "Isn't he coming?"

"No, he's not." Phillip gave a brief explanation of the circumstances, which seemed to satisfy Smithson, and added crisply, "Right, Mr. Smithson. Carry out your withdrawal."

The return to the beach was made without trouble. The Cossacks did not come in pursuit and, apart from a few isolated shots from Durbanville's Minié, Phillip heard nothing. The shots came at long intervals and evidently served their purpose in discouraging pursuit, as Durbanville had promised they would. Meeting the second party of Marines, under their Sergeant, about half-way down the cliff, Phillip learned that two boat-loads of wounded had already put off to the ship and he was tempted to relinquish command to Smithson and retrace his steps in order to make an attempt—however useless—to bring Durbanville down. But one boat had to come back, for a second load; his responsibilities could not yet be delegated, and he stumbled on down the steep, uneven path, now bathed in pale, watery sunlight. He could see the *Trojan* close inshore, watched first one boat and then a second go alongside and then saw his own boat returning, with O'Hara in the sternsheets. There was still a moderately heavy swell running but the wind, he realized with relief, had dropped. The crackle of musketry from the cliff top sounded fainter and soon ceased altogether but, as his party gained the beach, he saw that a small band of mounted Cossacks were galloping along, keeping the British party in sight. Half-a-dozen of them dismounted and essayed a few shots from the summit of the cliff but the range was extreme and their shooting—by Henry Durbanville's standards, at any rate—poor, so that they soon desisted and stood by, watching helplessly, as the Marines filed down to the waiting boats.

"You are coming, sir, aren't you?" Smithson asked, a note of concern in his voice as if, now that the moment had come, he sensed Phillip's inner conflict and his reluctance to return to the ship without Henry Durbanville.

Phillip hesitated, aware that what his conscience bade him do was both foolhardy and foredoomed to failure . . . and would be so judged by his superiors, if his conduct

171

were ever the subject of inquiry. Yet his conscience plagued him relentlessly and he knew that he must satisfy himself on Durbanville's account before he could hope to enjoy peace of mind. The *Trojan,* under Martin Fox's command, ran no risks now—Fox could take her into Eupatoria and land the troops under Major Leach, the two French surgeons and the nuns. No doubt the *Rapide* would be waiting there for the latter, so that he need not concern himself with the question of their transport to Kameisch. Phillip glanced up at the cliff top and saw that the Cossacks had vanished. This decided him and, turning to Smithson, he said curtly, "No. I am going back to see if anything can be done for Captain Durbanville."

"But what *can* be done, sir?" Smithson objected. "You said yourself that he had a leg shot away."

"I know, Mr. Smithson." Phillip sighed. "All the same my conscience won't allow me to leave him up there alone to die. I must go back." Now that he had made up his mind, he felt a lifting of his spirits and he shook his head firmly to Smithson's offer to accompany him. "No, I'll go alone . . . one man might escape notice, a party might bring the Cossacks back. Besides, I have no right to risk any more lives in what I realize may well prove a hopeless task. So embark your Marines, if you please, in Mr. Grey's boat." He led the way and Smithson followed him reluctantly.

"Sir——"

"Yes, Mr. Smithson?"

"At least permit me to wait for you, sir, with this boat," the Marine Lieutenant pleaded but again Phillip shook his head. "No. You and your men have done enough—all of you and you've done extremely well—but now return to the ship, if you please, and leave this to me. It is my responsibility and mine alone."

"Permit me to disagree, sir," Smithson persisted. "I'll
172

obey your orders, of course. But I beg you to change your mind."

Phillip relented a little. "I would if I could, Mr. Smithson, believe me. But I truly do not think I can." He turned to Midshipman Grey, who had been a silent but interested listener to this exchange. "Mr. Grey, I am returning to see whether it is possible to aid Captain Durbanville, who is severely wounded. When you report to Mr. Fox, ask him to give me a couple of hours. He can remain where he is with the *Trojan* for that time but tell him to keep a sharp look-out, in case the enemy bring back their gun battery. If they do, he is to take the ship out of range. When I require a boat I'll signal for one—and I can use hand signals, now that it's daylight. We'll keep them simple . . ." he detailed the signals he would use and continued, "But make it quite clear to Mr. Fox that his first concern must be the safety of the ship and her crew and that he is *not* to send a boat in response to any signal of mine if, by doing so, he considers it might endanger either. If, for any reason, he is compelled to haul-off, he may leave me the cutter at his discretion and with a volunteer crew . . . you understand?"

"Aye, aye, sir. But, sir . . . ." Grey was at his side, his tone pleading, "May I not accompany you? I was at school with Durbanville and I would appreciate it very much indeed if you'd take me, sir. Lieutenant Smithson will, I am sure, convey your instructions to the First Lieutenant and my cox'n could take command of the boat. Also, sir"—the boy reddened under Phillip's silent scrutiny—"I haven't been ashore. I've been with my boat all the time, so I'm quite fresh. And you *will* need someone to help you carry Durbanville down to the beach— you can't do that single-handed, sir, can you? If he's . . . if he's had a leg shot away, he'll have to be carried, won't he, sir?"

If he were in any state to be moved, Phillip thought,

173

but he smiled down at the pink-cheeked midshipman. "You advance a great many reasons in favor of my acceding to your request, Mr. Grey," he observed. "And you are, of course, right on the score of the last one—save that I fear we may not find it possible to carry Captain Durbanville down to the beach. His injuries are severe—he may have succumbed to them, poor fellow."

"But may I come, sir?" Grey begged. "In case he's alive? I'll make myself useful, sir, truly I will."

Phillip eyed him thoughtfully. "You appreciate what may be involved, if you do?"

"You mean that it may not be possible for us to get back here ourselves, sir? Yes, I do. But the Cossacks seem to have gone and that makes the chance worth taking, doesn't it, sir?"

"Very well, Mr. Grey, your request is granted," Phillip told him. If it were possible to move Durbanville, he thought, then he would need help. He glanced at Smithson in mute apology and the younger man smiled. "I did not want you to go alone, sir," he confessed. "And Mr. Grey's uniform has the advantage of being less conspicuous than mine."

"Thank you," Phillip acknowledged. "Then embark your men, if you please, Mr. Smithson. And perhaps you would permit us the use of two of your muskets, in case of need."

"Certainly, sir." Smithson passed on the order to his Sergeant and then draw himself up and saluted. "I'll convey your instructions to the First Lieutenant and—may I wish you both a safe return?"

"You may indeed and I thank you." Taking a Brown Bess from the Sergeant of Marines, Phillip echoed Smithson's smile, his own a trifle wry. "Remember, if you please, that Mr. Fox is to give us two hours—no longer. If we have made no signal or have failed to return here, to the beach, within that time, he is to take the *Trojan* to

Eupatoria so that the troops may be landed. After that he will be under the orders of Captain Lord George Paulet of the *Bellerophon*."

"Very good, sir." Smithson barked an order and his Marines started to file into the waiting boat but, before it could put off, there was a brief altercation and a single red-jacketed figure jumped ashore and, brushing past Smithson, came to a halt at Phillip's side.

"Commander Hazard"—Phillip, a trifle to his surprise, recognized the young military surgeon who had so unwillingly assisted Henry Durbanville with his floggings. "I did not fully comprehend what you intended to do. But if Captain Durbanville is wounded and you are going to his aid, it is my duty to accompany you, sir. I trust you will permit me to do so?"

Phillip hesitated. The young man had more than done his duty already, he thought, attending to the wounded members of the shore party, and he looked exhausted but . . . "If you wish," he assented reluctantly. "Although I fear there may be little or nothing you can do for poor Durbanville. His wound seemed to me to be mortal."

"Nevertheless, sir, I should like to do what I could. As military surgeon, it *is* my duty."

His name, Phillip recalled, was Vernon. He nodded acquiescence. "Then come with us, Mr. Vernon . . . and thank you." He waved to Smithson and, as the boat finally put off from the beach, led the way back to the cliff path.

In daylight, the climb was easier and took less than the twenty-five minutes the first ascent had taken but all three climbers were beginning to feel the strain by the time the head of the pathway came in sight. Phillip halted to regain his breath and, having done so, explained the lie of the land to his companions.

"I see, sir." Young Grey was looking eagerly about him. He was admirably composed but his voice betrayed his excitement as he gestured ahead of them. "The Cos-

175

sacks *do* appear to have gone, don't they? I mean, they would surely have fired on us if they were still in position, would they not?"

It was possible, Phillip reflected but, on the other hand, it was equally possible that they were waiting in ambush at the top of the cliff. As if reading his thoughts, Surgeon Vernon diffidently suggested advancing under a flag of truce and took a crumpled white handkerchief from his jacket pocket. "If I tie this on to the muzzle of your musket, Commander, they would heed it, surely? We are, after all, on a mission of mercy."

"Perhaps," Phillip conceded but without conviction. His experience of Cossack patrols had hitherto led him to place little reliance on their respect for flags of truce or, indeed, for anything in the nature of aid to the wounded. However, he allowed Vernon to attach the handkerchief to the barrel of his Brown Bess and, when this was done, motioned his companions to stay where they were and, as he had done earlier, covered the last few yards bent double, his musket—belying its symbol—at the ready. A careful scrutiny revealed no Cossacks and he straightened up, waving to the other two to join him. When they did so, he turned his glass on the rocky escarpment which had given Henry Durbanville shelter, seeking for some sign that he was still alive. But he was well hidden and Phillip knew that there was nothing for it except to climb up once more to his lonely stronghold—to hail him might bring the Cossacks back.

"Wait here, both of you," he ordered and silenced the young surgeon's protest with a crisp, "If you're needed, I'll wave." He turned to the midshipman. "Keep your eyes skinned, Mr. Grey."

Robin Grey, firmly grasping his musket, flashed him a quick smile. "Aye, aye, sir." He, too, had had experience of the Cossacks' treatment of wounded, Phillip recalled, and significantly had no white banner on his weapon. He echoed the boy's smile and set off on his climb, moving with caution and pausing occasionally to sweep the surrounding countryside with his glass. As he neared the summit of the escarpment he realized that he could see the white ribbon of a post road and frowned, seeking to get his bearings. It was the post road from Perekop to Simpheropol, of course—it could be no other—and was the road by which the Russian reinforcements from Odessa had travelled to Prince Menschikoff's headquarters at Simpheropol. The road by which, only a short while ago, Madamoiselle Sophie must have travelled with her husband, Prince Andrei Narishkin ... he stifled a sigh. In darkness, when he had previously ascended this escarpment, he had been unable to see the road and had not guessed how close it was ... he slipped his Dollond from his breast pocket and studied the road minutely, taking in that fact that it was deeply rutted and pock-marked with holes, evidence—if evidence were needed—of the heavy traffic it had borne during the past months.

But now, bathed in the strengthening sunlight, the dusty road was deserted and, replacing his glass, Phillip continued on his way. He saw the body of Guardsman Leeston first, pathetically spread-eagled on the rock face and, guided by this, dragged himself the last difficult five yards to Henry Durbanville's hiding place. The boy still lay full length in the rocky crevice, his greatcoat covering him and both rifles placed ready to hand. But he did not move or give any sign that he was aware of Phillip's approach so that, until he touched the young Guards officer's extended hand and felt its warmth, he imagined that the man he had returned to rescue must be already dead. The touch roused him and instinctively sent the hand Phillip had touched groping blindly for the rifle.

"Durbanville ... it's Hazard. Lie still." The warning reached the semi-conscious Durbanville. He turned, his lack-luster eyes momentarily lighting in relieved recognition, his fingers ceasing their vain search for the Minié.

"You . . . came back. You . . . shouldn't have . . . troubled, I . . . haven't got much longer." His voice was so weak as barely to be audible and Phillip had to lean closer in order to make out what he was trying to say. "I'm afraid . . . you're a . . . sentimentalist, Commander."

"Probably," Phillip agreed, without resentment. "But now we——"

"It was good of you," Durbanville put in. "And I confess I'm . . . grateful. To die . . . alone is . . . a frightening prospect. I . . ." memory returned and he asked suddenly, his voice a little stronger, "Did your Marines get down to the boats all right?"

"Yes—without a single casualty," Phillip told him. "You held off the Cossacks for us magnificently."

"I said I could." Henry Durbanville's cracked, almost bloodless lips curved into a gratified smile. "Now I'm watching the road in case they come back."

"They've gone," Phillip said gently. "And three of us have come to take you back to the ship. Your Army surgeon, young Vernon, volunteered to come and patch you up."

"Good of him. But you cannot move me, Hazard, and Vernon . . . can't patch me up," the boy demurred. "Don't you . . . understand, my . . . my leg's half off? For God's sake, I . . . don't want a sawbones. I told you that, Hazard, I said it was no use, I . . ." his voice trailed off into sudden, abrupt silence, as if the effort to talk had been too much for him and his eyes lost the brightness which had briefly illuminated them, glazed over and then wearily closed. Phillip moved him carefully into a more comfortable position and, rising, clambered to the edge of the crevice to wave an urgent summons to the two men waiting below.

They both joined him, young Grey skipping over the rocks with enviable agility. "No sign of a soul, sir," he reported. His glance went to the unconscious Durbanville but he offered no comment and added, looking about him with interest, "What a capital position this is! Why, it even commands the road, does it not? Shall I carry on as look-out, sir?"

"Yes, if you will," Phillip agreed. "Keep the cliff path under observation, as well as the road—and keep under cover. That road is the post road to Simpheropol and I don't imagine it will be deserted for long. Let me know of anything you see." He turned to Vernon who had slipped into the rock crevice beside Henry Durbanville and was examining the boy's wound, his face expressionless. "Well, Doctor . . . what do you think of his chances? Can we get him down to the beach?"

The surgeon did not look up, his fingers busy with the length of cord secured about the lower part of the young Guards officer's left thigh, which had acted as a tourniquet. "He's pretty far gone, sir, and I'm afraid this leg will have to come off. I doubt if he'll survive being moved, still less the shock of amputation—he's lost a lot of blood already. I cannot amputate here but I *could* splint the leg and we might try to get him down. But . . ." he shrugged. "Frankly, I don't give much for his chances."

"He'll die for certain if we leave him here," Phillip pointed out. He looked back, over his shoulder, to where the *Trojan* still faithfully held her off-shore position and then anxiously consulted his pocket watch. Almost forty minutes had elapsed since they had left the beach; it would take at least another forty—or possibly even longer—to return there, with the added burden of Henry Durbanville. But they could not leave him, to a lonely and inevitable death . . . he sighed. "Splint the leg, Doctor, and we'll rig a makeshift stretcher with his greatcoat and those rifles. Do you want any help?"

The surgeon shook his head. "No, I can manage." He

179

added, as if in answer to Phillip's unspoken warning, "I shall be as quick as I can."

"Good man," Phillip acknowledged. He wished that they could take the body of Durbanville's servant down with them also but knew that this was out of the question —poor Leeston would have to lie where he had fallen. There was no means of burying him here, unless his body were placed in the crevice now occupied by his master and. . . .

"Sir—Commander Hazard, would you come over here, if you please?" Midshipman Grey's voice, controlled but holding a note of urgency, broke into his thoughts. Phillip moved cautiously across to where the boy had taken up his position, well out of sight at the far end of the rocky crevice.

"Yes, Mr. Grey—what is it?"

"Over there, do you see, sir—that dust cloud above the road?" The midshipman pointed. "I've no glass but could a cloud like that be raised by enemy cavalry, sir?"

Phillip took out his Dollond and focused it in the direction Grey had indicated—that of Perekop, to the north west. The dust cloud was a long way away but, as he watched, it slowly resolved itself into a long column of mounted men—cavalry, as young Grey had suspected. The pale sunlight glinted on their lance-tips and behind them, Phillip saw, came gun limbers, which were stirring up most of the dust, followed by an almost unbroken line of plodding, grey-coated infantrymen. A considerable force was on the move, he realized—reinforcements destined for the Tchernaya valley perhaps or . . . he scanned the road ahead of the cavalry column and saw that just ahead of it, a second road branched off to the right. The road to Eupatoria, his mind registered and he waited, not really expecting the advancing cavalry to take it. But they did so, a squadron putting their horses to the gallop, which brought them to the turn-off ahead of the main

180

body. When this, too, turned in the direction of Eupatoria he knew that they could have only one objective. An attack was to be launched against the town—a major attack—aimed to overwhelm its small garrison at a time when they might be expected to have suffered some disorganization, as a result of the recent storm.

Phillip drew in his breath sharply, wondering how badly the storm had hit them, how many of the warships lying at anchor in the exposed bay had, like the *Rapide*, been driven ashore or wrecked. There were two first-rates at Eupatoria, he knew—Lord George Paulet's *Bellerophon* and the French *Henry IV* of 100 guns. Surely neither of these could have failed to ride out the storm? But . . . he peered again into his glass, attempting to assess the size of the enemy force. How many other ships, like his own *Trojan*, carrying reinforcements, had failed to make port, failed to land the troops they carried? He could delay no longer, he knew; he must get back to the *Trojan*, take her with all speed into Eupatoria and warn the garrison commander, Captain Brock, of the coming attack. If necessary he must signal Martin Fox to proceed without him and. . . .

"Sir, they are enemy cavalry—cavalry and guns—are they not?" Young Grey's voice was awed.

"Yes," Phillip confirmed grimly, "They are indeed. On your feet, youngster—there's no time to be lost. Cut down the cliff as fast as your legs will carry you—I'll signal for a boat to take you off. Inform the First Lieutenant that a mixed enemy force of several thousand—cavalry, artillery and infantry—is advancing along the road from Perekop, almost certainly with the intention of attacking Eupatoria. I estimate that they will be in a position to attack by . . ." he frowned, trying to judge the speed of the column and the distance it had to travel. The infantry would slow it down, of course, to marching speed and, if they kept to the road—which seemed probable—then this would add

181

four or five miles to the actual distance. "By nightfall, at the latest, though possibly before. Mr. Fox is to give this information to Captain Brock and land our troops immediately." He added a few brief instructions and saw the midshipman's eyes widen.

"Aye, aye, sir," he acknowledged dutifully, on his feet now and drawing himself to attention. "But what about you, sir—and Durbanville and the surgeon?"

"We shall follow you," Phillip told him, his tone one that did not encourage question, "with what speed we can. But do not wait for us, Mr. Grey. The information you bear is of the greatest urgency and must be conveyed to Eupatoria without delay." He hesitated, aware of his duty, wondering how he could justify his decision and yet obstinately determined not to change it. "A second boat— the cutter—may be sent for us, at Mr. Fox's discretion," he added, "if we're seen to reach the beach in time. We can sail ourselves into the bay or he can come back to pick us up, *after* he has landed our troops and delivered my message. Is that clear?"

"It's clear, sir, but"—young Grey swallowed hard, torn between the habit of obedience and his own personal feelings. "May I not stay to help the surgeon with Henry Durbanville, sir, instead of leaving you to do so? After all, sir, you're in command of the *Trojan* and——"

Phillip cut him short. "I appreciate your offer, Mr. Grey, but your legs are younger than mine and I have a limp, as you may have noticed. You'll make the descent in half the time it would take me ... and time is of importance. So cut along, will you please—now?"

"Aye, aye, sir." The midshipman turned and, obeying his instructions to the letter, flung himself recklessly down the steep escarpment. Reaching its foot, he made for the cliff path with scarcely a pause and went racing down towards the beach, showing little regard for his own safety. Phillip clambered to the summit of the escarpment and, heedless now of any possible enemy watchers, made his signal to the *Trojan*. She had steam up, as he could see, but in addition to his request for a boat, he warned his second-in-command to prepare to sail immediately, receiving an acknowledgement by semaphore from her deck, which was repeated a moment or so later by a flag hoist. He waited until he saw a boat put off for the beach and then descended to join Vernon, who was still kneeling beside his patient. Briefly, he explained the enemy troop movements he had seen and the action he had taken and the surgeon nodded, without looking up, as he continued to work on Durbanville's splint.

"Is he ready?" Phillip asked.

"As ready as I can make him, Commander." The Army surgeon rose, tight-lipped. "He regained consciousness, unfortunately, a little while ago but I managed to get some rum into him, which may help to deaden his pain." He bent and deftly thrust one of the Minié rifles into the sleeve of the bloodstained greatcoat with which the wounded boy had been covered. Phillip followed his example with the other and, between them, they lifted the limp body from the crevice and laid it on their improvised stretcher. Henry Durbanville stirred, muttering something but did not open his eyes and the surgeon added, looking up into Phillip's face, his expression wry, "It's going to be the devil's own job to get him down from here and I can't promise you that he'll ever reach the ship alive. This may well be an unnecessary sacrifice on your part, Commander Hazard."

"Sacrifice?" Phillip questioned. "Of what, pray?"

"Of your command and perhaps of promotion—certainly of the honor and glory of being able to convey a timely warning to the Eupatoria garrison. And for the sake of a man"—Surgeon Vernon's gesture in Durbanville's direction was expressive—"whom few of us have any reason to like, you least of all, I should have thought."

He shrugged. "You could have gone with your midshipman and left me here with Captain Durbanville, since it is *my* duty, as medical officer, to remain with him—not yours. But you stayed—why, Commander Hazard? I should like to know."

Phillip reddened. No doubt others would ask him this same question—Lord George Paulet, Admiral Lyons, the Commander-in-Chief, Admiral Dundas, and probably their Lordships of the Admiralty, if the matter should be brought eventually to their attention. They would expect an answer and he would have none to give them, no excuses to offer, still less a rational explanation of his conduct. His duty had been plain but he had ignored its call. He had chosen to stay, instead of returning to the ship entrusted to his command because . . . Phillip looked down at Henry Durbanville's white, shuttered face, touched already by the shadow of death, and expelled his breath in a long-drawn sigh.

Because, like Leach, he had misjudged the boy, he asked himself—because he disliked him, yet had been compelled to respect him for his courage this morning?

"You've given me no answer, sir," Vernon prompted.

"All right, no doubt I should not have stayed," Phillip admitted reluctantly. "But I felt I owed him something—a chance, however slight. He earned that, up here this morning when he covered our withdrawal. And the debt was mine, not yours . . . the more pressing because, as you say, I had little reason to like him." He bent to pick up one end of the stretcher they had fashioned. "Come, Doctor, we are wasting time. Let's get him down to the path. If you go ahead of me, I'll lower him down to you."

With difficulty, frequently slipping themselves, they contrived alternately to slide and drag their awkward burden to the foot of the escarpment. Durbanville's eyes opened before they had completed the first ten yards of the descent but, in spite of the fact that he must have been enduring a great deal of pain, he did not utter a sound. When at last they were on level ground, Vernon held the flask of rum he carried to the boy's bloodless lips and he swallowed a few sips before turning his head away.

"Please . . ." his voice was a tortured whisper. "I can't . . . stand any more. Leave me, for . . . pity's sake! Why don't you leave me?"

"You heard what he asked you, Commander Hazard," the surgeon observed flatly. "There's still time for you to go—look!" He pointed below them to the beach, on which the *Trojan*'s gig had just grounded and Phillip saw Midshipman Grey go stumbling across the shingle to meet it, breathless and spent but gamely determined not to slacken speed until his objective had been reached. The coxswain splashed ashore to assist him and Vernon added, "You could order them to wait for you. I'll stay with Durbanville."

He was right, Phillip knew. The boat commander, Midshipman O'Hara, was looking up to where he stood, as if expecting a signal—he had only to raise his hand. "Young Grey is there," he said. "It will take me twice as long as it took him to get to the beach—and he knows what to do. The First Lieutenant will also know, when the youngster delivers my orders . . . and he can be relied upon to carry them out, whether or not I'm aboard. It is essential that the Eupatoria garrison should be given warning of the attack which is about to be launched against them—and that our troop reinforcements, which may be sorely needed, are landed with the least possible delay. You must see that, Doctor. I have instructed Mr. Fox, as I told you, to send the cutter to pick us up."

"The decision is yours, sir," Surgeon Vernon returned stiffly. "I was merely endeavoring to offer you the chance to change it. And I must again warn you that, in my professional opinion, Captain Durbanville has very little hope of reaching even your cutter alive."

"He's alive now, Doctor," Phillip pointed out, suddenly angry, as much with himself as with his companion. "Let us see whether we can get him down to the beach—that is what we came to do, is it not?" He lifted the two rifle butts and the surgeon, flushing, picked up the other end of the improvised stretcher. As they set off down the steep cliff path, Midshipman O'Hara's boat put off for the ship, with young Grey aboard. The boat was alongside the *Trojan*'s midship chains before the stretcher party had covered half the distance separating them from the beach and, a few minutes later, with a curious sense of loss, Phillip watched his ship get under way. From her deck, as she set course for Eupatoria Bay, a semaphore signal told him that Martin Fox had received and understood his orders. The cutter was lowered according to his instructions and two of her crew, jumping ashore before she grounded, ran up the path to relieve Vernon and himself of their burden. Both men grinned at him in unconcealed pleasure and relief—unlike Surgeon Vernon and, perhaps, his naval superiors, Phillip reflected wryly, they saw no reason to criticize or condemn his absence from his ship or, indeed, to remark on it. One said, knuckling his brow, the pleased grin widening, "Glad to see you, sir. We was afraid we'd lost you for a while."

"Thank you, Matlock," Phillip acknowledged, recognizing him as a maintopman and not a regular member of the cutter's crew. In answer to his unspoken question, the seaman added, "The First Lieutenant called for volunteers, sir, to man the cutter. That's why I'm here. And Mr. O'Hara sir—he jumped the gun and brought her in, instead of Mr. Fisher." He looked down at Durbanville's unconscious face and asked wonderingly, "Is the poor young gentleman still alive, sir?"

Surgeon Vernon, fingers on the wounded boy's wrist, inclined his head. "Yes," he said, avoiding Phillip's eye, "Thanks to your Captain, he is."

Reaching the boat, willing hands lifted the stretcher and laid it carefully across the midship thwarts and Midshipman O'Hara, his own grin as wide as his men's, touched his cap in salute. "Welcome aboard, sir. You're just in time."

"In time?" Phillip echoed, puzzled. "What do you mean, Mr. O'Hara?"

"Look, sir!" O'Hara pointed. At the head of the cliff path, Phillip saw, a dozen Cossacks had reined in their panting horses and were reaching for the carbines slung from their saddles. A few ill-aimed, half-spent musket balls spattered into the water as the cutter ran through the shallows and then, with her mainsail and jib hoisted and filling, she drew away, heeling sharply as O'Hara brought her on to the port tack and the full force of the lively breeze caught her. It was an off-shore breeze, which would mean beating into the bay, Phillip realized, and the *Trojan,* under engines, was already almost out of sight . . . they would not catch up with her now, however skilfully O'Hara handled the cutter. Well, he had made his decision, back there on the rocky escarpment where Henry Durbanville had held the Cossacks at bay, and he could only abide by it. Martin Fox would deliver his warning and would report to Lord George Paulet—if questions were asked concerning his absence he, and not his First Lieutenant, would have to answer them.

He leaned forward, to look at Durbanville and, to his surprise, saw that the wounded boy was smiling at him. The smile was brief; a moment later his eyes closed and it faded, as Henry Durbanville again lapsed into merciful unconsciousness but . . . it was enough. Not enough, perhaps, to justify the foolhardy decision he had made in any eyes save his own but enough to satisfy his conscience, Phillip thought. Feeling suddenly very tired and lulled by the pleasantly lively motion of the cutter he, too, closed his eyes and permitted himself to relax.

O'Hara's voice roused him—he had no idea how much later—from his doze. "We're almost in the anchorage, sir, and ..." the boy's voice sounded shocked. "Oh, dear heaven, sir, look!"

Phillip sat up, instantly alert. Well might young O'Hara be shocked, he thought, for the sight which met his eyes would have shocked the most hardened seaman. Broadside on the beach to the south-east of the town lay a line-of-battle ship, her upper decks awash and a mass of wreckage surrounding her. Her masts were, however, still standing and, from the main her ensign, tattered but still flying, proclaimed her French. With a feeling of stunned disbelief, Phillip recognized her as the 100-gun *Henri IV,* the most modern steam-screw liner in the French Fleet. Not far from her was another French ship, also a steamer, denuded of her masts and the incoming swell swirling over her. Then, as he swept the rocky coastline with his glass, he saw a two-decker, wearing the Turkish flag, well aground and lying on her starboard bilge scarcely a cable's length astern of the *Henri IV.* There were others, some too badly damaged to make recognition possible and Phillip counted five before, his hands shaking, he turned his glass on those which were still afloat.

The 80-gun *Bellerophon* and the 50-gun sailing frigate *Leander,* were, he saw to his heartfelt relief, among this number. The *Bellerophon* had three anchors out and her lower yards struck, the wreckage of several small boats and other flotsam rising and falling on the tide between her and the *Leander,* whose jib-boom had apparently been carried away. Phillip was also able to recognize three small frigates of Admiral Lyons' steam squadron—the paddle-steamer *Cyclops* and the steam-screws *Magaera* and *Spiteful*—also afloat but all three showing signs of storm damage, their boats stove in and the 6-gun *Spiteful* with a heavy list to port, and men on deck working her pumps.

188

Finally, her spick and span appearance in marked contrast to the scene of desolation about her, Phillip's glass found his own ship. The *Trojan* had come to anchor close to the wharf which served the Eupatoria garrison for the landing of stores and a line of scarlet-jacketed figures, now drawn up there, bore witness to the fact that Martin Fox had lost no time in putting the troops on shore. As he watched, Phillip saw two more boatloads of uniformed men leave the ship's side and make for the jetty. They came alongside and he watched them disembark and— ant-like figures, at that distance—form up with the rest and march away. They looked like Marines but, even with the aid of the Dollond, he could not be sure.

"Make for the *Trojan,* Mr. O'Hara," he ordered, aware of anxiety. "I'll report aboard the *Bellerophon* later."

"Aye, aye, sir." O'Hara put the cutter's helm up and the small craft came about, skimming close-hauled under *Bellerophon*'s stern and demanding all the skill of her young commander in order to avoid collision with some pieces of wreckage floating on the littered surface of the water.

As they drew nearer to the town, Phillip counted another five vessels aground, three of them with masts still standing and their crews on board but the other two dismasted and deserted. All five were British transports and he found himself wondering with dismay, how those other transports—including the *Prince*—had fared, lying off Balaclava and forbidden the shelter of the harbor. If the gale had wrought such havoc here, in what had always been considered a reasonably safe anchorage, how much worse must be the toll taken of the transport fleet exposed to its full fury beneath the towering cliffs outside! He drew in his breath sharply, recalling several of the ships he had seen there by name—the *Niger, Retribution, Vesuvius, Trojan*'s sister ships in the steam squadron, the *Vulcan,* the *Sampson.* And Admiral Lyons' flagship, the *Agamemnon* . . . she had not been at Balaclava when he had last called

189

there—dear God, how many days and nights ago had that been?—but she might have returned. Phillip shuddered involuntarily, as he caught sight of yet another leaking, battered vessel, her crew despondently at work clearing away the chaotic mass of spars and rigging with which her upper deck was strewn. At least, he told himself grimly, as O'Hara gybed to give her a wide berth, at least one decision he had made was now proved to have been the right one—by riding out the gale at sea, the *Trojan* had suffered less damage than most of the ships at this anchorage and he was thankful that he had remembered Eupatoria Bay's vulnerability to southerly gales.

"There's the *Rapide,* sir, I do believe." Young O'Hara pointed, smiling and, following the direction of his gaze, Phillip echoed his smile.

"Yes," he agreed, "and in fairly good shape, by the look of her." And perhaps, he thought, looking back as the cutter left her astern, he would be able to claim the rescue of the *Rapide* as a mark in his favor, should his absence from his command ever become the subject of official inquiry. Turning, he glanced down at Henry Durbanville, still lying limp and unconscious across the cutter's thwarts, his blood-soaked greatcoat wrapped about him and the two Minié rifles, which had served him so well, at his side. Surgeon Vernon, crouched beside the wounded boy, looked up to meet his gaze and said quietly, "He's alive, Commander Hazard . . . but only just. That leg will have to come off as soon as we get him back on board the ship and, if he survives it, then you'll have been vindicated, and I shall be proved wrong." He smiled and added, to Phillip's surprise, "I hope I *am* proved wrong, sir, believe me."

There could be no doubting his sincerity and Phillip thanked him, strangely moved by his admission.

The cutter was within hailing distance of the *Trojan* now and, from her deck an alert midshipman sang out a

190

challenge. "Aye, aye ... *Trojan!*" O'Hara answered, as tradition decreed, his reply an indication that the commander was aboard his boat. With a deft thrust of his tiller, he brought the cutter in below the entry port, at which the side party was mustering and, as Phillip swung himself up the accommodation ladder with the swift ease of long practice, Martin Fox came to meet him.

"Welcome aboard, sir!" he greeted formally but his face wreathed in smiles. "I see that you brought Captain Durbanville back. I'll order a bo'sun's chair rigged for him, shall I? Or can he be lifted aboard?"

"Better let the surgeon decide," Phillip answered. "He's with him. But perhaps you'd pass the word to Surgeon Fraser that he's likely to require an immediate amputation, would you please? And then come to my cabin. I'm anxious to know what's going on. Did you land our Marines?"

Fox inclined his head. "On orders from *Bellerophon,* yes, sir. And there's a request from the garrison commander for seamen volunteers and guns . . . I'll tell you about it when I come below ... Major Leach, by the way, is fully recovered."

Five minutes later, he joined Phillip in his cabin, the steward at his heels with a jug of coffee liberally laced with rum, and a plate bearing an appetizing piece of tongue. Fox waited until the man had set down his tray and then began his report.

"We made our number to the *Bellerophon* as we entered the anchorage, Phillip, and I informed Captain Paulet by signal that we carried troop reinforcements and information of an impending attack on the town by a large enemy force."

"You did not go aboard the *Bellerophon,* then?" Phillip asked. The First Lieutenant shook his head.

"No. She ordered us by signal to anchor off the wharf, put our troops ashore and also our Marines, and to convey our report of enemy troop movements to Captain Brock immediately. I carried out these orders and sent Midshipman Grey ashore, with Major Leach in the first boat, so that he could make a full report on the enemy force you and he had observed to Captain Brock in person. I thought the Captain might wish to question an actual eyewitness. Grey is still ashore but since then I have received an officer of the garrison, who came aboard to express the thanks of his commander and, as I mentioned, to request any guns and seamen gunners we can spare, to assist in warding off the attack. It seems the garrison has been greatly depleted by sickness and also because Captain Brock has had to send four hundred Marines of the original defending force to Balaclava, on Lord Raglan's orders."

"I see." Captain Dacres had told him this, Phillip recalled, frowning, when he had ordered the *Trojan* to Eupatoria.

"The *Bellerophon* has landed all her Marines," Martin Fox went on. "And more than half her seamen. She is seriously undermanned and was, I gather, fortunate not to have been driven on shore in the storm, as the others were. You've seen how many, of course . . . the *Henri Quatre* among them."

"Yes. It was a sickening sight," Phillip agreed, conscious of a chill about his heart which even the scalding coffee could not dispel. "What answer did you give concerning our men and guns?"

Fox shrugged. "I did not commit myself—I felt the decision must be yours, Phillip. But I assured Lieutenant James, the officer from the garrison, that we would do everything in our power to help them. He volunteered the information that the position, *before* the gale struck, was sufficiently precarious for the *Bellerophon,* the *Leander* and two of the steam frigates to have their boom-boats out, in constant readiness to evacuate the garrison, in the

192

event of their being unable to hold the place. But"—his tone was grim—"as you probably noticed, all the *Bellerophon*'s boats have been swamped or have broken adrift, the *Spiteful* and the *Cyclops* are leaking badly and the *Leander* has suffered considerable damage. Most of the French transports, as well as five of ours, have been driven ashore and wrecked and the Turkish two-decker went down with all hands. If the garrison cannot hold off this attack, it looks very black for them, I fear. And from what young Grey told me, it's likely to be an attack in very considerable force, is it not?"

"It is," Phillip confirmed. He described briefly what he had observed from the summit of the escarpment. "They were a long way away, which made it very difficult to estimate numbers but I would put it at several thousand— five or six, possibly even more, since we may only have seen the van. Their advance was slow but, as no doubt Grey told you, I should expect them to reach here before nightfall. Perhaps even by late afternoon ... which does not give us long to get our guns ashore, does it?"

"You're going to send them ashore, then?" Martin Fox looked relieved. "They've asked for ten thirty-two pounders."

"What else can we do?" Phillip was on his feet, shaking off his weariness. "We can't give them support from the sea. Tell me, how is the wharf equipped? Are there sheers and can we bring the ship alongside, to enable us to use them?"

"There are sheers and I'm assured that the depth of water is more than sufficient for us. Lieutenant James can provide working parties to assist our men to haul the guns into position and—he's an artilleryman, incidentally—he says he has a powder wagon and some horse-drawn carts, to take ammunition. He has also promised to send us horse teams for the guns. They'll have to travel some distance." Fox sighed. "From what James has told me, I understand that the defenses consist of Captain Brock's headquarters, a fortified house in the center of the town, and a series of palisades and earthworks extending from the lazaretto at the south-western end to the magazine, on the eastern extremity of the bay. He says they are soundly constructed, with loop-holing and breast-works and the gun positions are good, with plenty of sandbags and gabions."

"Is he still on board?" Phillip demanded. "I'd like to find out how he proposes to site our guns."

"He's in the gunroom." Fox, too, was on his feet, pushing impatiently at the bandage wound about his head and Phillip asked, "How is the head, Martin?"

"Causing me no trouble, except that the bandage keeps slipping and is an infernal nuisance. In any case, it was only a scratch." Martin Fox turned, to meet Phillip's gaze, his own suddenly apprehensive. "Phillip, our friendship has lasted for a good many years and has stood the test of time, has it not?"

"Of course it has. Why do you ask?"

"I am perfectly fit to be entrusted with command of the shore party, I give you my word," Fox said earnestly. "And you, after all——"

"Did I question that, my dear fellow?" Phillip laid an affectionate hand on his arm. "You will also have to take charge of the landing of the guns, because I must repair aboard the *Bellerophon* to report myself to Lord George Paulet, seek his permission to disarm this ship and, as best I can, explain my absence from her quarterdeck when she made port. Call away my gig for me, would you please, while I have a quick word with Lieutenant James?"

Martin Fox flashed him a swift, boyish smile. "You will not have to explain your absence, Phillip—Captain Paulet is not aware of it."

"Not aware of it? What do you mean, Martin?" Phillip

stared at his second-in-command. "I don't think I quite understand. Surely you informed the *Bellerophon?*"

"What do you take me for?" Fox was still smiling. "We've always covered up for each other, have we not, since we were mids? My signal to the *Bellerophon* was made in your name and I took the—er—liberty of instructing young Grey to make his report to Captain Brock also in your name. Correctly, I venture to suggest—he would have received no warning of attack had you been on the quarterdeck all day, would he?" The First Lieutenant moved to the door of the cabin and stood holding it open for Phillip to precede him. "After you, Commander. I will call away your gig and make a signal to the *Bellerophon* right away, sir. And perhaps, when you have spoken to Lieutenant James, you would be good enough to tell me precisely how many guns we're to land, so that I may volunteer their crews?"

"One moment, Martin." Phillip held out his hand, conscious of an almost overwhelming relief. Good, loyal Martin . . . for what *had* he taken him? "I want to thank you."

"Thank me for what?"

"I . . . for covering up for me. And for being the good friend that you are. I'm grateful, believe me."

"I do. I also believe that you would have done the same for me, had our situations been reversed." Martin Fox wrung the outstretched hand and then mumbled, suddenly embarrassed, "There's no need for you to feel grateful, my dear Phillip. Not to me—I owe you a great deal. Er"—he looked down at the still half-filled cup and Phillip's barely-touched plate. "I can send James to you here, while you finish your meal. Damn it, you must be famished!"

He was, Phillip realized. He resumed his seat, gulped down the contents of his cup and then refilled it. He was enjoying the tongue when Lieutenant James knocked on the cabin door to request admission.

8

PHILLIP was received kindly enough by Lord George Paulet but the *Bellerophon*'s Captain was deeply distressed by the loss of so many of the Allied ships under his command and could think or talk of little else. Even Phillip's warning of the Russian advance on the town did not noticeably add to his gloom. He received it with a shrug of the shoulders and a resigned, "Well, this is only what both Captain Brock and I expected. If Lord Raglan had wanted us to hold this God-forsaken town, he would hardly have deprived us of the best fighting men in the garrison, would he? Damn it, Hazard, we had to send him three hundred and eighty Marines at the beginning of November . . . for the defense of Balaclava, I was given to understand. Balaclava!" He sighed. "Yet I hear rumours that it's to be abandoned."

Phillip murmured something, feeling acutely sorry for him.

"Normally I'd have been sorely tempted to advise Captain Brock and his garrison to abandon *this* place," Paulet went on grimly. "And taken them aboard our ships. But how can I do that now? I haven't sufficient ships left afloat to embark half Brock's men—I haven't even enough hands aboard my own ship to hoist in and repair my boats and the *Leander* is in much the same state. Believe it or not but I had to send a leaking barge, with a crew of five, to take off some of the *Henri Quatre*'s people . . . and they all but sank crossing the anchorage! You saw the *Henri Quatre,* of course, on the beach?"

"Yes, sir, I did. I was . . . horrified, sir."

Lord George Paulet spread his hands in a gesture of angry helplessness. "Well, I suppose, in the light of your report, Hazard, there's only one course open to us. We shall have to do all in our power to assist Captain Brock's garrison to repel the attack when it comes. Do you agree?"

Without hesitation, Phillip nodded. "I do, sir."

"In my case, that means nothing—I've supplied Brock with every man and every gun I can spare. But . . . you've landed troop reinforcements and you say you've been asked for guns and ammunition, as well as crews?"

"Yes, sir," Phillip confirmed. He enlarged on Lieutenant James's request for aid and added diffidently, "I took the liberty, sir, of ordering my First Lieutenant to prepare to land ten of our thirty-two pounders, pending your lordship's approval, since we haven't much time to get them ashore and into position. But if you wish, I can countermand the order and——"

"No, no, you did the right thing," Captain Paulet assured him. "We're in a desperate position and, if you care to take the risk of landing your guns, you must do so . . . and good luck to you! Apart from the three small steam frigates, yours is the only fully-manned ship we have and perhaps I ought to advise you to hold her in an effective state . . . but what would be the use?" His tone was bitter. "If the garrison suffers defeat, we cannot evacuate them between us, can we? I don't think I could stomach running out of here, with the few fit men that were able to reach me, and abandoning the wounded to the Cossacks. No, we must make a fight of it, we've no choice. I only hope your warning has come in time for the poor devils on shore to derive some benefit from it . . . though I hope

198

still more, of course, that you were mistaken and, by some miracle, the Russians are in retreat to Perekop."

"They did not look as if they were in retreat to me, sir," Phillip was compelled to point out.

Lord George eyed him glumly. "Alas, I'm sure you are right, my dear Hazard . . . it was just wishful thinking on my part. We're a thorn in Prince Menschikoff's side—we always have been. He wants to drive us out of Eupatoria and, as doubtless those swine of Cossacks lost no time in telling him of our losses during the gale, he probably sees this as a heaven-sent opportunity to launch a full scale attack on us."

"That seems more than likely, sir," Phillip agreed, wondering how he could take his leave. Time was passing all too quickly. "My lord, with your permission——"

Lord George's weary, anxious eyes met his. He said, as if Phillip's words had not reached him, "You heard what happened to most of the unfortunate seamen who managed to swim ashore, after their ships foundered or broke up, did you not? The Cossacks shot them, firing down on them from the top of the cliffs—they shot unarmed, shipwrecked men, Hazard, in cold blood! We could see them from here, before the light went and again in the early morning, and we were helpless to intervene, fighting to keep our own ships afloat. I had three anchors down, including a sheet anchor, and this ship was rolling so heavily, her yard arms were under water! Only the offset saved us from going on shore ourselves and, as I told you, our boats were all smashed to bits. There was nothing we could do to stop those infernal Cossacks, who massacred hundreds of poor fellows, right under our noses—they even fired on the few boats we were able to send to the rescue. But of course—you experienced the same thing, when you went to the rescue of that Frenchman, didn't you?"

"Er—yes, sir." Phillip wondered from whom the *Bel-*

lerophon's Captain could have heard this story and, answering his unvoiced question, Lord George Paulet smiled for the first time since receiving his visitor. "The *Rapide* brought-to almost across my bows, in order to give me a glowing account—in French and through his speaking trumpet, on the part of the Master—of what you and your people had done for him. It was the one heartening piece of news I've had since this infernal gale struck and I shall see that the Commander-in-Chief hears about it at the first opportunity, Hazard. I shall be sending a dispatch to him by the *Cyclops,* if and when she is able to sail . . . but I decided to delay until I can acquaint the Admiral with the news that our garrison has repulsed this latest attack. If the attack is *not* repulsed there will, I am afraid, be no dispatch from here."

"No dispatch, sir?" Phillip echoed uncertainly.

"No, my boy." The tired eyes lit with a defiant gleam. "Because I shall not be here to send it. I cannot put to sea, with most of my crew ashore. My only course will be to bring the *Bellerophon* close in and use what guns she has left to batter the defences into ruins, with as many of their captors as possible cowering behind them. Ah well . . ." he rose, holding out his hand across the immaculately polished cabin table. "I had best let you go, so that you can land those guns of yours. Your ship is moored to the wharf, you said?"

"Yes, sir." Phillip also rose.

"Then leave her there, under a strong guard and with steam up, in case all does not go well," the Captain ordered. "If you need coal, there's plenty—if you have men to load it and you'll have—what, eighteen or twenty guns still aboard?" He asked a few more brief questions and then nodded. "Then the *Trojan* will take off as many of the garrison as can reach her, if the attack cannot be beaten off, and the steam frigates can do the same. Those are the only instructions I can give you, Hazard. You will want to go ashore with your guns' crews, I imagine?"

Phillip's heart leapt and he said eagerly, "With your lordship's permission, yes indeed."

"For what it is worth, you have my permission," Paulet said. "You seem to be the sort of fellow the garrison needs ... perhaps you and your guns may contrive to tip the scales in their favor, who knows?" His handshake was firm and he added, as he walked with Phillip to the door of his cabin, "Place yourself under Captain Brock's orders and offer him my best wishes, when you see him. Au revoir, Hazard—and good luck!"

When Phillip returned once more to the *Trojan,* the work of unshipping the 32-pounder guns from her starboard battery was proceeding apace. His seamen, assisted by a party of soldiers and a few Marine artillerymen from the garrison, were going about their task with a will and already, he saw, half-a-dozen guns stood on their wheeled carriages on the wharf, rigged with slings and lines for towing. Two others were being hauled along one of the narrow streets of the picturesque little town by teams of men—some of them Tartar townsmen, he realized with surprise—and three horse-drawn ammunition wagons, fully laden, moved off as he climbed from his gig on to the wharf.

Martin Fox, seeing him, came hurrying over to join him. "All's going well, sir," he reported formally. "James promised to supply horse teams for the guns but, as they haven't appeared yet, I called for volunteers in the hope of saving a little time. Ah!" he broke off, pointing. "Here come the horses now ... and they look like captured Cossack ponies, don't they?" He called out an order to Lieutenant Sutherland, the Gunnery Officer, and then turned back to Phillip, smiling. "Sutherland's in his element. He's been to inspect the defenses and says the engineers are working like beavers, preparing sites for the guns. With a little luck and if those Cossack horses put their backs into it, we may have them in position before the enemy even sight the town."

"They're coming, I suppose?" Phillip asked, remembering Lord George Paulet's wishful thinking.

His second-in-command nodded. "Oh, yes, they're coming all right. Captain Brock sent out a mounted scouting party, as soon as Grey made his report. I understand, from young Grey—who has just reported back—that your estimate of their number and the speed of their advance wasn't very far out. The scouts observed a very large force of Cossack cavalry, which they put at between six and seven thousand, forty guns and something in the region of two regiments of infantry. But opinions differ as to *when* the attack will be launched. The officer who led the scouting party thinks they will wait until just before dawn but Captain Brock told Grey that almost certainly some of the Cossacks will endeavor to probe the defenses before the light goes."

"Let us hope the scout is right," Phillip returned, but without conviction, for Captain Brock, he knew, had a great deal of experience of Cossack cavalry attacks. "If he is, then that will give us the night to prepare to receive them." He glanced up at the sky, bathed in the rosy glow of a superb sunset and smothered a sigh, as he passed on Lord George Paulet's orders for the *Trojan* and the gist of what he had said concerning the situation. Fox's expression underwent a swift change.

"I did not realize the position was so grave," he said.

"No, nor did I, Martin." They were both silent as they watched another 32-pounder gun being lowered to the wharf. The men on shore, as if they, too, were acutely conscious of how little time they now had, dealt with it swiftly and, hauled by one of the shaggy horse-teams, sent it trundling on its way up the street, the gunlayer and his crew, told off by Sutherland, anxiously endeavoring to hold their weapon steady on a carriage which had not been designed to take it along roughly stone-paved streets. Yet these same men, Phillip reminded himself, had safely hauled heavier guns than these from Balaclava, up six miles of rutted track to the Heights above Sebastopol . . . and had done so without horses. He called out a word or two of encouragement and then said to Martin Fox, "Well, I had better go and seek out Captain Brock, I think. My compliments to Mr. Laidlaw and tell him, if you please, that he and Mr. Burnaby will be in command of the ship. Lord George wishes us to keep steam up, so we shall have to replenish our coal bunkers, as soon as the guns are out. He told me there was coal on this wharf."

"There is, plenty of it," Fox confirmed. "In those sheds over there. Are we just to help ourselves?"

Phillip shrugged. "Yes, why not?" He added instructions for the posting of guards and look-outs and was about to move away when Martin Fox stopped him. "Oh, by the way, sir—Surgeon Vernon went ashore while you were aboard the *Bellerophon,* to return to his unit. He asked me particularly to remember to tell you that young Durbanville's leg was taken off and that he came through it well. And I was to tell you also that you were right—I imagine you know what he was talking about?"

"Yes," Phillip answered. "Yes, I know, thank you, Martin. And what about my Queen's Hard Bargain—O'Leary? Is there any word of him, do you know?"

"Only that *he* still has his leg."

"I'm glad—and glad about Henry Durbanville too, I must admit." He laid a hand lightly on his First Lieutenant's shoulder. "See you later, Martin. I am instructed to place myself under Captain Brock's orders but no doubt he will permit me to visit our gun positions—of which you will be in command, of course."

"Aye, aye, sir," his second-in command acknowledged. "Good luck to you!"

"And to you, Martin."

"Take Grey with you, sir. He knows how to get to Captain Brock's headquarters," Fox suggested. "And thanks—I fancy we may need every bit of luck we can get, if the attack does come before dawn."

It came—launched, as Captain Brock had forecast, by the Cossack cavalry—just as the sun sank in a blaze of glory in the western sky. The Cossacks galloped up across the wide, open plain to the north of Eupatoria, wave after seemingly endless wave of savage horsemen, bent low in their high-peaked saddles, the afterglow of the sunset touching the tips of their fifteen-foot lances to blood-red and their appearance calculated to strike terror into the stoutest heart. They advanced arrogantly, without drawing rein and then, from a range of eight hundred yards, opened up a brisk fire with their artillery on the town's defenses.

It was evident that they had not expected these to be fully manned and still less anticipated that their fire would be returned by so many guns and with so much spirit. The recently constructed palisade, linking the various strong-points, had suffered some damage during the storm which it had been impossible, in the limited time, to repair and—proof of the close watch kept by the enemy's scouts and spies—a number of fierce assaults were made on each of the damaged sections. But the palisade stood firm and the naval guns, including the *Trojan*'s 32-pounders, well supplied with shot and shell and strategically placed at intervals so as to cover gaps in the long earth-wall—wrought havoc with every succeeding charge.

Phillip, who had, at Captain Brock's invitation, ridden out with him on one of the captured Cossack ponies when the enemy were first sighted, was conscious of a thrill of pride as he watched his men's steadiness and the rapidity and accuracy of their fire. Only eight of his guns had been properly sited when the attack began, the remaining two still some distance behind the defensive perimeter, their crews struggling vainly to haul them up to the sand-bagged emplacements prepared for them. But the eight, out-ranging the smaller calibre Russian field-pieces and handled with a great deal more skill, sufficed gradually— together with a naval rocket battery in their sector—to turn the tide of battle in favor of the defenders. When the attack had been pressed home, with ferocious courage, for nearly an hour, the light faded and first one of the Cossack gun batteries was glimpsed, limbering up, then a second and a third ceased fire and withdrew out of range.

"Well, Hazard," Captain Brock observed, scanning the scene with his glass. "They seem to have had enough, for the time being. Obviously they thought they would take us by surprise, with our men out in boats, endeavoring to take off the crews of the wrecked ships—as, indeed, they might well have done but for you. I am grateful for the timely warning you brought us, more grateful than I can begin to tell you . . . and also for your guns and ammunition. Your fellows did well—you must keep them in good practice, for I have seldom seen thirty-two pounders better handled."

"Thank you very much, sir," Phillip said, gratified. Praise from Captain Thomas Saumarez Brock was praise indeed, he thought, as they rode together along the line of defences, Brock pausing here and there to receive reports of casualties, or to watch the Cossacks' withdrawal across the plain.

Captain Brock had come out as supernumary Captain on board Admiral Dundas's flagship *Britannia,* Phillip recalled, and—like Captain Dacres of the *Sanspareil*—he was a member of that élite inner circle of captains and commanders who had served as junior officers in the *Blonde,* under Sir Edmund Lyons when, in 1829, the frigate had been the first British ship of war to enter the Bosphorus and Black Sea for twenty years. In addition, the commander of the Eupatoria garrison had been on board the *Sampson* when she had made her audacious survey of the Black Sea ports just before the outbreak of the war with Russia and he was considered one of the leading naval authorities on the enemy's seaward defenses, as well as on their strategy and tactics. Why, despite this, he had been left in Eupatoria ever since the Allied landing, over two months ago, was a question which only Admiral Dundas could answer but . . . Phillip studied him covertly, wondering whether or not Captain Brock resented the stagnation of his present command.

The Captain lowered his glass and observed, uncannily as if he had read Phillip's thoughts, "It *is* of considerable importance that we retain possession of this place, you know. It has a larger and better harbor than Balaclava and, if we were ever compelled to abandon Balaclava, we might be left with Eupatoria as our only operational base on the whole of the Crimean peninsula. Or, at any rate"—his tone was dry—"that is Admiral Dundas's belief. Lord Raglan, judging by the way in which he has seen fit to deplete my garrison recently, may not share it but, *if* he does not, his lordship has not confided the fact to me. My orders are to hold Eupatoria at all costs and I must seemingly do this with a makeshift force of British and French seamen and Marines—borrowed from the ships—and a few hundred Turks!" He glanced at Phillip, lips pursed. "Which may explain why I am glad to have an experienced campaigner like your Major Leach. But . . . lately I have heard a rumor that the Generals would like to quit Balaclava, now that it looks as if they must face a winter campaign. Have you heard anything of the kind, Commander Hazard?"

"Yes, sir, like yourself I have heard rumours," Phillip admitted, and gave him a cautious resumé of what Captain Heath had told him. "But Admiral Lyons—on whose Staff I had the honour to serve for a short time—holds a

206

strongly opposite view and so, I think, does Sir Colin Campbell, who commands the Balaclava defences."

"H'm, you interest me." Captain Brock, still searching the darkening plain with his glass, sounded thoughtful. "Sir Edmund is right, I am sure—he usually is—so I trust that his view may carry sufficient weight with Lord Raglan to prevail. We are forty miles overland from Sebastopol, as you know, but if the shipping at Balaclava has suffered anything approaching the damage we have suffered here, in the gale, we may yet find ourselves using this place as a winter base. A shore base, for the Army, I mean," he added, sensing Phillip's bewilderment. "The roadstead has proved quite unsuitable as an anchorage for sailing vessels, with the threat of gales always present in winter, so the sailing ships will have to go home and their Lordships will have to send us steamers, in their stead. I ..." he broke off, gesturing into the darkness ahead of them. "Do you see that?" He shouted a crisp order to a group of French seamen by the sandbagged palisade and one of the men sent up a flare. By its glow, a little band of Cossacks was revealed, attempting to steal up and catch the defenders unawares but a few musket shots quickly dispersed them.

"They will keep up this sort of thing for an hour or so." Captain Brock spoke with the confidence of experience. "Then they will retire to their camp fires to eat and sleep—Cossacks will ride all day but, at night, they like to sleep and rest their horses. They seldom attack in darkness, unless certain that their prey is defenseless—as, for example, were the wretched seamen, whose ships were driven ashore in the storm. So we may expect a lull quite soon and you will be able to stand your men down by their guns and let them eat and get what rest they can. My garrison cooks will provide a hot meal for them and you, perhaps, would dine with my officers and myself at our headquarters?"

"Thank you, sir." He sounded so calm and matter-of-fact that Phillip stared at him in some surprise and, again as if he had guessed his companion's thoughts, Captain Brock said, "In the early morning mist, the enemy will attack us once more in force, Hazard. If we can hold them then, we may count ourselves victorious . . . and I hope we can hold them, with the help of your guns and ammunition. You have two guns still to get into position, have you not?"

"Yes, sir."

"See to it, then, if you please," the garrison commander requested. "And perhaps you could let us have another wagonload of powder and shot—we are woefully short of munitions, I am afraid. I'll expect you at my headquarters in about two hours."

Phillip acknowledged the order and cantered back to carry it out. He found the *Trojan's* last two guns already being dragged into their emplacements, under Martin Fox's supervision and, having despatched a midshipman to the wharf to arrange for the unloading of further supplies of powder and shot, passed on the information he had gleaned from Captain Brock to his First Lieutenant.

"He was pleased with our shooting—pass that on to the guns' crews, will you please? And warn them to continue to keep a sharp look-out, until they see the glow of the Cossacks' camp fires . . . then, on Captain Brock's authority, you may stand them down. But they are to be at their guns, ready for action, well before first light. The Captain says we may expect another attack under cover of the early morning mist."

"Aye, aye, sir." Fox's eyes held a gleam of excitement. "It was extraordinary, that charge, wasn't it? Thousands of them, galloping hell for leather across the open plain! What did they expect to achieve? Cavalry are no match for guns."

"They apparently expected the defenses to be unmanned," Phillip told him. "And the garrison to be too short of ammunition to do them much harm. They have spies in the town, James said, who report regularly to the Cossack patrols. They . . ." out of the tail of his eye, he glimpsed a darker shadow among the shadows cast by the defensive earthworks, as the sweating men heaved and tugged the last 32-pounder on to its sandbagged platform and his warning shout came just in time. Both he and Fox emptied their pistols into the darkness and the Marine riflemen, positioned by the loopholes on either side of the gun, fired a scattered volley. A single, high-pitched scream of agony testified to their accuracy but then a score of dark bodies hurled themselves at the parapet, a few, with suicidal courage, managing to leap over it, hacking at the gunners with their sabers.

A wild mêlée ensued, with both Phillip and Martin Fox in the thick of it until finally Phillip, with the advantage of being mounted, managed to extricate his shaggy Cossack pony from the press of bodies and, rallying the Marines, led them back with bayonets fixed in a spirited charge. The attackers fled, as suddenly and as swiftly as they had appeared, leaving almost a dozen dead and wounded behind them and Phillip had to yell at the pitch of his lungs to stop his indignant gunners going in pursuit of their retreating foe. A big Gunner's Mate, a bloodied cutlass in his hand, said reproachfully as he obeyed the unwelcome order, "We could have had the lot of 'em, sir, if you'd let us go after them."

"They would have had you, more likely, my lad," Phillip returned. "There are quite a lot more of them in the darkness out there." As if in proof of his words, the sound of pounding hooves floated back to them and he added grimly, "You hear? About a hundred, I should say."

The Gunner's Mate shrugged his broad shoulders.

"Aye, sir, you're right. But they was after our gun, sir—trying to spike it, the heathen devils!"

"The gun's all right, Phillip," Martin Fox assured him breathlessly, after a swift inspection. He, too, listened to the sound of galloping hooves, now receding. "Well, they've gone, praise be! But it was a brave try and it almost succeeded. I'll double the look-outs, shall I?"

"Indeed you should, although I doubt if they'll try these tactics again. And pass the word for a surgeon, would you." Phillip dismounted, looking about him. Several men were nursing minor hacks and cuts but, to his relief, none of his *Trojans* admitted to serious injury. He ordered the uninjured back to the work of securing the gun and, calling for a lantern, went to where the enemy casualties lay. The first was an officer, a mere boy in an elegant Chasseur uniform and so too, he saw, when someone brought a shaded lantern, were three of the other dead . . . all four victims of the Marines' bayonet charge, judging by their wounds. A junior officers' prank, he thought, with a twinge of sadness, a do-or-die escapade devised, perhaps, in a spirit of adventure by boys having their first taste of action, whose cadet school training had made them despise the Cossacks' cautious reluctance to carry on the fight during the hours of darkness. Well, they had not lacked courage and, as his First Lieutenant had observed, the brave venture had almost succeeded. He was reminded suddenly of young Henry Durbanville and, conscious of an odd tightness about his throat, Phillip bent, in pity, over the first boy's body and gently closed the eyes, his fingers not quite steady, for all his determination to keep his emotions under stern control. War was an ugly business, when all was said and done and. . . .

"The surgeon's here, sir," Fox told him. "And Captain Brock's on his way."

Phillip recognized Surgeon Vernon, who was accompanied by a small party with stretchers. "Here they are,

Doctor." His voice, even to his own ears, sounded unpleasantly harsh. "I think five or six of them are still alive and you need not be afraid to touch them—they are Chasseurs, not Cossacks, most of them officers." He got to his feet and added quietly, "We will bury the dead."

Captain Brock listened, with raised eyebrows, to his account of the incident, as Vernon and his stretcher bearers busied themselves with dressing wounds and moving the injured, assisted by some of the *Trojan*'s seamen.

"A strange incident," the garrison commander agreed, when Phillip came to the end of his recital. "As you suggest, Commander Hazard, it was probably a young officers' escapade, of the kind some of our own midshipmen might well have planned, in this situation. We will give them Christian burial. I'll send you a chaplain or one of the Orthodox priests from the town, if I can get hold of one." He glanced at the gun, now in position with the rest of the *Trojan*'s battery, and smiled. "At least you did not lose your gun, which is fortunate, because we shall need it tomorrow morning."

"No, sir." It took an effort to return the smile but Phillip made it. "We did not lose our gun."

9

PHILLIP excused himself from the invitation to dine at Captain Brock's headquarters. The brief funeral service, conducted by a priest from the town, was soon over and he and Martin Fox remained with their guns' crews for the rest of the night, eating with them and snatching what sleep they could in the shelter of the palisade, while standing watch and watch with Anthony Cochrane and the young Gunnery Lieutenant, Sutherland. The look-outs were understandably nervous, having so nearly been caught off guard by the Chasseur officers' raid, but the night passed quietly, the distant glow of bivouac fires from the Cossack camp the only indication of the enemy's presence.

It was cold, with a chill wind from the east and a touch of frost in the air and, when the men were turned-up, an hour before dawn, Phillip ordered a double tot of rum to be issued with their morning brew of cocoa, served by the garrison cooks and brought up to the palisade in huge, earthenware containers, loaded on to hand-carts or ponies. Captain Brock was early astir, a calm, confident figure, ready with a jest or a word of praise as he made a tour of his defense lines.

"A Turkish army patrol caught a spy, attempting to leave town," he told Phillip, after he had inspected the *Trojan*'s gun battery. "Though what the fellow imagined he could tell the enemy that they don't already know

213

defeats me! Spies are constantly coming and going—with a mixed population of Tartars, Jews, Armenians, Greeks and Germans, as well as Russians and a number of Cossacks, it is hard to judge who is on our side and who isn't. In general, I must confess, most of them appear to prefer our occupation to the rule of their Russian Governor. A great many actively co-operate with us, besides supplying us with quantities of meat and grain, for which, of course, we pay and most of which we send on to Balaclava to feed Lord Raglan's troops." He smiled, without amusement. "Another reason, I suppose, why we must endeavor to hold this place. And we shall not have long to wait now—the wind has dropped and the mist is rising. Keep a sharp look-out—they'll come silently. These are the conditions they like best for an attack and you won't hear a bridle jingle."

"Aye, aye, sir," Phillip acknowledged, feeling his heart quicken its beat. "I have men standing by with rockets, to enable us to see our target."

The garrison commander nodded his approval. "It's worth trying, though I doubt if you'll see much if the mist is really thick." He hesitated. "Have you seen Major Leach, by the way?"

"No, sir. But perhaps my officers have." Phillip glanced at them but all four shook their heads. "Do you want him, sir? If so, I could send someone to look for him."

"Don't trouble, Hazard—I shall probably run into him myself." Captain Brock remounted his sturdy pony. "I like your Major Leach very much indeed and it is of great assistance to have a professional soldier of his caliber and experience, on whose advice I can call when I need it . . . as I frequently do! My garrison consists mainly of seamen and Marines, of almost as many different nationalities as the town itself can boast, and our combined knowledge of military tactics leaves much to be desired. So I hope I shall be permitted to retain the services of the Major and

214

his excellent Fusiliers, even if I'm compelled to let you and your *Trojan*s return to the Fleet." He smiled again, warmly this time, repeated his warning to Phillip to keep a sharp look-out and continued on his way.

Five minutes after his departure, the first Russian guns opened fire, on the eastern extremity of the defense works and from alarmingly close range. Phillip took his stand by one of the shoulder-high loopholes in the palisade, between Numbers Three and Four guns, peering into the misty darkness but—apart from the firing to the east—he could see or hear nothing. The sky was tinged with faint, grey light now but this served only to increase the obscurity of the swirling curtain of mist which, rising over the flat plain, completely hid any movement taking place upon it from the anxious watchers in the Eupatoria defense works.

At Phillip's side, Anthony Cochrane said, a slight tremor in his voice, "They're coming, sir, I could swear it. Shall we send up a flare?"

"No, not yet. Where's the First Lieutenant?"

"Here, sir." Martin Fox came to join him at his loophole and both listened intently. Phillip heard—or imagined he heard—the muffled thud of hoofbeats on the frost-hard ground but was unable to decide from which direction they came. More cannon opened to the right of the line but, as yet, none fired on his position. Were they, he asked himself, attempting to bring their field pieces to point-blank range, depending on the stealth and silence of their approach to take his battery by surprise? Were they hoping to maim or slaughter his guns' crews, before they could fire a shot in reply? A flare, while it might help him to locate them, would also serve to reveal his position to the enemy and . . . he stiffened, hearing the chink of metal quite distinctly now and—between the spasmodic crackle of musketry and the roar of the guns to the east—another sound, which puzzled him at first. Could it be the scrape of wheels on rock? There was a patch of rough, rockstrewn ground, he remembered suddenly, about four hundred yards—three hundred and fifty, perhaps—to his left front. And if wheels were passing over this, then the enemy field guns had not yet unlimbered and his guess as to the strategy they were seeking to employ might well be right. The mist which was affording cover for their approach must also, he knew, to a certain extent confuse them. Even with their knowledge of the ground and their spies' reports, the advancing Cossacks could not be quite sure how near to the curving line of the defense works they had come and might therefore have come closer than they had intended. Phillip gripped Martin Fox's arm.

"Did you hear that? Wheels passing over rock?"

"That was what it sounded like, Phillip." Fox, too, had noticed and remembered the rocky patch of ground to their front and he gestured in its direction. "There's a hillock just beyond and to the left which would give them good cover—probably the point they're aiming for but they've come too far and must wheel. Shall we open with Numbers Six and Eight and chance it? They're both loaded with grape." He broke off as the boom of cannon drowned his words, coming from the direction of the magazine, and then went on, his mouth to Phillip's ear, "The range of the hillock is three hundred and seventy yards—I worked it out last evening, when we were siting the guns."

"Very well. Tell Mr. Sutherland to open fire."

The First Lieutenant sang out the order and the alert Sutherland acknowledged it promptly, himself running forward to lower the elevation of his Number Eight gun. The gun opened, its flash momentarily blinding them, with Number Six doing likewise a few seconds later. Neither shot was on target but the next two were and a third, firing shell, from the gun under Anthony Cochrane's command—by what Phillip had afterwards to admit was an

216

almost incredible piece of good fortune—fell short, to score a direct hit on one of the enemy guns. This had been in position, ready to fire and the British shell, bursting amongst the unfortunate crew, virtually wiped them out, aided by the explosion of the gun itself—or of the piled ammunition behind it, Phillip could not be sure which. At all events, when the smoke cleared a little, he saw that the field piece had disintegrated into a heap of misshapen metal, surrounded by grey-coated bodies.

To their credit, the Cossack gunners managed, despite this setback, to bring four of their field-cannon into action. Taunted by the triumphant cheers of the *Trojan*'s guns' crews, the four 12-pounder pieces fought a courageous but unequal duel with the naval battery and not until another gun had been put out of action by a direct hit did the remaining three withdraw. Even then, they unlimbered just out of range, and fired a few defiant shots before galloping back across the plain, to be swallowed up in the now swiftly dispersing mist. Their part in the battle over, at least for the time being, Phillip ordered his men to cease fire. He was on his way to offer them the praise they had earned when an elderly French naval officer, with a bandaged arm and without his shako, came running up with a breathless request for aid.

"Zey are breaking t'rough, Monsieur," he stammered, in barely comprehensible English, gesturing vaguely in the direction from which he had come. "I beg you . . . 'elp us. We are wiz'out ammunition and ze crew of our gun . . . all are wounded."

"Let me go, sir!" Fox offered eagerly. "With a relief gun's crew." Phillip hesitated, reluctant to let him go but . . . he could offer no valid reason for refusal and his second-in-command, taking his brief nod for consent, quickly gathered a spare gun's crew and a munition limber and vanished with them into the smoke of battle at the French officer's heels.

217

Phillip returned to his vantage point at the loophole and, able to see more clearly now, watched in horrified amazement as two squadrons of Cossack cavalry charged past his line of vision, to hurl themselves at what appeared to be a breach in the defensive palisade. They were too close and at too much of an angle for any of his guns to range on them but they were met by a well directed volley of musketry, and then by a resolute line of seamen and Marines, with fixed bayonets. None got through and, beaten back, they were forced to retire, leaving their dead and wounded behind them.

"I hope, sir," Anthony Cochrane said, leaning a smoke-blackened face close to his, "that Mr. Fox's Frenchmen are as steady as those fellows over there."

Phillip nodded, tight lipped, fervently echoing his hope. "It will be over very soon, I think. They've fought well, no one can deny them that, but they're beaten. Their two attempts to surprise us have both failed and they've suffered heavy losses . . . unless their commander is a callous madman, he must order them to withdraw."

His prediction proved to be correct. The mist cleared and the Cossack force could be seen, retreating across the open plain. They did so in scattered groups at first, but finally in large numbers, some carrying wounded across their saddles and followed by gun limbers which moved at walking pace, piled high with other casualties.

Victory was complete for Eupatoria's defenders and the weary men, realizing now that they had been successful in beating off the attack, expressed their feelings in spasmodic cheers as they received the order to stand down. There was no sign of Martin Fox but a jubilant Major Leach came to exchange congratulations with Phillip and his officers, and the *Trojan*'s gunners, recognizing him, gave him an extra cheer. He and his Fusiliers had been among those facing the Cossack cavalry at one of the points their guns had managed to breach, having, Leach confessed

218

with engaging modesty, had to make a fifty yard-sprint in order to get there in time to form up with a line of Turkish sailors. He had no news of Martin Fox when Phillip questioned him but stated, with certainty, that at no point in the defensive line had the enemy succeeded in breaking through.

"They are savages, these Cossacks," he observed. "And I've never held them in great esteem but, by heaven, Hazard, I have to admit that today they fought as bravely as any troops I have ever come across. They almost got through to our magazine, early on in the attack . . . you heard them, I expect, battering away at point-blank range over to your right? They brought in a six-gun battery, without a soul seeing or hearing them, until they opened up. And then it was touch and go, until Captain Brock got a howitzer over to them and reinforced the defenders with some very gallant seamen from the *Leander*."

"Were the original defenders French Marines?" Phillip asked, still worried by the continued absence of Fox and his party.

"No, they were ours, I understand," Leach answered. "Oh, by the bye"—he put his single arm about Phillip's shoulders and smiled at him with genuine affection—"Vernon tells me that you brought young Durbanville in . . . well done, Hazard! I am most relieved that you did, for . . . oh, for a great many reasons I need not go into now. He's lost a leg, I believe, but is expected to live—is that right?"

"I was told so, yes, sir, though I haven't seen him since the surgeons finished with him. He's on board the *Trojan*."

"And you will be taking him with you when you leave, I suppose? Well, give him my regards, if you please. He has good stuff in him, that young man. It's a pity about his leg—I think he might have made a good soldier, given the chance, don't you?"

"Yes," Phillip agreed. "Perhaps he would."

Leach wrung his hand. "I must report to Captain Brock. Good-bye and the best of luck to you, my friend, if we shouldn't meet again ... although I hope we shall. And I trust you will find Lieutenant Fox unscathed."

"I trust so, too. Good-bye, sir. I also hope that we may meet again."

When the Major had gone, Phillip left Anthony Cochrane in charge of the guns' crews, to await the arrival of Captain Brock's admirably organized commissariat service, with its promised supply of hot cocoa and a meal, and set off in search of his missing party, accompanied by Midshipman Grey. Despite Major Leach's assertion that the magazine at the eastern extremity of the fortifications, had been defended by British Marines, he decided to walk over there. It had been the only part of the defensive line that had been in desperate need of help—or the only one that he had heard of—and so it seemed reasonable to assume that Fox had gone there. And, if the position had been badly damaged by the enemy's guns, he decided that the *Trojan*'s party would most probably have stayed down there, to assist with its repair.

Half-way to his objective, Grey stopped him, pointing. "Isn't that one of our fellows, sir, coming up from the town?"

Following the direction of the boy's pointing finger, Phillip recognized the big Gunner's Mate, Thompson, who had wanted to pursue their attackers the previous night. Recognition was mutual and the man quickened his pace, coming towards the two officers at a rapid jog-trot. His expression, Phillip saw, with a sudden premonition of what was to come, looked glum and anxious.

"Well," he demanded, his tone clipped. "What happened to your party, Thompson? And where is the First Lieutenant?"

"Mr. Fox was wounded, sir." The petty officer drew

himself up, passing a big, red hand over his heated brow. "I . . . I'm afraid he's pretty bad, sir. He wouldn't let us take him to the hospital—kept on saying he must get back to the ship. So we carried him down to the *Trojan,* and the Surgeon's caring for him now. That's why we didn't report to you sooner . . . it took us a while, you see, sir, because it's a tidy step from the magazine down to the wharf."

"You were at the magazine? Was anyone else wounded?"

Thompson shook his head. "Not of our party, sir—just a few cuts and slashes, nothing to speak of—but there were two Frenchmen killed and about ten or eleven wounded." Phillip turned towards the road leading into the town and both Grey and the Gunner's Mate fell into step beside him. "There's a short cut, this way, sir," the seaman pointed out.

As they hurried down the steep, cobbled path which ran between rows of white, stone-built houses towards the wharf, Phillip endeavored to get a coherent account of what had happened to Fox and his party. But Thompson, despite his splendid physique and his repeated insistence that he was fit and unscathed, was considerably shaken and it took much patient questioning on Phillip's part, before he was able to elicit and piece together the full story of what had occurred.

Martin Fox, it seemed, had led his small party to the aid of the hard-pressed Frenchmen with exemplary courage, and had received numerous saber cuts and a pistol ball in the chest. "I didn't see how it happened, sir," poor Thompson volunteered miserably. "Though I saw Mr. Fox go down once and then pick himself up. When we got there, you see, sir, a whole bunch of them Cossacks leaped their horses right into the middle of us—they must have seen us coming, I suppose. Their field-guns was right underneath the palisade, and they'd pounded away at it until they laid part of it flat. They was trying to get through to the magazine, someone told me, meaning to blow it up. We never got the Frenchmen's gun back into action, sir—or at least, not until the Jacks from the *Leander* came and helped us to drive the Cossacks out. And by then it was too late, of course, the enemy were away, guns and all. That was when I seen the First Lieutenant, sir. A couple of our lads had picked him up and were doing what they could for him, which wasn't much. I knew he was hurt bad, sir, when I went over to him."

"You didn't call a surgeon?" Phillip asked, his throat tight.

"No, sir." The petty officer shook his head. "There was a Surgeon's Mate with the *Leanders* but he was attending to the French lads and Mr. Fox said not to trouble him. 'Take me back to the ship, Thompson', he kept saying, over and over again. So that's where we took him, sir. And when we got him aboard, he sent me to report to you, sir. 'Go and find the Captain', he said. 'Because he'll be wondering where we've got to'."

Martin had been conscious then, Phillip's mind registered. He had been conscious when he was carried on board the *Trojan* and he was now in the competent hands of Angus Fraser, who would save him, if anyone could. He clung to this hope as, with Grey and Thompson panting at his heels, he rounded a bend in the narrow, deserted street and glimpsed the *Trojan*'s masts rising above the line of red-tiled rooftops.

"Seems funny to think them Frenchmen ran out of powder and shot for their guns, don't it, sir?" Thompson's voice broke into his thoughts. "When they was right on top of the main magazine, so to speak, and you'd have thought they only had to help themselves?"

The question was now of purely academic interest, Phillip reflected wryly. To his surprise, the big Gunner's Mate added flatly, "After it was all over, sir, one of them

222

Frogs—Frenchmen, I mean, sir—he said as the magazine was empty, that the whole lot had been issued, down to the last keg of powder! I don't believe that, do you, sir?"

Phillip answered noncommittally but, recalling the wrecked transports and Captain Brock's urgent request for powder and shot from the *Trojan,* he was less certain than Gunner's Mate Thompson that the Frenchman had been wrong. One, at least, of the transports had been a munition carrier, according to Lieutenant James, and very little of her cargo was likely to be salvaged from her battered hull, lying half-submerged on the rocky shore only a short distance from the *Henri Quatre.* Well, if the magazine *was* empty, it made Captain Brock's victory the more remarkable ... and the more courageous, for Eupatoria's spies had also been defeated. Phillip stifled a sigh, his mind shying away from the thought that the defense of an empty magazine might have cost the life of his best friend. Martin Fox was not dying, Thompson had not said so, only that he was badly hurt and he had been conscious when they had carried him on board the *Trojan* ... he quickened his pace, conscious of a sick feeling in the pit of his stomach.

"Sir——" Midshipman Grey was beside him. "I'll run ahead, shall I, sir, and find out how the First Lieutenant is?"

As he had run down the cliff path—could it only have been yesterday?—with warning of the attack which had just been driven off, Phillip reflected, conscious now not only of nausea but of his limp, which always affected him when he was tired. And he *was* tired, dear heaven how tired he was!

"Thank you, Mr. Grey," he said, careful to control his voice. "I should be obliged if you would."

"Aye, aye, sir." The youngster sped off on his self-imposed mission. He was waiting, with Laidlaw, at the entry port when Phillip and the weary Thompson boarded the ship. Neither spoke for a moment and, looking from one to the other of their two distressed faces, Phillip knew that what they had to give him could only be bad news. "Sir——" Laidlaw began but Phillip cut him short, glimpsing Surgeon Fraser behind them.

"Thank you, Mr. Laidlaw ... Mr. Grey. Carry on, if you please." He joined Fraser, a mute question in his eyes, and the Surgeon said quietly, "He's dying, I'm afraid. I've done all I can to ease his pain but that is all I can do. The pistol ball is lodged in one of his lungs and it would only hasten the end if I tried to remove it. But he's able to talk a little and he's asking for you, sir."

"Thank you, Doctor." It took all the self control Phillip possessed to speak normally. "Where is he?"

"In his own cabin, sir. That is where he wanted to be." The Surgeon laid a hand on his arm and added kindly, "You look just about all in yourself. May I get you a tot of whisky or brandy, perhaps?"

Phillip shook his head. "No, thanks, I'm all right. I'll go to him at once. Are you coming?"

"Aye, just to take a quick look at him." Surgeon Fraser stood aside, to allow Phillip to precede him. "I hear that the attack was successfully repulsed."

"Yes, it was." They descended the after-companionway and, at its foot, Phillip paused for a moment, bracing himself. "You are quite sure nothing more can be done for Mr. Fox, Doctor? I'm not questioning your professional judgement but——"

"I am quite sure." The Surgeon met his gaze steadily, pity and regret in his kindly grey eyes. "I wish I were not so sure, believe me. Poor fellow, he has other wounds—sabre cuts, some cracked ribs and a smashed collar-bone. I could patch those up but I cannot remove the ball from his lung, nor can I staunch the hemorrhage it is causing. That pistol must have been discharged straight at him, from a distance of a couple of feet." He sighed. "From

224

what the other men in Mr. Fox's party have told me, it must have been a very hot engagement while it lasted. But none of the others are badly hurt."

"That's something," Phillip said. Of the whole party, it had to be Martin Fox, he thought bitterly, the one man, above all others, that he—and the *Trojan*—could least afford to lose but . . . controlling himself, he inquired about Henry Durbanville.

"He is making quite good progress. Still shocked, of course, but I think he'll pull through." Reaching the door of the First Lieutenant's cabin, Surgeon Fraser assumed a cheerful smile before opening it. "Commander Hazard is here to see you, Mr. Fox." He dismissed Fox's servant, who had been in attendance, his blunt, capable fingers feeling for the pulse at the injured man's wrist and then he again stood aside, yielding his place to Phillip. "Send for me, if he needs me," he requested, lowering his voice and then, raising it once more, "You are doing fine, Mr. Fox, just fine. Your pulse is improving and so are you."

Martin Fox, heavily bandaged about the chest and propped up with pillows, eyed him quizzically, a faint smile playing about his lips. But he did not speak and, when the Surgeon had gone, his smile faded.

"Who is deceiving whom, I wonder? Because I fear he's wrong, Phillip. He has told *you* the truth, hasn't he? Oh, don't trouble to deny it"—as Phillip attempted to evade the question—"I knew, hours ago, that there wasn't much hope for me. I'm not in pain—the good doctor has filled me so full of laudanum and his own Scotch whisky that I can feel very little."

"Ought you to talk, Martin?" Phillip demurred, shocked by his pallor and labored breathing and by the feverish brightness of his eyes.

"I must talk to you, my dear Phillip. There are matters to settle . . . a letter I must ask you, if you will, to send home to my mother, to which, perhaps, you could add a few lines. But be careful what you say, I do not want to upset her . . . she is not young and her health is poor."

"I'll be careful," Phillip promised.

"Thank you. The letter is here, with some other papers, but I made no Will. Perhaps you could attend to that for me as well? Not that I've much to leave but . . . I'll dictate it, if you like. My servant set out pen and paper for you on my bureau, did he not? I asked him to."

"Yes, he did." Phillip picked up the pen, his hand not quite steady. The writing of the Will did not take long and, when it was done, Fox signed the single sheet of paper and entrusted it, as well as the letter, to his care. After that, they talked, the wounded man's voice growing gradually fainter, as his strength drained from him. He talked of the past, recalling events which had taken place years before and reliving shared adventures, when both had been lively midshipmen, serving in the *Maeander* frigate under Captain Henry Keppel, in the China Sea and in Borneo and Sarawak, and later in Australia.

"Those were good days, weren't they, Phillip?" Martin Fox was smiling. "I don't regret any of them and I certainly don't regret having made my career in the Navy. They say Captain Keppel's coming out here, from the Baltic Fleet—had you heard? In the *St. Jean d'Acre,* steam-screw and a hundred and one guns. I'd like to have seen our 'Little Captain' again. When you do, give him my respectful regards, won't you?"

"Of course I will. But don't be too sure—you may deliver them yourself."

"You *and* old Fraser?" Fox accused reproachfully. "Why, Phillip, my dear chap—do you imagine that I am afraid to die? I am not, I promise you. I believe in God and in a life, of some kind, hereafter, so how can I be afraid? I regret it, I admit but . . . it's a chance one takes in war. And I have seen a great many other men die, better men than I am, and so have you . . ." he started to

226

cough and Phillip saw that the cloth he held to his mouth was heavily stained. He leaned forward anxiously but Fox waved him away. "Do you suppose," he asked, when at last the coughing had subsided, "that Captain Crawford will resume command of this ship, Phillip? If he does, will you remain as her First Lieutenant?"

Phillip shrugged. "I don't know, I haven't thought about it."

"Think about it, Phillip. She's a good ship," her First Lieutenant said softly. "And there is scarcely a man of her company I'd change. Not now, not under *your* command. You have commanded the *Trojan* well, it's a thousand pities you cannot keep her."

"You know I shan't be given the chance. I've been fortunate, all things considered, to have held the acting command for so long. And to have had you, to back me up, Martin. *That* made all the difference." Phillip forced his stiff lips into a smile. "Having you as my friend, as well as my second-in-command."

"I have valued our friendship very highly," Fox told him gravely. He talked on, of Captain North, of Mademoiselle Sophie and the Baroness von Mauthner, and then, his tone oddly regretful, of Catriona Moray. "I should have liked to see her again, Phillip . . . more especially since you said that your intentions towards her weren't serious. Mine, I believe, might have been if she had given me any encouragement, for I held her in great esteem. Perhaps you will tell her so, if you should ever have the opportunity or if you write to her."

"Yes, of course I will," Phillip promised, feeling suddenly ashamed because, in his blindness, he had not guessed the truth and because, in Constantinople, he had monopolized Catriona. "Martin, I think you should try to rest. Talking cannot be good for you and——"

"Does it matter what is good—or bad—for me now?" the injured man asked. "And I want to talk. There are so
227

many things to tell you." He continued to talk but now his memory was failing, Phillip realized, and the ghastly coughing became more frequent. The Surgeon came twice, unbidden, to visit him and, on the second occasion, warned Phillip that it could not be much longer and urged him to rest. Obstinately he refused, leaving the cabin only when a staff officer came aboard, with a message from Captain Brock to inform him that he could withdraw his guns and their crews from the defense works the following morning.

"Guns, powder and shot and virtually every man of the *Henri Quatre*'s company have been taken off," the officer said. "By noon tomorrow, all being well, we shall have conveyed the men, at least, to the town—perhaps, if you will be good enough to provide these—with the assistance of your boats, Commander, so that we may shift some of her guns as well."

Phillip promised him what assistance was required and returned to his vigil in the small, cramped cabin that had been his during Captain North's command.

Martin Fox died in the early hours of the following morning, slipping quietly and almost imperceptibly from semi-consciousness into his last and final sleep, his fingers, which had been gripping Phillip's hand, suddenly relaxing their hold. Rising stiffly from his seat beside the cot, Phillip stood looking down at the still, calm face and then, wearily, went to his own quarters to compose a letter to his friend's mother.

There were two other sons, he knew, and four daughters but Martin had been the eldest and the pride of his mother's heart. The letter took him a long time and, when he had sealed it, he hesitated, wondering what he should write to Catriona Moray. But there would be time for that later. He flung himself, fully clothed, on to his cot and slept. . . .

10

MIDWAY through the Forenoon Watch on 19th November, the *Trojan* dropped anchor off Balaclava and, in response to an order from the signal station on shore, Phillip entered the harbor in his gig, to be received on board the *Sanspareil* by Captain Leopold Heath.

It was now almost a week since the gale had struck the Crimean coast with such devastating fury and a certain amount had been done to repair the damage to those ships which had survived its onslaught. Many of the less fortunate had vanished, broken up by the pounding seas but several still lay, like stranded whales, at intervals along the rocky, inhospitable shore and, turning his glass on them, Phillip wondered how many of their officers and men had been saved.

Within the small, land-locked harbor, the congestion was now worse than it had ever been, he saw, and, with few exceptions, most of the vessels lying inside the entrance or tied up to the wharves bore signs of the terrible ordeal they had endured. They lay, in lines of up to six or eight ships, broadside on to each other, some dismasted, others with rudders missing and boats stove in, a few barely afloat. Even the *Sanspareil*, her tall masts towering impressively above those of the frigates and transports, lay with her forefoot high and dry on shore and her shattered bowsprit foul of one of the stone-built houses which circled the inner harbor, looking for all the world as if some giant hand had picked her up and flung her there like a discarded toy.

"And so it felt to all on board, I'm told," Captain Heath said, his tone wry, "Imagine it—a ship of this size, with two anchors down!" He led the way to the stern cabin, apologizing for the absence of Captain Dacres. "He's resting but he'll join us in a little while. Poor, dear fellow, he is far from well. You will see a great change in him, Hazard, but . . ." he sighed. "He is still in official command of this ill-fated port and refuses to ask for sick leave, although what happened here during the gale almost broke his heart. As, indeed, it has broken mine . . . but I'm being a bad host. Sit down, my dear Hazard, and I will send for coffee. Unless you would fancy something stronger? No—then coffee it shall be. We are expecting Admiral Lyons sometime before dinner, so I suggest you stay and make your report in full to him, because he will certainly want to see you and hear all you are able to tell him of the situation in Eupatoria."

Over coffee, Leopold Heath embarked on a harrowing account of the toll taken, in ships and seamen, by the gale which had struck Balaclava, with hurricane force, during the hours of darkness on 14th November. "We, I suppose, were lucky. After discussing the matter with Commander Powell of the *Vesuvius,* I decided to bring the *Niger* into the harbor and he followed my example. By some miracle, we both entered safely but I should not like to try it again as long as I live!" He went into graphic and horrifying detail and then continued, "We lost the *Prince* and the *Resolute,* the *Rip van Winkle, Wild Wave, Progress, Kenilworth, Wanderer* and *Malta.* All were lying outside the harbor, all parted from their anchors and were driven on to the rocks, where they have gone to pieces. From all these ships, thirty men were saved. The rest went down with their ships."

"The *Prince*!" Phillip exclaimed, in shocked surprise. "You say the *Prince* is lost, sir?"

"Yes, the *Prince*, with vast quantities of winter clothing for the Army and a crew of a hundred and fifty three," Captain Heath confirmed bitterly. "She lost one anchor and cable and was dragging on the other but she was apparently holding her own, with her full power of steam, when either her commander or her crew yielded to panic, for she was seen to be cutting away her mizzen-mast. The rigging fouled her screw and she drove ashore like the rest. The *Resolute* followed her and"——he sighed deeply—— "she is much on Captain Dacres' conscience, as she is on mine, for her Master made the most strenuous efforts to persuade us to give him permission to enter the harbor, the day she arrived. It was not in our power to give him permission—our orders had not been changed. Nor were they, until the storm was at its height . . ." he talked on, sadly describing the loss of each ship and Phillip listened in numb silence.

He was speaking of the narrow escape of the steam frigate *Retribution,* with the Duke of Cambridge on board, when Captain Dacres came into the cabin. He looked ill and strained and he stared at Phillip without recognition, until his second-in-command prompted, "Hazard, sir—acting Commander of the *Trojan,* which has just returned from Eupatoria."

"Ah, yes, of course—welcome aboard, Mr. Hazard. Forgive me, I'll be with you in a moment but I must have a word with Captain Heath. Sit down, please."

"Thank you, sir." Obediently, Phillip resumed his seat and Dacres turned his white, tortured face to Leopold Heath and said wearily, "I have composed an urgent request to the Commander-in-Chief, Leo, for shipwrights. God knows where he's likely to obtain them but I've told him of our disastrous losses and explained that this harbor is now filled with crippled ships and, without help of

231

some kind, I cannot possibly repair a quarter of them. Some, I suppose, can be towed to Sinope or to the Bosphorus .... I have asked for any steam tugs the Admiral can spare."

"You've had no rest, sir," Heath reproached him.

"For heaven's sake, how can I rest? My sleep is haunted by visions of dismasted transports and rudderless frigates and, God help me, I can still hear that poor devil Lewis, beseeching me to allow him to bring the *Resolute* into harbor! And all I could do was advise him to follow the example of the commander of the *City of London* and get up steam at once and take his ship to sea. You heard his reply, did you not?"

"No, sir." Leopold Heath crossed to the table, poured out a cup of coffee and put it into his chief's hand. Dacres thanked him but set it down untouched, as he went on tonelessly, "Lewis said, 'I have the working stock of powder on board, I cannot go. What would be said if it were required and I was not on hand? The whole siege might be stopped and I should be responsible'. Now his cargo is under twenty fathoms of water and—God rest his conscientious soul—so is he ... but still they tell me I must keep this harbor clear, in case it has to be evacuated! Merciful heavens, Leo, how many more ships must we lose, how many more men's deaths must I have on my conscience, before these confounded soldiers believe that it is quite out of the question to abandon Balaclava now?"

"Perhaps, sir," Heath offered consolingly, "Sir Edmund may have succeeded in persuading Lord Raglan that, in these circumstances, it *is* out of the question."

"Perhaps he may," Captain Dacres conceded, but without conviction. "It's a pity some of the Generals did not have their tents blown down and——"

"I was about to tell Commander Hazard that the news we received from the main Fleet anchorage was not quite as bad as we had feared," his second-in-command put in,

232

catching Phillip's eye and obviously anxious to change the subject. Reminded of his visitor's presence, Captain Dacres courteously pushed a handsome silver box of cigars across the table towards him. "Forgive me, Hazard . . . I am not myself. Indeed, I wish I were anyone else at this moment. No doubt Captain Heath has given you an account of what happened here, so that you will understand why."

"Yes, sir, he has. I'm deeply sorry, sir."

"So am I." Captain Dacres took a cigar from the box, but did not light it, twirling it absently between his fingers. "However, as our good friend Captain Heath pointed out, the effects of the gale were not quite as appalling at the Katcha anchorage as they were here. The ships of war are all safe, according to Commander Reynolds of the *Beagle,* who called here on his way to the Bosphorus and dispatches. He said the *Sampson* was dismasted and the *Terrible* suffered some damage to her stern but the liners are all right. Five transports were driven on to the beach but their crews were all saved by boats from the Fleet. We saved thirty men here, that was all . . . thirty! And the rescuers risked their own lives, hauling the poor fellows by rope up the cliffs. We could launch no boats, alas . . ." he spread his hands in a helpless gesture, letting the untouched cigar fall unnoticed, and then, after eyeing Phillip thoughtfully for a moment, he frowned, "The *Trojan*—good heavens, I sent you to Eupatoria, did I not?"

"Yes, sir," Phillip confirmed.

"Is your ship damaged? You must have sailed straight into the storm." His eyes widened in astonishment when Phillip shook his head. "Ah, then you made port in time?"

"No, sir. We rode out the gale at sea, under our engines, as you advised the *Resolute* to endeavor to do. We lost one of our sixty-eight pounders, when it broke loose on the quarterdeck and we were unable to secure it, and

233

we shipped several tons of water but that was all. We were in less danger, as it happened, than the ships at the Eupatoria anchorage, which suffered almost as severely as you did here . . ." Phillip supplied details, while Captain Dacres continued to regard him with incredulously raised brows.

"I'm glad to hear the *Bellerophon* is safe but . . . you say the *Henri Quatre* was wrecked! Dear God, a three-decker, less than five years off the stocks and a steam-screw at that, anchored in a protected roadstead . . . it's unbelievable! Do you hear what the boy's saying, Leo? Perhaps, after all, we have less to reproach ourselves with than I had imagined, for at least we did not lose our only liner. Tell me more, Hazard—how did the *Henri Quatre* run on shore? And were *Bellerophon* and *Leander* able to send boats to her aid?"

"Forgive me, sir," Captain Heath intervened, "But I suggested that Hazard should make his full report when the Admiral joins us. Evidently he has quite a story to tell."

"Evidently. Well, Mr. Hazard, we will wait to hear it until the Admiral comes aboard but, in the meantime, I must congratulate you on preserving the *Trojan* undamaged." Captain Dacres eyed him with approval. "Captain Crawford will be immensely relieved to know that his ship is safe."

"I . . . did you say Captain Crawford, sir?" Phillip was aware that his voice sounded unnaturally loud but the mention of Captain Crawford's name had come as an unexpected shock. Yet it should not really have been unexpected, he chided himself—it had always been on the cards that *Trojan*'s Captain would return to resume his command. He had even discussed the possibility with poor Martin before he died . . . "Is he—is the Captain here, sir?"

"Indeed he is—did not Captain Heath tell you? The

Avon brought him, a few hours after you sailed for Eupatoria ... fully recovered, I am glad to say. And he reproached me very bitterly for having sent his ship out into the teeth of the gale with—forgive me, Mr. Hazard—a comparatively inexperienced junior officer in acting command. But . . ." the port commander smiled. "I can only suppose that he does not know you well or realize your professional competence. Perhaps you did not serve under him for long?"

"I have not served under Captain Crawford at all, sir," Phillip began. "You see, sir . . ." he was interrupted by a midshipman, who entered, cap in hand, to announce that the Admiral had been sighted.

"I will receive him, sir," Leopold Heath offered but his senior obstinately shook his head. "Good God, Leo, I'm still capable of dragging myself to my own entry port and, as long as I am, I won't have you trying to molly-coddle me. All the same, I shall be grateful for your arm . . . wait for us here, if you please, Mr. Hazard. And you'll dine with us, of course?"

"Thank you, sir." Phillip waited, containing his impatience and wondering whether Captain Crawford—who had also served as a midshipman under Sir Edmund Lyons in the 'thirties—would be with him. He heard the shrill sound of the boatswain's mates' pipes, as the Admiral was paid the customary honors and, a little later, the sound of voices on the deck outside. He recognized the Admiral's and then, as the cabin door opened, heard Captain Dacres say, with deep feeling, "Thank God . . . and thank *you*, sir! You have taken a well-nigh unbearable burden off my shoulders."

From his face, and that of Leopold Heath, which was wreathed in smiles, Phillip guessed that the Admiral had somehow contrived to persuade Lord Raglan to change his mind concerning the need to evacuate Balaclava—a guess which was confirmed, when Sir Edmund Lyons

235

answered gravely, "I've won you a respite, my dear Sidney, and for the moment, that is all it is. But we must continue to hope ... I had strong backing from Sir Colin Campbell this morning, incidentally. *His* support turned the scales in our favor. But it will cost us forty more heavy guns for the Naval Brigade."

"A small price, sir, in my view," Dacres assured him.

"A view the Commander-in-Chief is unlikely to share but ... I agree." Admiral Lyons, too, was smiling. He looked chilled and tired, Phillip thought—as well he might, after the long ride from Lord Raglan's farmhouse headquarters on the Heights—but, as always, his courage and optimism were infectious. Even Captain Dacres, sick man though he was, seemed to take on a fresh lease of life in the Admiral's presence as now, almost cheerfully, he motioned Phillip to join him. "Mr. Hazard, sir, who has been in acting command of the *Trojan* and has just come from Eupatoria. By a remarkable feat of seamanship, he took her, with troop reinforcements for Captain Brock, to Eupatoria, when the gale was at its height, and safely made port with, I understand, only the loss of a single gun. He has a report for you, sir."

"I am quite sure he has! Well, my dear Phillip, I am delighted to see you." The Admiral's handshake was warm, his blue eyes affectionate as they rested on Phillip's face. "You shall regale me with an account of your adventures as we eat. I breakfasted before dawn, and, I confess, I am devilish hungry now ... but it was worth the inconvenience of an uncomfortable ride in the darkness. You will have gathered, no doubt, from all the smiling faces about you, that we are—for the time being, at any rate—to continue to hold and to the best of our ability, defend Balaclava?"

"Yes, sir," Phillip assured him. "It is quite a victory, sir."

"A small victory," Admiral Lyons amended. "But ...

236

it had to be won, and the panic counsellors defeated, not for the first time, as you will recall." He accepted a glass of Madeira from his host. "Jack told me he had seen you in Constantinople, Phillip. It is a great joy to me to have him here . . . in fact, I have shifted my flag to the *Miranda* temporarily, so that we can catch up with each other's news and enjoy each other's company for a short while." He raised his glass. "Did he give you any of this stuff?"

"Indeed he did, sir, and it was much appreciated." Phillip glanced round, seeing many familiar faces among the members of the Admiral's Staff. Captain Crawford, however, was not among them and Sir Edmund, as if he had spoken his thoughts aloud, said, eyeing him quizzically, "If you are looking for your Captain, I fear you will be disappointed. We saw the *Trojan* as we rode down from the Heights and, when we reached the harbor, I offered him the use of my barge, so that he might go out to her. No doubt, in your absence, your First Lieutenant will do the honors."

"My First Lieutenant was killed, sir," Phillip told him quietly. "He was mortally wounded during an enemy attack on Eupatoria and——"

"An attack on Eupatoria?" The Admiral asked, with a swift change of tone.

"Yes, sir. It was successfully repulsed, sir."

"Tell me about it, Phillip."

Phillip took the dispatches with which he had been entrusted from the breast pocket of his frock coat. "From Captain Brock, sir, for you. And I have a personal letter for you from Lord George Paulet. The *Cyclops* was sent to the Fleet anchorage, sir, with full reports for the Commander-in-Chief."

The Admiral thanked him and read the letters, his white brows furrowed. Over dinner, he kept Phillip at his side and questioned him minutely, with Dacres and Leopold Heath occasionally interposing queries of their own.

237

Afterwards, the talk became general and was of Balaclava and its defenses, of Fleet news and then, inevitably, of the storm and the appalling losses it had caused, Phillip's news of the loss of the *Henri Quatre* evoking murmurs of shocked disbelief from those who had not been aware of it.

The meal over, the Admiral and his staff lingered for only a short while. Sir Edmund took Captain Dacres aside, talking to him earnestly in a low voice. Phillip, in common with the rest, had no idea what was the result of their conversation but Leopold Heath confided, as the Admiral prepared to make his departure, "He is trying to persuade Dacres to take sick leave . . . and I hope, more than I can say, that he will agree to do so. Not, let me hasten to add, that I am anxious to succeed him as commander of this port but because I am very much afraid that, if he stays here much longer, it will be the death of him. You've seen how desperately ill he is."

"Yes, I have, sir," Phillip agreed sympathetically and Captain Heath gave vent to a long sigh. "Well, the Admiral must have been at his most persuasive this morning, to have talked Lord Raglan and the Generals round, so let us hope he will be equally successful with my chief. Incidentally, talking of chiefs, Hazard, now that yours has returned to resume command of the *Trojan*, have you any idea of what your next appointment will be? Has the Admiral said anything about your rejoining his Staff? Because should you be unemployed, I would be more than pleased to apply for your services, if I do take over from Captain Dacres. You would not be at sea, of course, but you would be reasonably certain of promotion and, from my point of view, a capable assistant, who isn't afraid of work, would be a great asset. Think about it, will you?"

"Thank you very much indeed, sir," Phillip answered, with genuine gratitude. "The Admiral has said nothing concerning my future, so I don't yet know what he may require of me—if he requires anything at all. But, until he does, I think perhaps I had better go back to the *Trojan* and pay my belated respects to Captain Crawford."

"Yes, perhaps you had. Au revoir, Hazard, and good luck to you." Captain Heath clapped a friendly hand on his shoulder. "Remember there's a berth for you here, if you need one ... the only thing I cannot promise is that you will enhance your popularity if you accept it!"

Phillip thanked him again and found himself wondering, as he joined the rear of the procession which had formed up to escort Admiral Lyons to his barge, whether the Admiral now had any need for him on his personal Staff. His previous appointment to the *Agamemnon* had been temporary—almost as temporary, he thought regretfully, as his command of the *Trojan* had been ... and, perhaps, even his acting rank which had not, as far as he knew, been confirmed. For his promotion to become official, Admiral Dundas, as Commander-in-Chief, had to recommend it to Their Lordships and, if he had failed to do so, then ... he shrugged resignedly. He was back where he had started, as the *Trojan*'s First Lieutenant, since poor Martin's death had left the appointment unfilled, although this, too, would depend on whether or not Captain Crawford wished to retain his services. Crawford might have an officer of his own choice in mind or he might prefer to promote Duncan Laidlaw. Judging by what he had said to Captain Dacres on the subject of inexperienced junior officers, he. . . .

"Phillip! I've been looking everywhere for you. Hold hard." Phillip turned to find the Admiral's nephew and Flag-Lieutenant at his elbow. "The Admiral wants you." Lieutenant Algernon Lyons grinned, enjoying his surprise. He had succeeded Cowper Coles as Flag-Lieutenant and was an efficient and extremely pleasant young man, whom everyone liked. He laid a hand on Phillip's arm. "What were you trying to do—slip off to the *Trojan*,

239

without as much as an adieu to any of us? Aren't you interested in your new command, my dear chap?"

"My . . . my *what*?" Phillip stared at him incredulously. "Algy, did you say command?"

"I did indeed. Didn't my uncle mention it at dinner?"

"No."

"Well, he intended to and I know he wants to tell you himself, so I won't spoil it. But look lively, there's a good fellow—we're late and he's had a pretty tiring day."

Feeling a trifle dazed, Phillip followed him to where the Admiral was taking courteous leave of Captain Dacres. "Ah, Phillip . . ." Lyons motioned him to board the waiting barge. "We will take you out to the *Trojan*. I have some news for you."

As the barge pulled away, skimming swiftly across the evil-smelling water of the inner harbour, the Admiral said, "I had intended to tell you during dinner that the Commander-in-Chief has endorsed my recommendation for your promotion, but we were interrupted."

"Thank you very much, sir. I am deeply indebted to you, believe me, for I do not think the Commander-in-Chief would have approved my promotion without your backing, sir." Phillip tried to swallow the lump which had risen suddenly in his throat. "After Captain North's death, sir, the Admiral told me that——"

Sir Edmund Lyons cut him short. "Nonsense, my dear boy, that is all in the past. You have more than earned a step in rank and you seem also to have proved, during the last week or two, that you are capable of holding a command of your own. Well, I am going to give you one." He smiled. "Admiral Dundas has accorded me the privilege of choosing some of the Captains who, in future, will be serving under me. You know, of course, that I am to succeed him as Commander-in-Chief when he hauls down his flag?"

The lump in his throat vanished and Phillip echoed his

240

smile. "Yes, sir." The transfer of command would, he knew, be welcomed enthusiastically by every officer and seaman in the Black Sea Fleet, for the Rear-Admiral was their hero. "When, sir?"

"Sooner than I had expected, Phillip—probably before the end of December." The Admiral spoke quietly and, for an unguarded instant, a flicker of what might have been reluctance or even fear shone in his blue eyes. But it swiftly faded. "Looking back on a life of responsibilities not always courted but, please God, never shrunk from, this will be the heaviest responsibility of all. I can only pray that I shall be worthy of the trust reposed in me by Her Majesty's Government and by the men I shall command." He broke off and then went on, with a change of tone, "There will be a number of changes in the composition of the Fleet. Some of the sailing ships-of-the-line will be sent home—*Britannia, Trafalgar, Queen* and *London*—and they will be replaced by steam-screws. The *Royal Albert* is to be sent out to receive my flag and, I hope, she will be joined by Captain Keppel's *St. Jean d'Acre* and Lord Clarence Paget's *Princess Royal,* from the Baltic Fleet. In addition to steam ships-of-the-line, I have long urged Sir John Graham and Their Lordships to send us more light draught sloops and gunboats of the *Arrow* class, for these, as you know, are ideal for the type of operation called for in these waters. We should have a respectable number of them by spring, when it is my intention not only to blockade the enemy's ports but to attack and, where possible, seize them."

Phillip's heart lifted, quickening its beat. For too long, he thought, the Black Sea Fleet had been inactive, its ships of war used to transport troops and stores, to protect convoys, to beat wearily back and forth outside Odessa and Kertch, as well as Sebastopol, in an attempt—not always a hundred per cent successful—to disrupt the enemy's sea-borne trade and prevent them from sending troop reinforcements to Prince Menschikoff.

"My son Jack has his heart set on leading a small steam squadron into the Sea of Azoff when it is free of ice," the Admiral continued, a note of paternal pride sounding briefly in his voice. "He has already drawn up a plan of operation, with which I can find no fault—provided we get the sloops and gunboats for which I have asked. Menschikoff obtains vast supplies of grain and stores, as well as troops, by road from that area and will be able to hold Sebastopol indefinitely if his supply route remains unmolested. Well, we shall molest it, we shall molest all his communications! Given a number of small, fast, heavily armed squadrons of sloops and gunboats, driven by steam, we can harass the enemy from Odessa to Trebizond, Phillip, and make a valuable contribution to the successful conclusion of this war. At present, apart from supplying men and guns for the siege and ferrying troops we are, as a battle Fleet, contributing little. As I say, it is my hope that in the spring there will be a significant change in the composition of the Fleet, as well as in the part it will play . . ." he talked on of the future and of the plans he was endeavoring to make and Phillip listened eagerly, as the barge crew propelled their craft with deep, even strokes of their long oars, down the narrow inlet beneath the shadow of the towering red sandstone cliffs which hemmed it in and then into the open sea, steering towards the line of anchored ships silhouetted against the glow of the setting sun.

Two ships had joined the line since he had brought the *Trojan* in, Phillip noticed, and one of these caught and held his eye. She was a steam-screw sloop-of-war, ship rigged and ram bowed, of sturdy rather than graceful design, with a tall, slender funnel sat at an angle between her main and foremasts and her boats on davits astern and on either quarter. In the fading light he could not see much more but, in view of what the Admiral had just been telling him of the request to the Board of Admiralty for light draught steam-screws with a comparatively heavy armament, his interest quickened. She was new, her design differing in several respects from those with which he was familiar but on the whole, he decided, he liked the look of her. She might lack the beautiful lines of a Symonite sailing brig but she was workmanlike and compact, obviously ideal for the type of operation which the future Commander-in-Chief was planning. As he stared at her with rapt attention, Admiral Lyons laid a hand on his shoulder and the barge crew, at a crisp order from their commander, rested on their oars.

"Her Majesty's sloop *Huntress*, Phillip," the Admiral said. "The first of her class to be built at Woolwich and, I most fervently trust, the first of many to join my flag before spring. She carries two sixty-eight pounders on slide carriages and twelve thirty-twos . . ." he went into technical details, to which not only Phillip but the rest of his officers listened with approving interest. Then, smiling, he requested the barge commander to go alongside the new sloop, and turned to Phillip. "Well, do you like her?"

"Indeed I do, sir, very much," Phillip assured him enthusiastically.

"Her commander unhappily died on the voyage from England, so I am appointing you in his place, Phillip. Go aboard and read your commission at once—you can make your farewells to the *Trojan* later." Still smiling, Admiral Lyons waved aside his stammered thanks. "I shall make time to inspect you as soon as I can but now I have a mountain of paperwork awaiting me on board my own ship, so I shall not tarry. God go with you, boy."

A voice from the *Huntress*'s upper deck hailed them and, at a nod from the Admiral, the barge commander answered it with a shrill, "Aye, aye—*Huntress*!" and, as

243

he brought his craft smartly up to the midships chains, the side-party assembled and fell in at attention.

Phillip, conscious of a feeling of intense happiness and pride, stepped aboard his new command to the customary pipe and, from her deck, his hand raised in salute, he watched the Admiral's barge pull away.

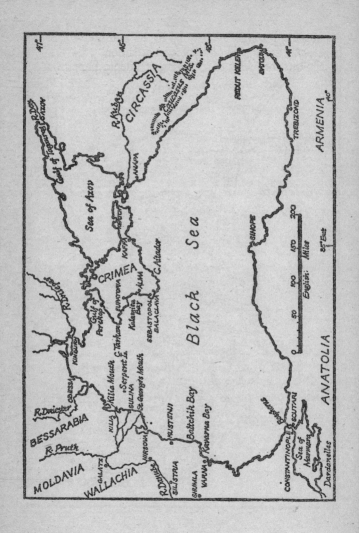

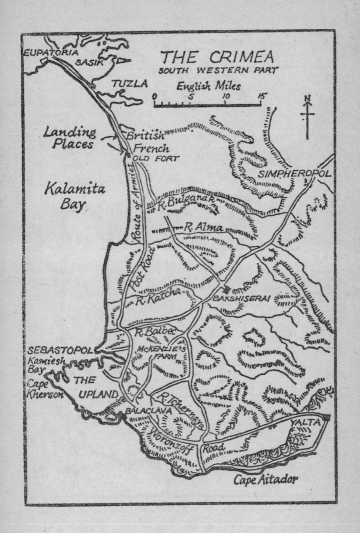

THE CRIMEA
SOUTH WESTERN PART

English Miles
0   5   10   15

N

EUPATORIA
SASIK
TUZLA

Landing Places — British
French
OLD FORT

SIMPHEROPOL

Kalamita Bay

Route of Armies

R. Bulganak

R. Alma

Post Road

R. Katcha

BAKSHISERAI

R. Balbec

McKENZIE'S FARM

SEBASTOPOL
Kamiesh Bay
Cape Kherson

THE UPLAND

R. Tchernaya

BALACLAVA

YALTA

Voronzoff Road

Cape Aitador

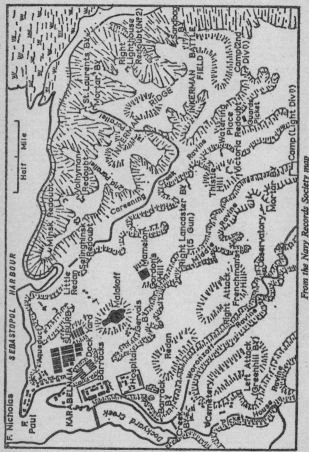

From the Navy Records Society map

BOOKS CONSULTED

ON THE CRIMEAN WAR

(General)

History of the War Against Russia, E. H. Nolan (2 vols., 1857)

History of the War With Russia, H. Tyrell (3 vols., 1857)

The Campaign in the Crimea, G. Brackenbury, illustrated W. Simpson (1856)

The War in the Crimea, General Sir Edward Hamley (1891)

Letters from India and the Crimea, Surgeon-General J. A. Bostock (1896)

Letters from Headquarters, by a Staff Officer (1856)

The Crimea in 1854 and 1894, Field-Marshal Sir Evelyn Wood (1895)

The Destruction of Lord Raglan, Christopher Hibbert (1961)

Battles of the Crimean War, W. Baring Pemberton (1962)

The Reason Why, Cecil Woodham Smith (1953)

Crimean Blunder, Peter Gibbs (1960)

The Campaign in the Crimea, 1854–6: Despatches and Papers, compiled and arranged by Captain Sayer (1857)

Letters from Camp During the Seige of Sebastopol, Lt.-Colonel C. G. Campbell (1894)

The Invasion of the Crimea, A. W. Kingslake (1863)

With the Guards We Shall Go, Mabel, Countess of Airlie (1933)

Britain's Roll of Glory, D. H. Parry (1895)

Henry Clifford, V.C., General Sir Bernard Paget (1956)

Biographies

The Life of Colin Campbell, Lord Clyde, Lt.-General L. Shadwell, C.B. (2 vols., 1881)

A Life of Vice-Admiral Lord Lyons, Captain S. Eardley-Wilmot, R.N. (1898)

(Naval)

The Russian War, 1854 (Baltic and Black Sea) D. Bonner-Smith and Captain A. C. Dewar, R.N. (1944)

Letters from the Black Sea, Admiral Sir Leopold Heath (1897)

A Sailor's Life Under Four Sovereigns, Admiral of the Fleet the Hon. Sir Henry Keppel, G.C.B., O.M. (3 vols., 1899)

From Midshipman to Field-Marshal, Sir Evelyn Wood, V.C. (2 vols., 1906)

Letters from the Fleet in the Fifties, Mrs. Tom Kelly (1902)

The British Fleet in the Black Sea, Maj.-General W. Brereton (1856)

Reminiscences of a Naval Officer, Admiral Sir G. Giffard (1892)

The Navy as I have known it, Vice-Admiral W. Freemantle (1899)

A Middy's Recollections, The Hon. Victor Montagu (1898)

Medicine and the Navy, Lloyd and Coulter (Vol. IV, 1963)

The Price of Admiralty, Stanley Barret, Hale (1968)

The Wooden Fighting Ship, E. H. H. Archibald, Blandford (1968)

Seamanship Manual, Captain Sir George S. Naes, K.C.B., R.N., Griffin (1886)

The Navy of Britain, England's Sea Officers, and *A Social History of the Navy*, Michael Lewis, Allen & Unwin (1939–60)

The Navy in Transition, Michael Lewis, Hodder & Stoughton (1965)
Files of *The Illustrated London News* and *Mariner's Mirror*.
Unpublished Letters and Diaries.

The author acknowledges, with gratitude, the assistance given by the Staff of the York City Library in obtaining books, also that given by the Royal United Service Institution and Francis Edwards Ltd.

Pinnacle Hits!

CHARTING THE CANDIDATES, '72, by Ronald Van Doren. A Pinnacle special! A probing analysis of all the 1972 candidates for the presidency, with Chart Indexes for each candidate.
P075—$1.25

THE DESTROYER: CHINESE PUZZLE, by Richard Sapir and Warren Murphy. Third in the smash series starring Remo Williams in an international plot.
P078—95¢

DIAMOND RIVER, by Sadio Garavini di Turno. The incredible true story of one man's quest for a fortune, and his discovery of an Amazon paradise.
P079—95¢

LEAP IN THE DARK, by Donald Gordon. An exciting suspenseful novel about the flight of a new SST, and of the lives of its crew.
P080—95¢

LOVE, AMERICAN STYLE, 2, by Paul Fairman. Four lighthearted episodes about the many faces of love. Original stories based on the popular ABC-TV show.
P081—95¢

HAZARD'S COMMAND, by V. A. Stuart. Philip Horatio Hazard in his most exciting naval adventure of men at war on the high seas.
P083—95¢

DEATH MERCHANT: OPERATION OVERKILL, by Joseph Rosenberger. The second in this hot new action series starring Richard Camellion, only man to leave the Mafia and live.
P085—95¢

WHERE SHADOWS LIE, by Miriam Lynch. A spellbinding Gothic tale of suspense, in the new large type. The drama of a young girl's quest for love.
P086—95¢

RELAXERCISES, by Joan Fraser. The quick and easy way to fitness and beauty. Fully illustrated with photographs and line drawings. Be happier and healthier!
P088—$1.25

BURN AFTER READING, by Ladislas Farago. An exciting history of World War II espionage and counter-espionage by one who was there! Important non-fiction.
P090—95¢

DOWN THE TUBE, by Terry Galanoy. The fascinating and funny story of the multi-million dollar business of making TV commercials. How TV commercials turn *you* on! P091—$1.25

HOW TO "MAKE IT" 365 DAYS A YEAR, by Paul Warren. The one indispensable guide for the man-about-town, or the would-be man-about-town. Be more attractive to women—watch your life change!
P092—$1.25

THE CANARIS CONSPIRACY, by Roger Manvell and Heinrich Fraenkel. The story of the secret plot to overthrow Hitler's Reich, and of Wilhelm Canaris, spymaster extraordinary.
P093—$1.25

HANNIE CAULDER, by William Terry. A new Western—wild, rugged, sexy! Soon to be a major motion picture from Paramount starring Raquel Welch.
P094—95¢

ORDER NOW TO KEEP AHEAD!

To order, check the space next to the books you want, then mail your order, together with cash, check or money order, to: Pinnacle Books, Mail Order Dep't., Box 4347, Grand Central Station, New York, New York 10017.

Order No.	Title	Price
___P003	CATACLYSM, The Day The World Died	95¢
___P004	THE EXECUTIONER'S BATTLE MASK	95¢
___P005	BLOOD PATROL	95¢
___P006	THE GUNS OF TERRA 10	95¢
___P007	1989: POPULATION DOOMSDAY	95¢
___P008	MIAMI MASSACRE	95¢
___P009	KILLER PATROL	95¢
___P010	THE GODMAKERS	95¢
___P011	KILL QUICK OR DIE	95¢
___P012	CAST YOUR OWN SPELL	95¢
___P013	THE VEGAS TRAP	95¢
___P014	THE FEMINISTS	95¢
___P015	THE DEAD SEA SUBMARINE	95¢
___P016	STAY YOUNG WITH ASTROLOGY	95¢
___P017	THE EXECUTIONER: CONTINENTAL CONTRACT	95¢
___P018	TALKING TO THE SPIRITS	95¢
___P019	THE AVENGER TAPES	$1.25
___P020	TO CATCH A CROOKED GIRL	95¢
___P021	THE DEATH MERCHANT	95¢
___P022	THE GREAT STONE HEART	95¢
___P023	THE DEADLY SKY	95¢
___P024	THE DAY THE SUN FELL	$1.25
___P025	COME WATCH HIM DIE	95¢
___P026	SLATER'S PLANET	95¢
___P027	HOME IS WHERE THE QUICK IS: MOD SQUAD	95¢
___P028	EVERYTHING YOU NEED TO KNOW ABOUT ABORTION	$1.50
___P029	THE EXECUTIONER: ASSAULT ON SOHO	95¢

Order No.	Title	Price
___P066	NAKED, AS AN AUTHOR	95¢
___P067	GUNS FOR GENERAL LI	95¢
___P069	THE PENTAGON	$1.95
___P070	BRAVE CAPTAINS	95¢
___P071	CONGO WAR CRY	95¢
___P072	THE DESTROYER: DEATH CHECK	95¢
___P073	101 BEST GROWTH STOCKS FOR 1972	$1.25
___P074	DUELING OAKS	95¢
___P075	CHARTING THE CANDIDATES	$1.25
___P076	THE EXECUTIONER: CARIBBEAN KILL	95¢
___P078	THE DESTROYER: CHINESE PUZZLE	95¢
___P079	DIAMOND RIVER	95¢
___P080	LEAP IN THE DARK	95¢
___P081	LOVE AMERICAN STYLE, 2	95¢
___P083	HAZARD'S COMMAND	95¢
___P085	DEATH MERCHANT: OPERATION OVERKILL	95¢
___P086	WHERE SHADOWS LIE	95¢
___P088	RELAXERCISES	$1.25
___P090	BURN AFTER READING	95¢
___P091	DOWN THE TUBE	$1.25
___P092	HOW TO "MAKE IT" 365 DAYS A YEAR	$1.25
___P093	THE CANARIS CONSPIRACY	$1.25
___P094	HANNIE CAULDER	95¢

Pinnacle Books, Box 4347, Grand Central Station,
New York, New York 10017

Gentlemen:

Please send me the books I have marked. I enclose_____

_____as payment in full. (Sorry, no CODs.)

Name_____

Address_____

City_____State_____Zip_____